PAST IMPERFECT

ALISON G. BAILEY

Past Imperfect
Copyright © 2014 Alison G. Bailey
All rights reserved.

Cover design by Robin Harper, Wicked By Design
https://www.facebook.com/WickedByDesignRobinHarper

Photography by Abigail Marie, [non`pa*reil] Photography
www.nonpareilphotography.com/

Interior book design by Angela McLaurin, Fictional Formats
https://www.facebook.com/FictionalFormats

Edited by Linda Roberts
lindafayroberts3@gmail.com

ISBN: 978-0-9914744-2-4
CREATESPACE ISBN: 10: 0991474422

To those who feel broken and alone. You are neither.

CHAPTER 1

THE PRESENT

Brad

I can't keep my leg from bopping up and down while I sit here and wait. Every part of my body that has a gland is sweating. I've never been this nervous in my entire life. Standing, I start to pace, alternating between checking my watch and the entrance. She'll be here any minute. I have everything planned out to perfection tonight.

I've rented the private patio at our favorite restaurant in downtown Charleston, the Peninsula Grill. I had them remove all the tables except for the one we'll be sitting at. The area is secluded and away from the noisy activity of the restaurant and street. Small white lights snake up and around each palmetto tree that surrounds the area. In the center, a table for two is dressed with white linen, crystal champagne flutes, and pristine silverware. In the middle of the table there's a crystal vase with a dozen orange tiger lilies and some sort of purple flowers. Being a graduate of Clemson University, her favorite colors are orange and purple. Tiger lilies are her favorite flower. I just told the florist orange tiger lilies, purple, and make it look perfect.

1

Checking my watch for the five hundredth time in the past ten minutes, I steal another glance toward the entrance. I can feel my breathing speed up and my palms feel as if I have dunked them in water. If she doesn't get here in the next few seconds, I'm going to be a hyperventilating-sweaty-impeccably dressed mess. Just as I let out a deep breath I hear her soft voice float through the air.

"Brad," she says breathlessly with just a hint of surprise in her tone.

God, I love the way my name sounds coming out of her mouth. Her incredibly talented mouth that's surrounded by her full pale pink lips. The bottom lip is slightly more plump than the upper one. When she's concentrating hard on something, her teeth graze across that bottom lip as it's sucked into her mouth. There is no better sight in this world than Mabry Darnell concentrating. Whenever she is *thinking* hard, I get hard. I can't help it. It's as if her mouth and my dick have this synchronicity. In fact, everything about us feels in sync.

From the moment she walked into my dad's law firm, she grabbed my attention. We are both first-year lawyers, which means we are low on the food chain in the firm. Even though it's my father's law firm, dear Dad doesn't believe in playing favorites, especially where I'm concerned. Mabry and I have spent a lot of late nights together preparing for cases. We flirted, got to know each other, and I asked her out. She kept refusing until she could no longer resist the charming masculinity that is Brad Johnson. We've kept things casual, but I knew from the second I laid eyes on her, my reaction was different. It was more than lust at first sight. I've fallen for this girl and need her in my life.

I've been with a lot of pretty girls, but Mabry is the first beautiful woman for me. When I say "beautiful", I don't just mean on the outside, although the outside is mouthwatering. Everything about her holds my attention. She stands about five feet six inches on shapely toned legs that lead up to her perfectly round ass, small waist, and one of the all-time best racks the good Lord has ever created. I've seen a lot of racks, so I consider myself an expert. Her shoulder-length chestnut brown hair frames a well-defined, but soft, square jawline, and when she smiles, smirks, or grins, her straight little nose crinkles up in the most adorable way, causing my heart to skip a beat every time. Her azure blue eyes pop against the backdrop of her creamy pale skin and are captivating. The outside is effortlessly beautiful and sexy, but what drew me in and has held me is what's behind those eyes.

The times she's dealing with a colleague or client those eyes match the tone of the meeting—warm and kind, or strong and serious. But it's in the quiet times when she thinks no one is looking that those eyes hold the most truth. There is something intriguing and sad behind them during those unguarded moments.

"Hey Sweetness," I say.

I walk over to her and pull her into my chest. I close my eyes as the smell of vanilla hits me. I pull back slightly and place a soft kiss at the corner of her mouth, letting the tip of my tongue skim across the crease quickly. I have to watch myself. Things with Mabry can go from zero to a hundred eighty in less than five seconds. Pulling back I stare into her beautiful eyes. I can't believe I found her. She's perfect for me. We have been "together" for three months and tonight is the night. I'm going to tell her how much I love her. I don't know at what point during the night I'm going to say it, I just know I'm ready to say it. I've never said those words to anyone before, so I want everything to be special tonight.

We walk over to the table and I pull the chair out for her. "What's all this for?" she asks.

"I just thought it would be nice to do something different, is all." I sit down across from her, taking her hand and lacing our fingers together.

"This is a little more than just *different*. It's not my birthday," she says as her lips form into a straight line at the same time her head cocks to one side. Then her eyes widen and her mouth goes slack. "Oh god, it's not your birthday, is it?"

"Sweetness, if it was my birthday eating dinner with you would be the last thing I'd be doing."

Looking up at me through her long dark lashes, she asks in a sultry voice, "What would you be doing?"

I lean in close so that we are nose-to-nose. "I'd have you spread across my bed tasting you." I hold her gaze for a moment before I look down and see the huge lump she's swallowing slide down her slender neck.

"Don't do that."

"Do what?" I smirk.

"Say stuff like that to me in public. You know what it does to me," she says shifting in her chair.

I lean back, happy with myself. I love to tease her and make her squirm. "Then you need to relax and enjoy. Don't question it." My voice now sounds slightly annoyed.

Mabry is very guarded. She's less so with me now, but still questions every nice thing I do for her. I hate it and at this point don't understand why she's still like that with me. She's suspicious that ulterior motives are attached. It strikes a nerve with me because I'm not like that anymore. I'm upfront and honest with people. I've learned my lesson the hard way.

"Fine. I'm sorry. I appreciate all the trouble you went to. You know you don't have to do this type of thing for me."

"I want to do this type of thing for you." We hold each other's gaze for a few seconds before hearing her name from across the patio.

He's tall, dark, and has douche bag written all over him. As he walks up to our table, Mabry gives me a tight smile and squeezes my hand before pulling hers away.

"Hey Ten," she greets Sir Douche.

"Hey, I thought it was you sitting out here," he says.

"I'm surprised you saw me out here especially with the restaurant being so crowded."

"I'd always be able to spot you no matter how many people were in the room," he replies, staring at her a little too long.

Who the hell is this guy?

I clear my throat, startling my date.

"Oh, I'm sorry. Ten this is Brad Johnson, a colleague." I cringe slightly at the reference. "Brad, this is Ten McGuire," Mabry introduces.

We shake hands. "Tin? Like Rin Tin Tin, the dog?" I ask.

He gives me a smug look, *the motherfucker*, and answers, "Short for Tennyson. It's a family name."

"Does your family hate you?"

Mabry gently kicks me under the table, causing my gaze to snap in her direction. "Brad!"

"What?"

"I'm sorry, Ten. Brad has a weird sense of humor."

Is she actually apologizing for me?

"That's okay. I get that a lot." Sir Douche throws another smug look my way before focusing on Mabry. "You were amazing in court today." Every muscle in my body tightens.

I notice a slight blush creep over Mabry's cheeks. "Thank you, but I didn't do anything, besides sit there."

"The research you did for the case was extremely well done and detailed. Maybe we can get together sometime and discuss your future."

Well, fuck me. Fuck you.

"Maybe," she says, with a slightly nervous laugh, glancing over at me.

An awkward pause takes over as his eyes roam down, landing on her chest, before shooting up to meet her eyes. My fists and jaw clench tighter.

"I should let you two get back to your business. Brad, it was nice to meet you," he says, never taking his eyes off of her. "Mabry, it's always great to see you."

He takes a step back and Mabry gives him a slight smile just before he exits.

Turning back to me she looks over with concern written across her face. "I'm sorry about that." I don't respond. I'm trying to get my temper under control so I don't blow the entire place up. I feel her hand wrap around mine. "Are you okay?"

"That's incredible."

"What?" she asks.

"The way Sir Douche can kiss your ass so thoroughly while you're sitting on it. What was that, Mabry?" I look over at her.

"A colleague coming over to say hi."

"Is that all it is?" My voice is low as I stare into her eyes.

"To me it is. Are you jealous?" There's surprise in her voice when she asks the question.

"Should I be?" My words sound colder than I mean them to.

"No. I'm not like that."

I look deep into her eyes, making sure what she's saying is true. It is. We've never discussed being exclusive, I just assume we are. Of course, we've never discussed what this is between us. I feel my pant leg rise as her foot travels up and down it. My dick starts to twitch and all thoughts of Sir Douche vanish.

I fumble with my keys, trying to unlock the door to my condo, as I pin Mabry against it. Our tongues take turns darting in and out of each other's mouths while she's undoing my belt. I finally get the door open and we stumble into the room, our lips never disconnecting. I close the door by shoving her up against it. My hips grind into her as my hands move to the back of her neck, my fingers tangling in her hair. Her hands move underneath my jacket and push it over my shoulders, tossing it to the side. She undoes my tie and quickly unbuttons my shirt, using the same movement as she did with my jacket. When her hand lightly grazes one of my nipples, a bolt of electricity runs through me and I almost come right then. Next, she works the button and zipper of my pants. Her hand moves inside and she grabs my dick releasing it from my boxers. I feel my knees buckle slightly.

I pull away in order to take a breath. Staring into her eyes I see desire mixed with the sadness that is always prevalent. I almost tell her I love her, but the words seem to stick in my throat. Grabbing the hem of her dress, I slide it up as my hands run over her smooth hips and torso. She lifts her arms allowing me to peel the dress off her completely and then it finds a spot on top of my shirt and jacket. My eyes roam down her body. She's wearing a black lace push-up bra, a pair of black four-inch stilettos, and that's it.

Fuck me, I love this girl.

I plunge my tongue back into its rightful place inside Mabry's mouth. My hands glide over her ass as her fingers move up and down my dick. The only sounds in the room are the moans coming from us and the occasional thud as I push her against the door.

"Talk to me," she whispers on my lips. Her tits push against my chest with each heavy breath she takes. Mabry likes dirty talk and it just so happens that I like to talk dirty. It's a win-win.

I kiss along her jaw until I reach just below her ear. "I'm going to fuck you, baby. You want to know how?" I whisper in a raspy voice.

"Yes," she moans.

"I'm going to take my tongue and lick down your body, only stopping to suck on your beautiful tits." I bring my hand up and pinch one of her hard nipples through the lace, causing her back to arch. "I dream about your tits, Mabry," I continue. "I'm going to lick all the way down to between your legs. Then I'm going to suck you hard just before I fuck you with my tongue."

"Inside. Now!" she yells out.

I slip off my shoes as she slips her hand into my pocket to grab the condom. Holding the foil packet between her teeth, she slides down the door until she's squatting in front of me, taking my pants and boxers with her. I place my palms flat on the doorframe to brace myself as I step out of my clothes. Looking down I see Mabry tear the packet, slip the condom out, and on to my dick, all the while looking up at me through her long dark lashes. She seems to enjoy doing this and who am I to deprive her of any joy.

She slowly sucks and licks her way up my abs and over my chest until she reaches my mouth. Our tongues make another once-around in each other's mouths before my hands shift behind her thighs, lifting her while pressing her against the door at the same time. I can feel the heel of her stilettos pierce my skin as her legs wrap around my waist. The slight jolt of pain turns me on even more than I already am. Her hands find their way into my hair and she holds on tight. Two hard thrusts and I'm buried deep inside her. Everything speeds up and intensifies, our breathing, my thrusts, and her moans. She tightens around me in every way and we come together. We both shiver and cling to each other like our lives depend on it.

Still inside her, I carry her to my bedroom and lay her back on the bed. I place soft kisses across her lips, down her jaw, and to the top of her tits.

"How is it possible?" I mutter as I continue kissing everywhere my lips can reach.

"What are you talking about?" she asks as her fingers run through my hair playing with the chunky style.

Looking up at her I say, "How is it possible that it gets better every time? It was pretty awesome the first time."

Tugging on my hair, she pulls me up so we are face-to-face. "I'm trying to up my game. I think you just like my choice of undergarments more and more."

"You do have excellent taste in that department. I like what's under those garments too, and what comes out of your mouth, and what's behind those eyes."

Now is the time to tell Mabry how much I love her. I haven't looked at, thought about, or wanted to be with another girl since we met.

Clearing my throat, I look deep into her eyes and say, "Mabry, the past few months with you have been fantastic. Spending time with you is my favorite part of the day. It doesn't matter what we're doing. All that matters is I can look up and see you by my side."

"Brad…"

"Mabry, I've fallen in…"

"I need to get up," she interrupts as she shoves on my chest.

"What? Is anything wrong?" I ask, pushing off and out of her.

Sitting up, she moves away from me and off the bed quickly. "I need to go to the bathroom," she says as she walks across the room, never looking back at me.

I watch as the door closes. I get up and remove the condom, tossing it in the trash can. I grab a pair of pajama pants and slip them on. The door to the bathroom suddenly swings open and Mabry comes rushing out wrapped in a towel.

Scanning the room she asks, "Where are my clothes?"

"Excuse me?" I stand in shock with my hands resting on my hips.

"I need my clothes. I didn't pay attention to where they ended up."

"Why do you need your clothes?"

"Because, the authorities don't look kindly on public nudity." She gives me a slight smirk that disappears in a nanosecond.

"You're leaving?" My shock wears off and I'm getting angry.

"I have an early day tomorrow. Besides, you know the rules. No overnighters," she says as she walks out of the bedroom and down the hallway in search of her clothes.

"What the fuck just happened here?" I follow behind her.

"We had a delicious dinner, an amazing fuck, as usual, and now I have to go," she throws over her shoulder.

I find her in the living room shimmying into her dress. I can feel my entire body tense up as I stand there with my arms crossed over my chest staring at her. "I want to tell you something."

She runs her fingers through her hair. "Yeah, well, can't it wait until morning?"

"It's not business related."

She stops the nervous searching for her purse. Looking me in the eye she says, "Don't get all hearts and flowers on me, Brad. You knew what this was when we started."

"Yeah, I knew what it was when we started, but somewhere along the way things changed. I love you, Mabry."

Her blue eyes fill with water, fear, and anger as she steps back. "Fuck you." Grabbing her purse, she turns on her heels and is out the door.

Mabry

I keep moving. I don't think or breathe until I'm safe and secure in my car. I take several slow deep breaths trying to get control of my anxiety before it swallows me up. I still feel on the verge of hyperventilating. Thank god Brad didn't follow me. I fight to keep the picture out of my head of him standing there looking vulnerable and sad. My throat stings and my eyes burn as I try to hold back my tears. I can't lose it, not here. I start the car and head home.

Things were going so well with us. Why did he have to ruin it? The main reason I finally agreed to go out with him was because I knew he had a reputation for being a player and he wouldn't be looking for anything serious or permanent, which is exactly what I wanted and needed. I can't have anything serious, not with Brad or anyone. He's supposed to be safe and uncomplicated. What's he thinking telling me that?

Walking into my condo I'm a bundle of nerves. I was able to calm myself somewhat on the drive home because I had to focus on the road, but now it's too easy for the thoughts to creep in. I have to do something to get my mind off Brad and what he said to me. Passing through the bedroom I kick my shoes off, toss my purse on the bed, and make my way to the bathroom. I turn the shower on full blast, letting the hot water steam up the place while I undress. I focus on every little movement I make, trying to keep my mind occupied. I can't let the thoughts in. Once they're in, they take over, and I can't control myself.

I step into the shower and immediately flinch when the scalding hot water pelts my skin, but I don't move away from it. I focus on how the hot beads prick my flesh. It hurts for only a few seconds before my skin gets used to the temperature. I scrub my skin a little more forcefully than usual and do the same with my hair. The roughness helps keep my mind focused. I step out of the shower, dry myself and my hair, and put on a T-shirt and a pair of pajama pants, before crawling into bed. I decide to watch some TV to help distract. I need to stay focused on physical things to keep from disappearing into my thoughts. I'm reaching for the remote when my phone chirps with a text.

I try to ignore it, pretend I didn't hear it, but then it chirps again. I know it's him. I turn the TV on and try to put the text out of my head. I flip through channel after channel, desperately trying to find something to take my mind off the damn text that I know is waiting on my phone. I play this game for at least fifteen minutes before I cave. I grab my phone with a shaky hand and swipe the screen.

Brad: I'm sorry. I didn't mean to freak you out. Please let me know that you're home safe.

I stare at the words for a few minutes. Pictures of his sad eyes flood my mind. I toss the phone to the bedside table as if it were on fire. I try to forget the text. I try to forget the words he said. I try to forget his hurt. I try so hard, but I can't keep the images and feelings away. I have to do something to stop them from consuming me. I run both hands through my still damp hair. I hesitate. I didn't want to do this, but I know it's the only thing that will help me right now. I wasn't prepared for what he said to me tonight. Hesitantly, I scoot down until the back of my head is in line with the edge of the headboard. My body automatically goes into the ritual of preparing itself for the impact—eyes close, fists clench, heels dig in, all muscles tense. I perform three rapid slams to the back of my head. Relief immediately washes over my body, my mind becomes clear, and my feelings numb.

CHAPTER 2

THE PAST

Brad

I was standing just outside the kitchen door. Mom and Dad were in the study, arguing. Both were lawyers, so they did it for a living. The only difference was when *they* argued there was a mean and calculating tone with the sole purpose of hurting each another. I don't remember a time when they didn't hate each other. I often wondered why they got married. They couldn't even be in the same room for very long before the sneers and snide remarks started. I'm not sure at what age my older brother, Peyton, and I were when we made a game out of it. We used to bet how long our parents would last in a room before the gloves came off.

Today's argument was about me. I had been sent home early from school for inappropriate behavior, which translated into getting caught with my hand up Tamron Boyd's dress. My two friends, Jeremy and Spencer, bet me that I couldn't get my hand up there. If my dad taught me anything it was to never back down from a challenge. Before school this morning I went up to Tamron, making sure the guys didn't see me talking to her. I told her about the bet, that I would split the money with her and then I gave her *the smile*. *The smile* usually got me what I wanted, especially from the ladies. She thought about it for a few seconds while staring at *the smile* and then agreed. So during recess Tamron and I snuck behind the building and she let me shove my hand up her dress while Jeremey and Spencer peaked at us from around the corner. Me and the guys never talked about how long my hand needed to be up there for it to count. Tamron seemed to like my hand where it was and so did I.

Tamron and I were both looking down at where my hand disappeared when I was suddenly yanked back. Mrs. Fisher told Tamron to follow her as she tugged me all the way into the school office. They insisted both my parents come to the school to talk with the principal because of the severity of my inappropriate behavior. I didn't understand what the big deal was. Tamron wanted my hand up her dress.

My parents' voices were getting louder, but were still muffled. I walked closer to the door to hear what my punishment was going to be. That was a bad idea.

"William, could you stay off of the phone long enough to discuss your own son?" my mom said through what sounded like gritted teeth. I heard the phone slam down.

"Okay, you have my full fucking attention now. Happy?" my dad barked back.

"I don't think it's too much to ask for you to be a father for ten minutes. Bradley has a problem and something needs to be done."

"So he stuck his hand up a girl's dress. He's a curious ten-year-old boy. What's the big deal? I'd be more concerned if he had shoved his hand down a boy's pants."

"You're a pig. It was embarrassing enough to be called down there, but I was completely mortified when I found out what he had done. There's something wrong. You need to have a talk with him."

"Why do I have to talk with him?"

"Because I don't have the time to deal with it. I have a million things on my plate already and I don't need to add a perverted son discussion. Besides, you're his father."

"Hold on. You don't have time? Well, ten years ago you should have thought a little more about your *plate* and how much shit it would be able to hold. You had an out then. Remember? I even drove you to the clinic to get rid of it, but then you changed your mind. You blew your chance to be free of the little bastard."

"It was a mistake, I was hormonal. I wasn't thinking clearly. I should have gone through with it," my mom said coldly.

"It was a mistake to get drunk and fuck you without a condom that night, but we all have our crosses to bear. One kid, that's all I said I wanted, just one, and you couldn't even do that right."

"I made a stupid mistake."

"Yeah, well, *your* mistake is now walking around feeling up girls at school."

A mistake? I stood completely frozen outside the door. Numb. Their voices faded from my awareness. I knew my parents were busy and didn't have a lot of time for me. It never crossed my mind that they simply didn't want me around in the first place.

I don't remember climbing the stairs to my room, but somehow I had made it there. I had been a mistake from the very beginning. *A mistake?* As I repeated the word in my mind, the feelings slowly seeped into my body. I felt an empty and lonely ache in the pit of my stomach. I was confused. Parents were supposed to think of their children as blessings. I had seen shows on TV where the parents were happy and proud of their children. I racked my brain trying to figure out what I had done to cause my parents to hate me so much. I kept coming back to the same conclusion. I was born.

I cringed as I walked up the driveway to my house and saw my mom's car parked there. She was home early from work. I wished baseball practice hadn't been called off today. It was just the two of us living in this huge house now. She and my dad had been divorced for two years. Mom filed a few weeks after I overheard them in the study that day. Dad wanted Peyton to live with him and Mom let it happen. I don't know if they asked Peyton where he wanted to live, but no one ever mentioned that I had a choice.

I walked in the front door and tossed my backpack down as I passed the dining room table on my way to the kitchen to get something to eat. The house was very quiet. I didn't know or really care where my mom was. I grabbed a bag of chips from the cabinet and a soda from the fridge before heading toward the game room to watch some TV.

As I turned the corner I heard a loud crash and then a moan coming from the study. A couple of seconds passed before I heard another moan. It was my mom. She sounded like she was in pain. Maybe she fell and hurt herself. I put the chips and soda down and moved toward the study. I heard another moan and then a thud. I picked up my pace and flung open the door.

At first I didn't comprehend what I was seeing. The desk lamp was laying broken on the floor along with some papers and pens scattered around it. My eyes moved up and across the desk to see my mom sitting on the edge of it, a huge pair of hands gripping her hips, and some guy's face between her legs. I stood still, not believing that I was watching some guy go down on my own mother. Neither of them had a clue that I was in the room. My daze was broken by another loud moan from her and muffled humming from him. Suddenly her eyes opened and she spotted me.

"Brad, get out of here and close the door!" she yelled, her voice a combination of pleasure and pain. She never pushed the guy away or told him to stop. She just kept yelling at me to get out.

I turned and ran out of the room and out of the house. When I hit the front yard I saw a van parked on the street that I hadn't noticed before. The words Turner's Pool Service were written across the side of it. What a fucking cliché she was. I just kept running. I didn't have anywhere to run to. My dad lived across town, so he was too far away. Of course that wasn't the only reason not to go to his house. He rarely asked me to come over to spend time with him. The times he did spend with me I think were just to keep up appearances. So I decided to keep running until I got the picture of my mom and that guy out of my head or I collapsed from exhaustion, whichever came first.

I'm in my father's office sitting across the desk from him, watching as he signs some kind of documents with one hand while palming his much younger assistant's ass with the other. He thinks he's doing a great job of hiding it from me. What a douche bag. I turn fifteen in a few months and mommy and daddy dearest felt that it was time I had a job. So here I am, waiting for daddy douche to impart his work philosophy to me, that is, if he can pry his hand away from the ass it's currently glued to.

"There you go, Kristina. Thank you for bringing those in for me so quickly," he said.

"It was my pleasure. I know how hard you've been working on this case and I wanted to make sure you got what you wanted and needed," she squeaked out.

They gave each other a quickie eye fuck, causing my stomach to churn. I almost hurled every bit of food I had eaten over the entire month. My father leered at the ass as it bounced across the room and out the door. His look then shifted to a hard serious glare in my direction.

"Okay, you'll be working here helping the staff with anything they need, sorting mail, running errands, that type of thing. You can come in Monday, Wednesday, and Friday after school." He focused his attention on the documents in front of him.

"I have baseball practice Monday and Wednesday after school," I said.

He glanced up. "Then you can come in after that and work for an hour or two, plus some on Saturday." He nodded his head slightly and returned to his work.

"Have I done something wrong?" I asked.

"What do you mean, Bradley?"

"Am I being punished? Is that why you're forcing me to work here?"

"I'm sorry. I didn't realize spending time with your father would be such a horrible experience." A smug smirk appeared across his face.

"Are you suffering from Alzheimer's, Father?" I asked sarcastically.

"Don't be a disrespectful little prick, Bradley. I won't tolerate it."

"I'm not being disrespectful. I'm being serious. The past fifteen minutes that I've been sitting here is the most time you've spent with me in ten years. Now, I admit years one through five are a bit hazy, but chances are they weren't much different, *Dad*."

He put his pen down and closed the file that had his attention. He stared up at me with ice blue eyes. Leaning forward slightly, he placed his elbows on the desk. He was trying to keep his temper under control. Friends, colleagues, and clients all thought William Johnson was a friendly, kind, and thoughtful man and father, but he was also one of the best actors around. The real William Johnson was cold, calculating, and heartless. I wasn't positive how a good father acted, but I knew for a fact mine didn't act like one.

"You're here to learn some responsibility now that you're older. Everything has been given to you. It's time for you to earn your keep. Take Miss Cox..." The irony of her last name and the fact that she more than likely sucked my father's in order to get her job was not lost on me. I couldn't help but smirk. "...she's been working here for almost two years while putting herself through school. She's an incredibly talented and intelligent young woman."

"Is she going to be my new mommy?" His face began turning a deep shade of red, starting at his neck and quickly rising to the top of his head. He looked like a cartoon character getting angry. The only thing missing was smoke shooting out of his ears. With a cocky glare, I held his gaze. He would never show his true colors in public.

He took a couple of deep breaths, trying to calm himself, and said, "You know where the mailroom is. Go find Tim. He'll tell you what he needs. I don't want to see you for the rest of the day. Now get out of my office." He turned his attention back to his work.

I hesitated for a few seconds. My father was a dick, has always been a dick, and will always be a dick. I knew that. I had no respect, like, or love toward this man. He was almost a stranger to me, but his coldness always hurt. I'm not sure why. It wasn't as if it was a surprise, but it never stopped me from needing and hoping that one day he would become my dad.

Mabry

Summer was one of my most favorite times of the year next to my birthday and Christmas. Living in Charleston we were surrounded by beaches, so every other summer we would spend our vacation here. We'd rent a house and stay at one of the local beaches for a week. Dad would spend most of the time fishing while my mom and I divided our time between the beach and the local shops. I loved spending time with my mom.

At ten years old a lot of my friends were trying to spend as much time as possible away from their parents, but not me. My mom had always been my best friend. She was so happy and fun. She loved to sing, dance, and bake. Whenever we were in the kitchen baking cookies, Mom would make up a song about the type of cookies we were baking and dance around singing it. There were times I laughed so hard my stomach would hurt. She was always a perfect mom. Every day before we went to the beach, she would pack a picnic lunch for us. We'd take chips and soda along with the sandwiches and brownies that we made together. We would talk about anything and everything.

"Mom, I know I already had a brownie, but could I have another one, pleeeease?" I asked, giving her my best sad puppy look.

"Of course you can, sweetheart. We're on vacation. No rules on vacation. I'm going to have another one too," she said.

We sat in silence staring out at the ocean while we finished eating our brownies. This was our last day of vacation. I think we were both a little sad. Even though we didn't live more than twenty minutes from a beach, it was awesome to be able to walk out your backdoor and directly onto sand.

"Mabry, you know I love you more than anything else in this world, right?" I saw out the corner of my eye that she was still staring out at the waves.

"Sure. I love you too, Mom."

Turning in my direction she made me look at her. "No matter what, I don't ever want you to doubt how much I love you, understand?"

The look in her eyes was different. I didn't know then, but that day would be the last time I saw my mom happy.

I woke up later that night to go to the bathroom. As I walked out of my room I could hear noises directly across the hall coming from my parents' room. As I got closer I could hear my mom crying. It wasn't normal crying. It sounded as if she couldn't catch her breath. My dad was trying to calm her down.

"Bren, you need to take deep breaths and stop crying."

"I've tried but I can't. It's too hard. I can't do it anymore, Thomas," my mom choked out.

"Do what, sweetheart?" Dad asked.

"All of it."

"Bren, you need to take your medicine every day."

"The medicine doesn't do a thing for me. There's no point in it. There's no point to anything."

"You have to take it regularly for it to help. Maybe you need to call and make an appointment with Dr. Jackson. You haven't seen her in a while," Dad said.

"I'm not going back to her. She's as useless as the pills she gave me." Mom's tone was turning angry.

"You can't get down like this. Mabry and I need you. You've been doing so well. I don't understand what's happened."

"I'm tired of pretending for everybody. I'm so tired, Thomas. I just want it all to stop. Maybe things would be better if I left."

I waited to hear what my dad's response was, but all I heard were the muffled cries of my mom. I assumed he was holding her. I went to the bathroom and did what I needed to do. I didn't know what was making my mom so sad that she would cry like that. I had never seen her that way. She was always so happy. I was scared. When I returned to my room, I crawled into the bed and pulled the covers over my head. I wanted to block out the sound of my mom's crying and the memory of her sad eyes.

Over the past two years Mom got progressively worse. I never saw her smile again after we returned home from the beach. She didn't make up songs or dance around. She didn't bake. One day she didn't get up to fix my breakfast or help me get ready for school. She still picked me up after school and soccer practice, but one day that stopped too. Everything about her just stopped. I didn't understand what was going on. Dad said she was tired and needed to rest. She stayed in bed most of the time now. When my dad worked late I would fix dinner for myself, mostly sandwiches. I would always fix a plate for my mom, but she never ate it.

Dad was working late today, so after soccer practice my friend and teammate, Sylvie, invited me to her house for dinner. It was fun having dinner at the Addison's house. Sylvie had two older brothers and her dad was really funny. I'd been eating by myself for so long I had forgotten what it felt like to talk about what happened at school and laugh around the table.

I climbed the steps to my front door. Before opening it, I turned and waved goodbye to Sylvie and her dad. I walked in and headed to my room. Since I hadn't been home for dinner, I figured I needed to check on Mom and see if she was hungry. I knew the answer would be no, as usual, but maybe today would be the day she started to feel better and got back to being her old self. I sat my backpack down outside my bedroom door and headed down the hall to check on her.

I knocked softy on the door, but didn't get an answer, which was usual. She was probably sleeping. That's about all she did nowadays. I knocked a little harder, but still no answer. I was sure she was in there. She hadn't left her room in a long time. I turned the knob and slowly inched the door open. Mom kept the room pretty dark. There was a little light spilling in from the bathroom, but that was all. It took a few seconds for my eyes to adjust. Looking over at the bed I could see there was a lump the size of my mom under the comforter. Dad always said when she was sleeping not to bother her, but I wanted to make sure she wasn't hungry.

"Mom," I whispered. She didn't respond.

As I walked closer to the bed, I felt a squishing underneath my feet as if the carpet was soaked. I looked down and saw there was a large dark stain that ran along the length of the bed. There was a weird smell in the room like rusted metal. I raised my hand and pulled back the comforter. The weight of it surprised me. It was heavy like when I'd help my mom hang it on the clothes line after washing it. I pulled on it, revealing my mom laying on her back. Her arms were raised, palms up, and placed on either side of her head that was turned to one side. The same dark stain that was on the carpet surrounded what I could see of her. The rusty metal smell was a lot stronger since I had pulled the comforter down. She was really still. Suddenly, all the lights in the room flashed bright and I felt two hands grab my shoulders and shove me into the hallway.

The door to my parents' room slammed in my face and I heard my dad scream. "No!! Don't leave me. Bren baby! I need you! Mabry needs you! Oh God, why!"

I stared at the door unable to move. I heard my dad's muffled voice. He was talking between gasps for air, telling someone our address. Then there was silence. I glanced down and saw deep red footprints on the carpet made by my sneakers. My entire body shook and tears gushed from my eyes. I was having trouble breathing. I took a step back, then another, and then one more before turning and running full force out of the house. I didn't know where I was running to. I didn't have anywhere to go. I picked up my pace when I heard the sirens and saw the ambulance speeding toward my house. I had to keep running until I got the picture of my mom out of my head or I collapsed from exhaustion, whichever came first.

Dad and I were sitting at the kitchen table eating pizza. We ordered out a lot now that Mom was gone. It's been two years since I found her. Dad tried to sell the house right after, but didn't get any offers. Their room has been completely redone: new carpet, new bed, new paint, but we never go in there. He sleeps either on the sofa or in the guestroom. All he does is go to work, for groceries, and he takes me to the occasional doctor and dentist appointments. That's about it. He moves and breathes. He exists, but he's not living anymore. I knew he loved and missed my mom a lot, but so did I. He had forgotten that I needed him too. I lost both my parents in one day.

"Dad, we're supposed to be at the field tomorrow at 8 am," I said, picking up another piece of pizza. He turned his head in my direction. The same glassy dazed look that had taken up permanent residence in his eyes met me. I knew he had no idea what I was talking about even though I had asked him a week ago if he would come to my last game of the season. "My soccer game, Dad. It's the last of the season. I asked you about it last week," I said, annoyance evident in my voice.

"I'm sorry, Mabry. I completely forgot."

"So, we have to be there at eight."

"I won't be able to make it. I have to work," he said robotically.

"Tomorrow is Saturday and you promised last week you'd do whatever you needed to do at work, so you'd be able to make the game."

"Well, I tried, but didn't get everything done."

"You didn't try. You just said you completely forgot, so how could you have tried when you can't even remember you still have a daughter who needs you at her last game?" I stood abruptly, shoving my chair, causing it to fall backward.

"Mabry, I'm sorry. It's just been so hard. I'll try to do better. I promise." His voice was shaky. It sounded so weak and small.

"No you won't! It's been two years since you've acted like my dad. I miss her too. I think about her all the time. I still smell the blood when I pass by that door. I can't get the image of her lying there out of my head. You're the dad. You're supposed to help me get through this, but you left me just like Mom did."

We stared at each other for a few seconds. Tears streamed down both our faces. He made no attempt to reach out, to hug me, or to comfort me in any way. All he did was stare at me with his dead eyes. I ran to my room, slamming the door as hard as possible. As I paced, I felt the anger that had started building at the table double in strength. I tried to breathe deeply to calm down, but it wasn't helping. I hated my parents for not loving me enough. I hated my mom because she didn't stay around to take care of me, and I hated my dad for not being strong enough to take care of me.

I had to focus on something else. I had to stop thinking about how much my parents hurt me. I needed some way to make this pain go away. I stomped over to my dresser, picked up my hairbrush, and started hitting myself in the head. With every slap of the hard bristles on my scalp came a little relief. I concentrated on the stinging sensation instead of my parents. After five hits my head throbbed, but my anger had disappeared.

Stay focused on the throbbing, Mabry. Think only about the throbbing.

I crawled into bed still in my clothes. I had to fall asleep before the physical pain stopped because once *it* stopped, the real hurt would be back.

CHAPTER 3

THE PRESENT

Brad

It's been three days since Mabry ran out of my place. I decided to give her some room to breathe and recover. The look in her eyes that night just before she bolted was something I won't forget. Mabry always has an underlying sadness in her eyes. They're beautiful and mesmerizing, but sad. After a month of being together I asked questions, hoping she would open up. I wanted to know everything about her, what made her happy and especially what had made her sad. That look held more than just a woman who was afraid of commitment, I just hadn't been able to figure out what.

Day one, post bolt, she managed to completely avoid me. I don't know how she did it. I mean, my father's firm is pretty big, but not huge. I thought at first she might have called in sick, but that wasn't Mabry. She's ambitious, and determined, plus being a first-year lawyer meant a sick day was not an option. Day two, the firm had an early morning breakfast meeting. This meant I did see her, but she wouldn't make eye contact with me. She's extremely stubborn. She was so dead

26

set on not looking at me that she almost ran into the door on her way out of the meeting. Today is day three post bolt and I am done giving Ms. Darnell space.

It's 6 pm on Friday and the office is deserted except for myself and Ms. Overachiever, who I just saw walk into the firm's library. I follow her and stop at the door. Shoving my hands in my pockets, I lean one shoulder against the doorframe and watch her. We are so perfect for each other, we're even dressed similar. She's wearing a black skirt that hits right above her knees and glides over the curves of her hips and ass as if it's painted on. I have on a pair of black suit pants. The sleeves of her gray silk shirt are pushed up to her elbows, same as my gray button-down shirt. My black and gray tie is loose and the first couple of buttons of my shirt are undone. Her shoes are the same black stilettos that I love piercing my flesh when her legs are wrapped around me. She walks to one of the tables and starts flipping through the case book. While searching for what she's looking for, she raises her hand and pushes some hair behind her ear. I watch as the tips of her fingers graze the shell of her ear and then return to flipping pages. Her lower lip slowly disappears into her mouth as her teeth hold it in place. As if on cue, my dick starts to twitch. I close my eyes and take in a deep breath.

Clearing her throat, voice shaky, she says, "I'm almost done in here if you need to use it."

I open my eyes and see the same look I saw the other night. She wants to bolt, but the overachiever in her is keeping her sweet little ass glued to the chair.

"I don't need to use the library."

"Then did you need something?"

"You," I say.

I push off of the doorframe and head toward her as she gets up to leave. I block her and she backs up from me, but the built-in bookshelves stop her from moving farther away. I get directly in front of her, placing my hands on either side of her shoulders. I lean in as close as possible without touching her. Her eyes are frantic. She doesn't want to look at me.

"Brad, I need to go. I have a lot of work to do."

"It's Friday, you have the entire weekend to work. Stop doing this," I say.

"What?" She still won't look at me.

"Avoiding me. Talk to me, Mabry," I insist.

"I don't have anything to say."

"Then you listen to me." Her eyes inadvertently dart up to mine and I capture her gaze. I lean in so close that I'm within a hair's-breadth of her face. "I've given you space for the past couple of days because I know when I told you I loved you it freaked you out."

"Stop saying that." She tries to shift her gaze away, but can't.

"Why should I?"

"Because we had a deal. We were supposed to stay casual, fun, and breezy. Nothing serious. You knew that going into this." Her breathing picks up.

"Things change, Sweetness."

"Not for me."

"Bullshit." The look of surprise on her face almost makes me smile. "I know you have strong feelings for me, Mabry."

"Of course I like you, Brad. I wouldn't have had sex with you if I didn't like you somewhat."

The corners of my mouth turn up into a slight grin. I lower the tone of my voice like when I talk dirty to her. "You more than like me *somewhat*, Sweetness. I see how your eyes immediately dart toward me when I walk into a room." I feel a shiver radiate off her body and I feel myself growing harder.

"Don't flatter yourself. I have a nervous twitch."

"I see the way your talented tongue slowly slides out and over your bottom lip while you watch me eat during the weekly breakfast meetings. You can't keep your eyes off my mouth. Tell me, are you thinking about how much pleasure it's given you?" Her gaze quickly zeroes in on my mouth as she releases a deep sigh.

"I have severely dry lips. I'm not thinking about you. I'm thinking about Chapstick."

"I bet I can help you get moist." She takes in one extremely deep breath that pushes her hard nipples against the silky material of her shirt and my chest. It takes my eyes a second to decide where they want to land, her lips, her eyes, or down her shirt where I can see the swell of her tits. I swallow hard before continuing. "I see the way you squirm in your chair when I walk by you."

"I have hemorrhoids. The condition runs in my family."

I can't help my laughter as I say, "I love your mouth." Mabry breaks eye contact and focuses on my chest. "What are you thinking about?"

"Nice tie."

"Thanks. Do you recognize it?" Her eyes meet mine. "It's the one I used the night we played Fifty. Remember, I tied you to the headboard and ate ice cream off your body?" I watch as she bites her lower lip slightly and swallows. "You have one more day, Mabry."

"Before what?"

"Before I become relentless." I look into her eyes to make sure she understands what I mean before pushing away and walking out of the room.

I stay completely still until I know he's out of the room. I slowly let out a breath and try to pull myself together. I have been with a few guys. Well, more than a few over the years, but no one has ever affected me like Brad. Everything about him turns me on, his body, his charm, his intellect, and his humor. Since the first time I saw him my body had a chemical reaction to him. I had been attracted to guys before, but what I felt toward Brad was different, deeper.

Obviously, the first thing I noticed was his physical appearance. I remember my first day at the firm. When I walked into the meeting he was in, I felt a charge of electricity even before laying eyes on him. Standing by the window, he was talking to a colleagues before the meeting started. He wore black dress pants, a crisp white button-down shirt, with a sapphire blue tie that matched the color of his piercing eyes. His dirty-blond hair was cut short, but not tailored. It looked as if he ran his hand through it a few times and let the strands land wherever they wanted. That coupled with the always present stubble that ran along his strong chiseled jaw gave him a bit of a bad boy edge even while wearing a suit. His chunky watch and Duke University ring caught the sunlight as he raised his coffee to his full lips. Brad screamed masculinity and sex. Even in his business attire I could tell his body was unbelievable because of the way he moved and the confidence that radiated off of him. The first time I saw him shirtless confirmed my suspicions. There was no part of his body that wasn't cut and toned. It was all a beautiful sight, but my favorite parts were his torso and arms. From the top of his shoulders all the way to his V was perfection. Just thinking about every ripple and indentation got me hot.

When we started working together there was a continuous charge between us. The first time he flirted with me, I nearly melted. The first time he kissed me, I knew I needed more. The first time we had sex was the first time I felt every part of it. With other guys I simply went through the motions. Sex was another way to numb myself from the hurt in my life. It helped a little, but at some point during the act my mind drifted back to the reason why I was lying under the guy. The very first time I was with Brad, I stayed focused on the present, on him, and how incredible he made me feel.

I could feel his intense gaze on me earlier even before I looked up. My body reacts to his presence. Just his voice almost made me come undone. I need to put a stop to things getting more out of hand than they already are. I need distance. I was stupid to have thought I could have something casual with him seeing as how he affects me, mind, body, and soul. There's something between us, a deep connection, as if we were supposed to find each other in this life.

At first, I thought I was safe with him because I had heard how he used women to pass the time away. When he was done he was done, nothing messy. Our relationship was supposed to be only physical, a release, and a distraction. Somehow it has never been just that, though. We go out to dinner, concerts, and movies. I'm not seeing anyone else, nor do I want to, and neither is Brad.

Jesus, are we dating?

My intention was to keep turning him down until he got bored and moved on, but he was relentless with his flirting, his sweetness, and charm. He turned out to be more than I expected. Brad makes me feel special, wanted, and connected to someone. I haven't felt any of those things since before my mom got sick. One day I gave in and kissed him. Since then it's been a constant struggle to keep him at arm's length because I crave him and I'm scared to death I'm starting to need him. But I can't have him.

Self-harming helps me keep my emotions under control. Since Brad and I started being friends with benefits, it's become harder to keep my emotions in check. Only a couple of weeks into our "arrangement" we were ending a meeting with a very attractive middle-aged female client. As we left the conference room I noticed she slipped her hand under his jacket and placed it on his ass. He didn't react at all. He simply stepped away from her reach. The intensity of my anger and jealousy surprised me. I hadn't felt anything that strong in a long time. My first instinct was to grab her and start yanking her bleached blond hair out. Of course, I didn't. I went into the bathroom and plucked as many strands out of my head as needed until I calmed down. I pull my hair when I'm away from home instead of banging my head. It's a quick fix and takes the edge off of my anxiety without drawing attention. I just pop into a restroom or close my office door, and pull as many strands as needed to get numb. I knew I should have ended things with him before now, but I couldn't bring myself to do it.

I walk into my office and grab my cell. I have to do something to show Brad that there is no point in him making an effort with me. He wouldn't give up simply because I ask him to. Besides, deep down I don't think I'm strong enough to keep him at arm's length for very long. I hadn't done a very good job of that before and that's why I'm in this mess. I glance at the time before scrolling through the numbers in my phone. He picks up on the second ring.

"Hey, you just made my day," he says in his deep baritone.

"Hey Ten. I hope I'm not catching you at a bad time."

"Mabry, there's never a bad time when you're involved." Ten is a bit much, but still he's nice enough.

"I know it's late to be asking you this, but I was wondering if you had any plans for tonight?" My voice is a little louder than normal. I glance up at my open door, hoping Brad overhears.

"Um... I did, but I'll change them."

"No, you don't have to do that."

"Mabry, I was just going to hang out with some friends, but I'd much rather spend the night with you." I can hear the smile of self-satisfaction in his voice. He really is kind of a douche.

"Okay, I still have about a half hour left of work to finish, how about you come by the office and we can walk to one of the nearby restaurants."

"Sounds great," he responds.

"Great, I'll notify the security guard you'll be coming. Just come on up to my office when you get here."

"Mabry?"

"Yes?"

"I'm really glad you called," he says in a low voice.

"Me too, Ten. See you in a little while."

I press End and close my eyes, taking in another deep breath. I knew Brad would be here until I left. He's not the type to leave me alone in this big building. I don't want to hurt him, but it's better he gets the message now that we can't have a long-term serious relationship.

Right at 6:30 there is a soft knock on my door. I look up to see Ten standing there in a light blue button-down shirt and khaki pants. He's really a nice looking guy with short black hair and dark eyes, but he's not as tall or as built as Brad. I've never seen Ten without a shirt on, but I can tell his body is nowhere near as sexy as Brad's. Ten doesn't ooze sex the way Brad does.

What's going on with me? I need to stop comparing the two of them. This is about pushing Brad away from me, not about me being attracted to Ten, which I'm not even the slightest bit.

"Hey, right on time," I say, looking up smiling slightly.

"I'd never be late coming to see you, Bright Eyes. Ready?" he asks, as he walks farther into my office.

"Sure." I put my heels back on that I had kicked off under my desk and grab my purse. Passing by Ten I feel his hand touch the small of my back. No shiver or catch in my breath. Absolutely no physical reaction. *Good.*

As we walk toward the elevator I hear a throat clearing. I glance back, knowing it's Brad. We make brief eye contact as I give him a tight smile.

"Mabry, my office, now!" Brad demands, his voice flat.

I nervously look back and forth between Brad and Ten. "Ten, you remember Brad?"

"Sure, how's it going?" Ten walks toward Brad with his hand extended. Brad turns back to his office completely ignoring him.

"We're just heading out to dinner. Can it wait until Monday?" I ask.

"No!" Brad yells over his shoulder.

Ten looks over at me. "Looks like it can't wait."

"I guess not. I'm sorry. I won't be long."

"I'll hold the elevator."

"Thanks," I say.

Brad's in front of his desk, arms across his chest, staring at me. The look on his face is intense. He's pissed. *Good.*

"Shut the door."

"Brad…"

"Shut. The. Fucking. Door." His voice is strained, controlled, and commanding. It makes my pulse speed up and causes shivers to run through my body. I love his commanding tone. I grab on to the chair beside me to steady myself. "Why is Sir Douche here?"

"I told you. We're going to dinner."

"No you're not." He holds me in place with his sapphire blue eyes.

"Excuse me? I'm a grown woman and can go out with whomever I want."

"Why are you doing this? I'm not playing these fucking games with you."

"I'm not playing, either. This doesn't have anything to do with you, Brad. Christ, you think the world revolves around you." I need to end this and get out before I cave. Brad is my weakness. "Have a good weekend. I'm out of here." I turn to leave when his words stop me.

"Don't go. I've never had anyone in my life like you, Mabry. You're mine." His voice is soft and low, causing my heart to skip a beat. I have to be strong.

I let out a deep sigh before turning to face him. My look matches the coldness of my voice. "I'm not yours or anyone's. We're not living in a lame romance novel. You and I were never more than fuck buddies. That was our deal. It's not my fault you went all pussy on me. Now if you'll excuse me, I need to go and get acquainted with my new buddy." I turn abruptly and leave his office as quickly as possible. I can't bear to see the effect my words have on him.

The elevator doors open as I get there. Ten and I both step in. Just before the doors close, I hear a loud crash coming from Brad's office followed by him yelling "Fuck!"

I pull up to my place later that night. The dinner with Ten was pleasant enough, but I felt uneasy the entire time. No matter how hard I tried, I couldn't stop thinking of Brad. Everything Ten said or did had me comparing him to Brad and Ten wasn't winning the game. He offered to follow me back here, saying that he wanted to make sure I got home safe, but I saw the look in his eyes, and he was definitely thinking about more than my safety. He talked for fifteen minutes trying to convince me to let him escort me home. I thanked him and told him I'd be fine on my own.

I close my eyes tight, trying to get the image of Brad out of my head before heading inside. As I approach my place I see him. He's leaning against my door. My breathing stops.

"What are you doing here?" I feel chills run through me.

He pushes off from the door and leans down, bringing his gorgeous face in line with mine. "Don't you ever say we are just fuck buddies again. We are so much more than that and you know it."

Our eyes lock for a few seconds before he simply walks away.

"I know…," I whisper as I watch him get into his car and drive off. *And it scares me to death.*

CHAPTER 4

THE PAST

Brad

"I don't know, guys. That's some crazy shit y'all are talking about doing," Spencer said.

Spencer, Jeremy, and I were sitting around the pool at my house a couple of weeks before we were to start our junior year in high school.

"Why are you being such a pussy, Spencer? We've been betting for years." Jeremy was the main mastermind behind our latest friendly wager.

"I know, but what you're talking about is more than shoving hands up skirts, touching tits, or seeing how far you can get your tongue down a girl's throat." Spencer rubbed the back of his neck and hesitated before he continued. "I mean shit like this is important to girls. I've heard."

"Girls want to lose it just as much as guys do, man," I explained.

I wasn't exactly an expert on girls, but out of the three of us I had gotten the furthest with them. As the guys and I got older, the risk factor of our friendly bets increased. We had already bet on French kissing, touching tits and ass, over as well as under clothes, blowjobs, and finger fucking, so there really wasn't anything left except snatching the V card. At first, I wasn't sure about doing this either. I talked a big game in front of the guys, but the other stuff didn't seem like it was too bad. None of us ever forced a girl to do anything she didn't want to do. Besides, girls used their pussy all the time to get what they wanted from guys, so it wasn't like we would be taking anything from them that they didn't want to give up. I've had girls, who supposedly liked both Jeremy and Spencer, offer me blowjobs if I let them stay at my family's beach house and take them out for a day of sailing. I had seen my mother employ the tactic as well as every female who worked for my father. They were all eager to fuck their way up the ladder and my stupid father fell for it every time. What a dumb douche.

It was senior year and Amanda Kelly was going to be my virgin trophy this semester. I'd noticed her before. She was hot after all, but I never bothered with her. Noah "Mr. Fucking Perfect" Stewart had always been around, so I assumed that they were together. I noticed at the beginning of the school year that she was alone a lot. One day at lunch I felt the chilly breeze between the two of them that got me kind of hot and I decided that the time to strike had finally come. What surprised me was how much I liked her. She was different from the other girls I had done this with. She was smart, funny, and acted like she really wanted to spend time with me without asking for anything in return.

I had put off the issue of sex for as long as I could. We had major make-out sessions, but I always stopped myself before it went further. I knew once we had sex it would be over with her and I wasn't ready for it to be over. But time was running out. Spencer had already lost.

He bet it would take him two weeks to get into Nicki's pants. He was such an idiot. He'd pick these ridiculous time frames that even I couldn't have met. He had been "seeing" her for over two months and still no action. I wasn't sure why he didn't cut her loose, he had already lost the bet. Maybe he felt like he had put so much time into her that it would pay off soon. He wouldn't get the money, but he would get fucked. Jeremy and I were still in the running. He had bagged Beth in a month and a half, two weeks shy of his target. I had to get this done today or I would lose and I hadn't lost one of these bets in a long time. I really wanted Amanda in my life and not just in my bed, but I knew she'd never be mine. Noah made that perfectly clear to me on many occasions. Plus, I saw the look in her eyes whenever he was around and I knew she would never shift it in my direction.

We headed up to my room after mommy dearest showed up abruptly. I wasn't sure of the real reason she came home early. I mean, the pool guy wasn't scheduled to come today. I closed my door and walked up behind Amanda. Wrapping my arms around her waist, I placed a soft kiss on her cheek. God, she smelled great, like raspberries.

"You know what," I said, playfully.

"What?"

"I gotta *girl* in my room."

"Somehow I don't think that is a rare occurrence," she said.

"I've never had a girl in my room, unless you count my mom and Miss Sally, and trust me, neither one of them have seen girl-dom in a long, long time."

She turned around in my arms, facing me. "Who's Miss Sally?"

"The maid. She comes a few times a week, but today is her day off." I gave her a wink.

Narrowing her beautiful teal-colored eyes, she asked suspiciously, "So, I'm really the first girl you've ever had in your room?"

"The one and only."

"Why have I been granted this honor?"

"Because, you're special to me," I said, smiling. It was the truth and now I was getting ready to do something she would never forgive me for.

We had listened to music, I had checked my email several times, and we talked about our plans after graduation. I'd be attending Duke University for my undergrad as well as my law degree, just like dear old dad. I wasn't thrilled about it, but I didn't have much of a choice. Amanda sensed my lack of enthusiasm for my career path. She really looked as if she cared and was sorry I wasn't happy.

Beautiful, don't act like you give a shit about me. I'm not worth it.

I needed to get this over with. The guys would be here soon. I got up from my desk and walked to the dresser to empty my pockets, still stalling.

"So you don't sound like you really want to be a lawyer. What do you want to be?" she asked, nervously. Amanda and I didn't do serious talks. I don't know why she picked today of all days to start one. I didn't need her caring about me. I had to break off this line of questioning.

Spinning around, I held my hands up, palms facing out, and said, "A dancer!"

She did a full-blown belly laugh. "You're crazy."

"Damn straight, Beautiful. Crazy for the dance." I gyrated my hips as I walked toward her. "I got the music in me and it's gotsta get out!"

I grabbed the hem of my shirt and slowly peeled it off, tossing it to the side. She was laughing, but I could see in her eyes that she really liked what she saw.

I continued to gyrate all the way to the foot of the bed. Leaning over, I grabbed her ankles, pulling her down toward me. Crawling up the bed and over her body, I hovered just above her, my hands on either side of her head. I leaned toward her slightly and asked in all seriousness, "Why are you laughing at my dream?"

"I'm not laughing at your dream. It's a very nice dream. I just never pictured you as Lord of the Dance," she said, trying hard not to laugh.

I stared at her for several seconds. She was beautiful, inside and out. She had no idea how much I loved spending time with her. She's the first female, hell the first person in my life who genuinely cared about me. And here I was getting ready to fuck her, literally and figuratively.

She'll never be yours, Brad. Just get it over with. The guys are headed over here.

Shit, Stewart's right. You're a Smurffucker.

"Oh yeah. The sequins, the jazz hands, the tights. It's what I live for," I joked.

"I apologize for mocking your dream."

"I am very hurt and offended. But I can think of twenty-five ways you can make it up to me, Wait, twenty-five and a half ways." I shot her a wink.

I dipped down close to her lips, but didn't kiss her. She got the message and grabbed the back of my neck, lifting her lips to meet mine. I shifted my body, lying down beside her, using my elbow for support.

As our lips connected, she ran her hands over my abs and up my chest, until they found their way into my hair. The feel of her hand touching my bare skin sent shivers through me and caused my dick to strain against my jeans. I moaned into her mouth several times.

The music stopped, replaced by heavy breathing and moans. Time was running out. I had to make my big move. "I really like you, Amanda," I said between kisses.

"I really like you too," she said between moans.

I cupped the side of her face and pulled my lips from hers, sucking on her bottom lip as I broke away. Looking down at her, I whispered, "You're special to me." I hoped she would see the sincerity in my eyes. She was *so* special to me.

I'm sorry I'm a ball-less prick.

"There's more to you than what you let people see," she whispered.

No there isn't. I'm a low-life just like my parents.

"God, I want you so bad," I whispered against her lips.

"You have me. I think of us as close friends."

Chuckling, I said, "You're so damn adorable." I paused for a moment. "I want to be with you."

More than you'll ever know.

I placed light kisses along her jaw, talking in between. "Amanda, you're so beautiful and sweet." My lips headed toward her neck. "...and hot." I moved to below her ear. "I'm going to explode if I don't get inside of you soon." I nipped at her earlobe, and then returned to her lips.

My hand slid down to her tits. Her nipples were standing at attention as my thumb ran over them. She wanted me as much as I wanted her. A part of me wanted her to put a stop to this right now, but she didn't say a word. She didn't resist in any way, so I stayed the course. Slowly, I nibbled across her jaw again. In a low gravelly voice, I said, "Take your shirt and bra off. I need to get my mouth on your gorgeous tits."

She did as she was told. My hand moved to her back, unclasping her bra. I slid the straps down her arms and off. Looking down at her exposed body took my breath away.

"Fuck, you're gorgeous," I panted. Not being able to wait any longer, my mouth descended on one of her nipples.

I moved my hand down, landing on the button of her jeans. I freed the button and slowly pulled the zipper down. I wanted to give her another chance to stop me. Her hand flew to the top of my hand. This was it. This wasn't happening today. I stopped and looked at her, hoping to convey how much I actually cared for her. Just when I thought she was going to pull away, she gave me a slight smile and moved her hand, giving me permission.

I nibbled, sucked, and licked my way down her body. All of a sudden, I felt her tense up. "Maybe we should stop. I mean you're... um... we're not alone," she said, her voice raspy and sexy as hell.

"It's okay. No one will bother us." I felt a shiver run through her body as I licked my way down to her hips.

Sitting between her legs, resting back on my heels, I grabbed the waistband of her jeans and slid them off. I bent down and kissed her inner thigh as my hands slid over the smooth skin of her legs. I nuzzled and kissed between her legs. She was already so wet I didn't need to do anything else to get her ready, but I had to taste her real quick. I slipped her panties to one side and plunged my tongue into her as far as I could.

"Oh god!" she moaned.

Between where my tongue was and her moans I almost came right then. "Does my tongue feel good inside you, Beautiful?"

"Incredible."

My fingers hooked the sides of her panties and I slid them off just before my tongue performed one continuous lick all the way up her body, and into her mouth. I wasn't going to be able to hold off any longer. One, because my dick was so hard it was about to tear through my jeans, and two, the guys were probably already downstairs.

The next several minutes were a blur and before I knew it we were done. All I could think about was how fantastic it felt from the first kiss to being inside her. I've been with a handful of girls and it's never felt like this. I mean, it always felt good, but as soon as it was over I was ready to go. With Amanda I wanted to stay. I looked into her eyes quickly and gave her a slight smile before sliding out of her. I removed the condom, tossing it in the trash, just before a noise came from the hallway.

"You locked the door, didn't you?" Amanda asked.

"I'm pretty sure I did." I threw on my jeans and slipped my shirt on as I walked to the door. I wasn't going to let them come in. They knew she was up here and I'm sure they heard us, so no need to see her for proof. Placing my hand on the doorknob, I turn it with every intention of stepping out into the hall and getting rid of the guys when asshole Jeremy came busting through, pushing me out of the way.

"Shit! I don't believe it. You won again," Jeremy said.

Go along, Brad. Show her what a low-life you are. She'll never be yours. You need her to hate you before you fall any further.

I laughed along with Spencer. The look in her eyes punched me in the stomach. From that point on I didn't know what I was saying. I went on autopilot until I left the room.

I was sitting in the kitchen staring at nothing, trying to get the image of Amanda out of my head while Spencer continuously gave Jeremy a hard time about losing the bet. I caught a glimpse of her when she came downstairs. I knew I could never take back or apologize for what I had just done to her, but I knew I could give her some peace of mind. I walked into the living room as she was gathering her things.

"I don't kiss and tell, so you don't need to worry. Stewart won't find out."

She hugged her backpack to her chest and without turning around, left. I stood frozen and numb. I knew she wasn't mine and never would be, but I could have pretended a little longer, maybe. No, I had to get out now before I fell completely, so I stood there and watched the best thing that had ever been in my life walk out the door.

Mabry

We were at the first big senior party of the year. Sylvie had gone off to hook up with someone and I was sitting here on the sofa with Stephen, watching as he got the bong ready for me to take a hit. He was the biggest pothead at our school. Although it was rare, I did use it on occasion. Today was the fifth anniversary of my mom killing herself. You would think after all this time this day would get easier. I remember after her funeral people kept telling me and my dad, time would heal our hearts. Bullshit. It all seems like just yesterday to me. At night I can still see her lying in her bed, with the odor of rusty metal overwhelming my sense of smell, reminding me of all the blood. So, on occasions such as her anniversary, I do what's needed to forget for just a little while. A tap on my arm brought me back to the present.

"Hey, Mabry, did you hear me?" Stephen asked.

"No. Sorry."

"You've taken hits off a bong before, right?"

"Actually no. I've just smoked joints."

"Well, it's pretty easy. I'll hold it for you. All you have to do is wrap your lips around it and inhale. Try to hold it in your lungs for as long as you can," he instructed.

Facing each other on the sofa, I did as Stephen said. I inhaled deeply and held it for as long as I could stand. I started to feel a slight tingling all over my body and the edginess that my nerves usually had started to subside.

"Wow! You are really good at that. You held it in like a pro, didn't even cough." I smiled lazily at Stephen's compliment.

A half hour later he and I were still sitting in our spots, but had put the pot to one side and were making out. His hands couldn't make up their mind where to go, they were all over me. I was pretty buzzed and sleepy, so I didn't object and let him do what he wanted.

"Mabry you are so fucking hot," he mumbled against my neck. "The way you wrapped those gorgeous lips around that bong… I bet they'd look just as good around my dick. Come on, let's go." He stood pulling me up and leading me to one of the bedrooms toward the back of the house.

Once we got in the room he locked the door and started to unzip his jeans. My head was in such a haze I didn't comprehend what he was up to.

"What are you doing, Stephen?" I asked, confused.

"You're gonna give me a blowjob."

I thought he was joking, so I giggled. "No I'm not."

"Um… yeah you are."

"No, I'm not," I said, defiantly.

"Come on, Mabry, you're no virgin. Besides, you owe me."

"True, I'm not a virgin, but I've never done that… I don't want that in my mouth," I said, pointing at his crotch as I scrunched up my face in disgust. "And exactly what do I owe you for?"

"I gave you a lot of my pot." He was standing against the door with his jeans undone and resting low on his hips. I could see how excited he was already.

"I don't care. I'm not doing it. Now let me go." I took a step toward the door.

"Isn't today the day your mom killed herself and didn't you have something to do with it?" he asked looking straight into my eyes.

"I found her," I whispered, my tone flat.

"I'd be happy to share the rest of my stash to help you get through the night if you do me this one little favor. I don't want to have sex with you. I just want to watch you suck me off. I promise, I won't come in your mouth."

My buzz was quickly fading and five-year-old memories were flooding back in. I just wanted and needed some relief, especially today of all days.

I was sitting on the bathroom floor at Sylvie's. She was already passed out on her bed. Since we knew we'd be out late at the party I was staying the night at her house. Not that it made a difference to my dad what I did. Nowadays, we barely spoke to each other. Basically, we mumbled to each other while passing first thing in the mornings and again at night. That is if we even saw each other. I can't believe what I did just a little over an hour ago. I had given up my V card the summer between my sophomore and junior year, but I had never given a guy a blowjob, and to think I did it because I wanted more of his weed.

God, does that make me a pot whore?

I just needed something to take the ache in my heart away for a little while. I missed my mom and dad so much, there were times when I couldn't bear the loneliness. I had to have something to take the pain away and fill the emptiness.

I started self-harming the day my mom died. I ran out of the house and kept moving until I was so exhausted that I collapsed. I had managed to get to a playground several blocks away from my house. I sat and waited for my dad to come get me and wrap me in his arms, letting me know things would be okay, but he never did. When I got back home and walked into the house, I saw the bloody footprints my sneakers had made still soaked into the carpet. My dad was sitting at the kitchen table looking straight ahead. He didn't make any move to come comfort me. He didn't even ask me where I had been.

He turned his lifeless eyes toward me and said, "She's dead, Mabry. She's not coming back."

I ran to my room, tears streaming down my face, and slammed the door. I leaned back against it and slid to the floor. As I sat there, I wondered why my mom left me and why my dad never found me. They said they loved me. I had so many thoughts and emotions running through me that it was hard to distinguish one from another. My muscles became tense and my breathing got faster and deeper. I felt heat and adrenaline take over my body. My fingernails dug into my palms as I reared back and pounded my head against the door once, twice, and then a third time. I lost count after that. The jolt I got whenever the back of my head connected with the hard surface unleashed the natural endorphins and gave me relief from the emotional pain that was consuming me. There was no physical pain, just a sense of being calm.

I was trying to apply as much force as possible while being as quiet as I could be. I banged my head against the edge of the bathroom counter, trying to calm the rage I felt for what I had done tonight. No one knew I self-harmed, not even Sylvie, and she was my best friend. The great thing about head banging was that you could hide any bruises, lumps, or bumps very easily.

After feeling sufficiently dazed, I stumbled back into Sylvie's room, crawled into the spare bed, and wondered how much longer I could do this before causing permanent damage.

CHAPTER 5

THE PRESENT

Brad

Today is day one of *Operation Relentless*. I've given Mabry a week to de-freak from my "I love you" statement. If she thought I'd be so pissed at her for going out with Sir Douche that I'd move onto someone else, well, then she seriously underestimates me. I will never give up on Mabry. I've always been alone and lonely. I had no idea just how lonely until she came into my life. Even though we agreed to keep things casual, I knew the first time I saw her that there was a connection. Since meeting Mabry, I've feel like a whole person and I sure as shit am not giving that up just because Sir Douche and her went out to dinner. He probably took her to one of those fucking trendy eateries with artisanal crap on the menu. He's such a pretentious, fucking, son-of-a-bitch, cock-sucking, douche bag hipster.

It's early Sunday morning and I'm sitting on the steps outside her place waiting for her to come down for her morning run. I'm making sure my Nikes are tied tight when the front door opens and she steps out. She's wearing hot pink really short shorts, a white sports bra, and pink and white running shoes. Her hair is in a high ponytail, sunglasses, and ear buds in place. She bounces down the steps, focusing on her iPhone without noticing me sitting there. She stops several feet ahead of me and stretches. She does a couple of lunges and then bends over, stretching the backs of her legs.

Fuck me.

I walk up behind her before she straightens up. "Mornin', Sweetness," I say with a huge grin on my face.

When she stands, her back grazes my chest and startles her. The heel of her right foot immediately slams down on my foot just before she whips around and kicks me in the shin.

"Fuck!" I yell, hopping back a few steps.

"Brad?" She removes her ear buds, sounding surprised and confused.

"The one and only." The pain in my leg starts to subside.

"Are you okay?" She's concerned. *Good.*

"I'm fine. It's nice to know you can handle yourself." I pace back and forth a few times, walking off the rest of the pain in my leg before landing directly in front of her.

"What are you doing here?" she asks.

"I'm here for our morning run, unless you'd rather do another activity to get our hearts racing." I wink.

"I thought I made myself pretty clear about this." She points a finger back and forth between us.

"Well, I *know* I made myself crystal clear about this." I mimic her movement with my finger. "Now, I'm here to get a workout. If you don't want to go inside to do it, then get moving."

I remove my sunglasses and Duke Baseball cap, handing them to her while I peel off my gray T-shirt and shove one end of it inside the back pocket of my red basketball shorts. Mabry's chest visibly moves faster and she licks her lips as she stares at my abs and chest. She's a huge fan of my torso. Her hands and lips have spent a lot of quality time in these areas.

Bending down close to her face, I speak in a low voice, "I hope I'll be able to make it through the entire run. Just the thought of your sweet little ass bouncing down the street in those shorts is making me hard." I give her *the smile* and walk away.

Once reaching the sidewalk, I turn and see her still standing in the same spot. "Mabry! Get your head in the game, baby. We got some sweatin' to do," I yell as I walk backward a few steps. Mabry stomps past me and slow jogs to warm up. I come up alongside her and ask, "You want me to stay in front so you can drool over my ripplin' back muscles?" She picks up her pace and moves past me, not saying another word for the rest of the run.

After our run I go home, take a quick shower, throw on a pair of jeans, and my sapphire blue polo. Mabry loves this shirt because it matches my eyes. Once I'm through dressing, I head to brunch at The Sweetwater Café downtown. Mabry meets with a few girlfriends the first Sunday of each month for their book club brunch. Fortunately for me, Melanie who works in our office, and Mabry have become friends and fellow book clubbers. After talking to Melanie one day at the office, I got all the info I needed about today. That's the power of *the smile*.

I walk in the door of the café and immediately spot Mabry at a corner table, with her back to me. She's with three other ladies, one of whom is Melanie. I don't know the other two. As I walk up, the two ladies I don't know visibly straighten and give me flirtatious smiles. They look at each other, their eyes enlarge when they realize I'm heading directly to them.

"Hey Sweetness and ladies," I say, my tone cheery.

Mabry looks up and blinks her long lashes a few times, as if she doesn't quite believe that it's me standing there. "Brad, what are you doing here?"

"You are just full of questions today."

"Hey Brad," Melanie squeaks out.

"Hey Mel." She giggles at my greeting.

Two throats clear simultaneously. "Mabry, aren't you going to introduce your friend?" the blonde asks.

Mabry looks at her friends, then me, then back to her friends before answering. "This is Brad. He works with me and Melanie."

The blonde extends her hand. "Well, look at you. I'm Sylvie." We shake hands.

"Nice to meet you, Sylvie." I give her a quick wink and she giggles.

"And I'm Christine," the redhead chimes in, extending her hand as well, and we shake.

"Nice to meet you, Red." She pulls her hand back, raising her shoulders as she giggles.

I get the distinct impression the ladies have been partaking of the brunch drink special, Mimosas. "Brad, please join us," Sylvie says.

"Oh yeah, Brad, join us," Mel agrees.

"Please sit down, right here." Christine slides the chair out that's between her and Mabry and then pats the seat.

"Brad doesn't want to join us for our book club meeting," Mabry protests. "He'll be bored."

"No I won't."

"No he won't. Besides it'll be great to get a male's perspective," Sylvie states.

"He hasn't even read the book," Mabry counters.

"I've read the book."

"He's read the book. Sit down, Brad," Sylvie orders.

"Waiter! Another round of Mimosas, please. Pronto," Christine announces.

As I take my seat I have four sets of eyes, three smiles, and a scowl aimed in my direction. Our drinks arrive and we place our order. Once the waiter leaves, the discussion turns toward the book.

"So our book this month, *Impossible Perfection* by A. K. Stewart. What did y'all think?" Sylvie begins.

"I loved it although it made me ugly cry from seventy-five percent on," Mel says.

Turning to me, Christine asks, "Brad, do you know what an ugly cry is?"

"Um… when you cry so hard that your face contorts into an ugly mess? Although, I can't imagine any of you ladies even coming close to being unattractive." I flash them *the smile*. Cue the next round of giggles.

"Unbelievable," Mabry mumbles under her breath.

"Oh, don't mind her, Brad, She's been wound up and frustrated all week," Sylvie informs.

A wicked grin involuntarily appears across my face as I look over at Mabry. "Well, maybe I could help unwind you." Three deep sighs in unison come from the other end of the table.

"So, the book… thoughts on the book?" Mabry asks, trying to divert attention away from us.

"The book, yeah. I loved it. Nathan was absolutely perfect. He's right up there with Christian, Caleb, and Kellan as best book boyfriend for me," Sylvie states.

I continue to stare at Mabry and fight the urge to reach over and grab her hand. I haven't touched her in a week and I crave the contact. I halfway hear the ladies chatter on, not paying attention to who says what.

"I wanted to slap that damn Abigail in the face, then punch her in the throat and then shake her."

"I know, right? Why did she keep pushing sweet perfect Nathan away? I swear I screamed several times for her to get her head out of her ass, already. He told her a thousand times he loved her."

"If there hadn't been all the push-pull the book would have been the length of a pamphlet."

"The twist almost had me throwing my Kindle against the wall."

"Oh and Brantley… he was hot as hell even though he turned out to be a Smurffucker. I think there's more to him. I hope the author writes a book about Brantley."

"Brad, what do you think about what Brantley did?" The sound of my name breaks me from my Mabry trance.

"I'm sorry. What?" I look toward the other ladies.

"What did you think about what Brantley did to Abigail?" Christine asks.

"Well, I'm sure he had his reasons. People aren't all bad or all good. I bet Nathan isn't as perfect as he appeared. Brantley probably has deep issues." I turn my focus to Mabry. "Maybe he tried to stay away, but craved her so much that he couldn't think clearly. He needed that connection with her. He felt lost and lonely, and couldn't imagine his life being anything but miserable if she wasn't in it."

There was complete silence at the table. Mabry and I lock eyes for a few seconds before she abruptly scoots her chair back. "Excuse me. I need to go to the ladies room."

"Excuse me too, ladies," I say, following after her.

As I round the corner I see her head into the ladies single restroom. I slip in behind her, closing the door and locking it.

"Brad, this is the ladies room," Mabry says in a low voice.

"I know."

"You're not supposed to be in here."

She walks to the sink and combs her hair with her fingers. She's wearing a gray jersey halter sundress, exposing her soft shoulders. Her favorite color, orange, shoots up from the hem onto the flowing skirt that hits just at her knees. Simple silver hoop earrings and sandals complete her easy sexy look. It's been a week since we had any physical contact. I can't resist any longer, so I move in close, wrap my arms around her waist, and nuzzle her neck. Her body immediately molds to mine, leaning back against my chest. The electrical volt that passes between us is overwhelming. My pulse picks up and I feel Mabry's doing the same.

I let my lips glide up and down her neck. "I've missed you so much, Sweetness."

"Brad, please...," she whispers.

"Please what?" I ask against her neck.

"Stop showing up."

"I was invited to the book club brunch."

"You crashed the brunch and charmed the panties off of everyone sitting at the table."

"Everyone? Does that mean I could move my fingers up your thigh, under your dress, and inside of you without the obstacle of those pesky lace panties you wear?" I inch my fingers up her inner thigh.

"Brad...," she moans breathlessly.

"You could watch yourself in the mirror as I make you come, Mabry. Watching you come is the most beautiful fucking thing I've ever seen." My hand disappears under her dress. "God, I've missed the feel of you."

"I've missed you too," she whispers.

I feel her hips rock slightly against my hand as it continues to travel up her leg. I'm so lost in her body, her scent, and her voice that my emotions just start pouring out of me. "I love you so much, Mabry."

My words snap her out of the moment. I feel her body stiffen and pull away from me. I remain standing in the same spot and watch her in the mirror as she walks across the room and turns to me. "Brad, I'm sorry. I can't do this. I told you from day one there can't be anything serious between us."

"Why? Why can't there be anything serious between us? You owe me a fucking explanation."

"I don't owe you anything. I've been upfront and honest from day one."

I turn to face her. "Bullshit! You've been anything but upfront and honest with me. You want me as much as I want you and I don't mean for just a quick fuck."

"Is your ego so big that you can't accept the fact that somebody doesn't want you?"

"Yeah, I can accept the fact that somebody doesn't want me, but I can't accept the fact that it's you," I say before walking away from her.

Mabry

I spend the rest of my Sunday cleaning my place, doing laundry, and trying to get Brad out of my head. I didn't see him for the rest of the day. I know I keep telling him to stay away, but deep down I don't want him to. I've missed being held in his arms and lying next to him. I've missed his flirting, charm, and that smile he believes gets him anything he wants. Which for the most part it does. I miss the way he makes me feel worth the effort. I've felt lonely in the past, but I've never had this ache inside like I do when he's not around. Both times I saw him today I immediately felt lighter and excited. He is so much fun when he flirts. And when he looks at me with those warm beautiful eyes that hold so much honest emotion and tell me how he feels is when I melt. I almost gave in to him when we were in the restroom. It felt incredible to have his arms around me again. I feel safe in them. I just can't subject him to my life in any real way.

I never knew what brought on my mom's depression. To me she was fine one minute, and the next she was lying in her own blood. She may as well have slit my dad's wrists that day too because he died along with her. I could never do that to someone I love, And I do... I do love Brad. What would I do if he got tired or bored with me, and left? I know he says he loves me, but he's been with a lot of women. Does he even know what being in love is? Would it be too much of a trigger to open myself up and be that vulnerable? It's hard enough now just pushing him away. If we were together and he left me, would I become just like my mom? No, I had to be strong and keep my distance from him. It was the best thing for both of us.

While repeating these thoughts, my anxiety builds along with the desire to bang my head. It's seeping into me and difficult to ignore. I've succumb to it so many times this week. The stress of seeing Brad every day is overwhelming. Knowing how much I need and want him, coupled with the intense anger that I still hold against my parents, had me caving to the relief the physical pain and the numbness give me. I need a distraction. I have to fight the pull of it. The other night was one of the worst times I'd had in a long while. After my date with Ten and seeing Brad at my door I came in and immediately started banging. I don't know the length of time in minutes that I banged my head against the edge of the counter. I never know the length of time in minutes. I measure the time frame in how dazed I feel. I thought once about setting a timer, an alarm, to keep it under some sort of control, but I never have. I scared myself that night. I banged so hard and for so long I think I blacked out for a moment. I remember the last strike and then waking up on the floor of the kitchen, with an intense throbbing in my head.

I've been sitting in front of my computer for the past half hour trying to do research on a case I'm assisting with, hoping to focus my mind on something besides my anxiety. My leg has not stopped bouncing the entire time. It's a struggle to read and comprehend these case studies, when I feel agitated and restless. I stand and pace the floor, hoping to get rid of some of this nervous energy. I walk to the kitchen, grab a bottle of water from the fridge, and head back to my computer. I can't sit. I'm too jittery. My breathing accelerates. I walk around the condo a few more times. I know what would calm me, but I resist the urge. I sit down but then immediately pop back up. My mind wanders back to seeing and feeling Brad earlier. I can still hear his low sexy voice.

I head to my bedroom and decide to change into a pair of pajama pants and a tank top. I run a brush roughly through my hair several times hoping that will be enough of a tug to calm me, but it doesn't work. My hands tremble and beads of sweat accumulate across my forehead. I can't take it any longer.

Maybe just one or two decent hits, and it will take the edge off.

I close my bedroom door and slide down it. I take three deep breaths before I lean my head forward slightly. With my hands by my side, I curl my fingers into my palms, letting the nails cut into my skin. My heels dig into the carpet and all my muscles tense up as I thrust my head and shoulders back against the hard wooden door.

Thud!

My neck snaps forward causing my teeth and jaw to clench. My hair rushes past my cheeks before settling back down on my shoulders. The effects of the first strike flow through my body taking the edge off my anxiety.

Thud!

Numbness sets in.

Thud!

Anxiety is almost completely drained from my body.

Thud!

As I bolt forward I catch my reflection in the full-length mirror across from me. I stare at the figure of the young woman sitting on the floor dazed, eyes glassy, and I don't recognize her. I've never watched myself do this before. I don't know if it just happened like that or I subconsciously stayed away from anything that my image could be reflected in, but this was my first glimpse of what I had been doing for years. Knowing and feeling it is one thing. Seeing it is an entirely different experience. The glassiness in my eyes is replaced by my tears. I watch them take over my face. Disgust replaces the numbness. What am I doing to myself?

The next morning I screech into the parking lot of the firm. I'm never late for anything, especially work. I haven't been able to get the image of myself last night off of my mind. That along with the headache I developed and continuous thoughts of Brad made for a sleepless night. I feel so groggy that I had a hard time getting ready this morning. I grab my suit jacket, briefcase, and purse before jumping out of the car. With my arms weighed down, I struggle with my keys, aiming the key remote at the car several times before it finally locks. I rush across the lobby, into the elevator, and up to the fourth floor where my office is, hoping my absence hasn't been noticed yet. As I step out of the elevator I'm met with sapphire eyes. Brad's at the receptionist desk, talking with Tina. I smile weakly at him.

"Good morning," I say, sounding as cheery as I possibly can.

"Good morning, Mabry," Tina greets.

"Any messages?" I ask.

"The Shackleford meeting has been pushed back to two," Tina answers.

I breathe a sigh of relief. That gives me time to catch up on what I missed this morning and try to get rid of this headache.

As I pass Brad I hear Tina say, "A picnic dinner at Middleton

Place Gardens sounds incredibly romantic."

My pace and breathing increase and I can't seem to get to my office fast enough. I know I told him we can't be together, but hearing those words coming out of Tina's mouth, directed at Brad, makes me feel as if I've been stabbed in the stomach. I knew he would move on someday, I just didn't realize someday would get here this soon. I need to get to my office before the tears start to roll. Once inside, I quickly close the door and toss my briefcase and purse on the chair, before I let the tears out. I'm trying my damnedest to push the anxiety, anger, and hurt down. The intense deep ache I have in my stomach almost has me doubled over in pain. I refuse to self-harm here. I was weak a couple of times and went to the restroom to pull my hair, but that won't take this pain away. Only hitting would and I can't do that here. I'm pacing, taking deep breaths when there is a soft knock on the door.

I'm a mess. No one can see me like this.

I run my hands over my face and through my hair before walking to the built-in bookcase. I grip one of the shelves, clear my throat, and say, "Come in."

I don't need to look to know who it is. My body reacts whenever he's within thirty feet of me.

"Mabry, are you okay?" he asks with concern in his voice.

"Yeah, I'm fine. Is there something you need?"

"I just need to know if you're okay." I feel him walk farther into my office and hear the click of the door as it closes. "You're upset. Did somebody say something hurtful to you?"

"No, not to me. I'm just tired and I have a really bad headache." I turn my head toward my desk, so he doesn't see how red and puffy my eyes are from crying. On my desk I notice a Starbucks Caffe Misto, a box of Krispy Kreme doughnuts, and a small vase with orange Gerber daises. "You did this?"

"Yeah." His voice is soft and low.

"Why?"

"I drove by your place this morning for some reason and saw your car was still there. You're always here before me, so I figured you were running late and wouldn't have time for breakfast."

"Krispy Kremes are my favorite. How did you know?"

"One time when you were at my place I had a box and you sucked down three."

A chuckle escapes me. "That does sound like something I'd do. Thank you."

I feel his approach from behind me. He places a soft kiss at the crown of my head, causing me to wince. It's still tender from last night. "Thank you," he says.

"For what?"

"For letting me take care of you this morning," he whispers before walking out the door.

CHAPTER 6

THE PAST

Brad

Even with all the people crowded into the frat house, I noticed her watching me. We had been eyeing each other off and on all night. I earned my undergrad degree and had just started my second year at Duke University. I was no stranger to the weekend frat parties, or to those who regularly attended them. But I had never seen this girl around before, which wasn't all that unusual. Duke was a huge university loaded with girls, one or two were bound to slip under my radar.

This girl wasn't my usual type. Not that I had a hard and fast set of rules. A pair of tits, an ass, a vagina, and a face that wouldn't make me gag was pretty much all I required. My tastes were not very discriminating. This girl was quirky but cute. Her straight jet black hair that stopped just under her jawline, pale skin, and heavy dark makeup gave her a Goth look. She was dressed in a long black skirt and tank top that hugged her small fragile-looking frame. I wasn't drawn to her in any strong way, but there was something about this girl that caught my attention. She came off as the quiet and shy type. For her to follow me around at a party seemed very bold and out of her comfort zone. You had to admire a person who took a chance.

Leaning against the wall, I took several swigs of beer while I occasionally glanced at Goth girl. Stephanie *what's-her-name* was standing beside me, rattling on about something. We had hooked up a couple of times last semester. Everything out of this girl's mouth sounded like a question, even her moans. It was like fucking Barbara Walters. I mean, she had a talented mouth, just not for speaking. Finally, the ringing in my ears from her blabbering stopped. Apparently, she had left me to find another guy's ear to talk off. Goth girl and I were blatantly staring at each other at this point, so I decided it was time to make my move. Who cares if she wasn't my type, I was more curious than turned on, so what the hell.

Hooking up with girls was a lot like snacking on Cape Cod potato chips. I really liked Cape Cod original potato chips. So much, in fact, that I could eat three large bags of them in one sitting. But, after that third bag, I'm tired of the Cape Cod chips. Maybe now I want to try a bag of spicy nacho Doritos. I don't normally care that much for spicy things, nor have I given them much thought, but the packaging was kind of cool and I might like munching on a different type of chip for a while until I crave the Cape Cods again.

I swallowed the last of my beer, tossing the bottle into the trash can as I made my way toward Goth girl. She visibly straightened, no doubt preparing herself for my approach. I walked up and stood in front of her, confidence and charm radiating off of me.

"Well?" I asked.

"Well what?" she said lifting her eyes to meet mine.

Close up, her large green eyes were mesmerizing. The shade was so dark they looked black. It was only when the light hit them at a certain angle that a flash of green would appear. She had them heavily lined in black and her dark lashes were coated with black mascara. Her skin was so pale, practically translucent, and her lips were painted with blood-red lipstick. Her body was lean, but her face was round, cherub-like. She was Goth, yet classic looking at the same time.

"I thought I'd give you an up close and personal view seeing as how you've been staring at me all night," I said followed by a slight grin.

"I thought you were staring at me." She nervously chuckled, casting her gaze down as if she were embarrassed by her comeback.

"I'm Brad Johnson."

"Hi, I'm Becca Hyams, Art major," she said as if it were her official title.

"Nice to meet you, Becca. I haven't seen you around campus before."

"I just transferred here from South Carolina, the state, not the university."

"Really? I'm from Charleston. Whereabouts in South Carolina are you from?"

"The upstate," she said hesitantly. I didn't push for answers because it really didn't matter to me. I wasn't looking to get to know her that well.

"You don't seem like the frat-party type."

"I'm here with my friend, Stephanie. She was talking to you earlier." She looked past me and around the room. "I'm not sure where she's gone off to and I'm kind of ready to go. I thought I saw her go down the hallway."

"If she went down that hall, then she's busy with someone. That's where the bedrooms are."

"Oh."

"I can take you back to your dorm."

She began to fidget with the hem of her shirt. "I actually just moved here this week, and I'm rooming with Stephanie, but she hasn't given me a key to the place yet."

"I have an apartment not too far from here. You could come home with me. I'm done here anyway."

Glancing up at me nervously, she said, "Um… I don't know you."

"Brad Johnson. You met me like five seconds ago. Wow, you're not very good for my ego. The ladies don't usually forget me that quickly or easily." I flashed her *the smile*. I wasn't sure why I used it on her. It was only reserved for when I *really* wanted something or someone, and in this situation, that didn't exactly apply. There were no ulterior motives asking Becca back to my place. I felt bad for her for some reason. She seemed so innocent and needy, but acted as if she didn't want to be a bother to anyone. I didn't have plans for this girl. I was just playing it by ear.

"Okay, I'll go. Thank you."

The power of the smile never ceased to amaze me.

We walked to my place in relative silence. It was weird but not awkward. It felt weird because I'm used to girls who shut up only when I shove my tongue down their throats. So far, spicy nacho Doritos were a nice change of pace. Once we arrived at my place, I played the good host by asking her if she wanted anything to drink. When she said no, I took her on the grand tour, which lasted all of five minutes. Since she didn't talk much and I still wasn't sure why I had asked her here, I decided it was probably time to call it a night.

"Becca, you can have the bed. I'll sleep on the sofa."

"I don't want to put you out of your room."

"Not a problem. I can sleep almost anywhere. Let me just grab some pajamas and I'll be out of your way," I said, heading into the bedroom.

I wasn't positive, but when I told her I'd stay on the sofa she looked disappointed. Did she want me to make a move on her? Did I *want* to make a move on her? If only I had had a few more beers there'd be no confusion. Even though my standards for screwing a girl were pretty superficial, on rare occasions my dick couldn't make up his mind. When that happened, beer number six was the tipping point. I got undressed and threw on my pajama pants, grabbed a pillow, and headed to my temporary sleeping quarters. Once in the living room I noticed Becca standing in the exact same spot I had left her in.

"Is everything okay?" I asked.

"Yeah, everything's fine."

"Well, goodnight then."

"Yeah, goodnight." She hesitated for a second before heading into the bedroom.

So weird.

My sofa and living room were the only things that were clear. The rest of my mind was fuzzy when I first opened my eyes. I didn't know if what was happening was real or a dream, but either way I was sporting a raging hard on caused by the soft hand stroking my dick. Once my eyes adjusted to the darkness, I was able to make out the silhouette of a small female kneeling on the floor next to me. It took me a second to remember her name. When I did, the confusion was evident in my voice. "Becca?"

"I'm not a virgin, if that's what you're worried about," she whispered.

"What?"

"It's just that other than Stephanie I don't know anyone here. I've been so lonely. I could just give you a hand job and nothing more if you want."

"I need a condom," I said.

"I'm on birth control."

"I still need a condom." There was no way I was going commando in a girl.

I've been involved in some weird kinky sex before. Not that being woken up by a female's hand on me was weird or kinky. It was the fact that this girl seemed scared of her own shadow, so her sudden boldness took me off guard. But I have never wasted a willing chick or a hard dick in my life, and I certainly wasn't about to start now. I grabbed her wrist, stopping her hand from moving further. I slid my hand under the sofa cushion, feeling around for a condom. I like to have them scattered around the place. You never know when the mood will strike. I found one and quickly rolled it on and then pulled her on top of me. As she straddled me, I lifted my hips slightly so she could slide my pants down. She had already taken her panties off, but still wore her black tank top. She lowered herself onto me and we began to move. We didn't kiss, we didn't speak, or touch anywhere else. We didn't even look at each other, we simply fucked in the purest sense of the word.

The next morning I woke up exhausted. It wasn't that Becca and I had screwed our brains out all night. We did it only one time, but it was the longest fucking fuck I'd ever had. She took forever to come undone. Every time I thought she was almost there, she'd fake me out. I've made girls come right on the spot with only a wink and a flash of *the smile*. Finishing off Becca had become more of a challenge than anything else. There was no way I would let a quiet, pasty, little semi-Goth girl get the best of me. Finally, I conquered the challenge and she had an orgasm, but my stamina was shot in the process.

I opened one eye, looking over to the other side of the bed. It was empty. This girl didn't talk much, she was willing to just satisfy me, and she left before I woke up. She just might be my dream girl. Just then I heard a noise coming from the other room.

So much for the dream.

I threw on a pair of jeans and grabbed a T-shirt, pulling it over my head as I walked out of the bedroom. I found Becca in the kitchen cooking.

"Good morning. I hope you don't mind, but I made some breakfast," she said with a slight nervousness in her voice.

"No, I don't mind. Is there coffee?" I asked in a gravelly voice.

"Oh, sure." She grabbed a mug and poured me a cup as I pulled a stool out from the bar and sat. Handing me the mug and a plate of food, she said, "I made French toast. I hope you like it."

"I had French toast?" I was astonished there was anything edible in my kitchen.

"Well, you had bread, eggs, and milk. That's basically French toast."

"The fuck you say?" I muttered, shoveling in the mouthwatering food.

She giggled. "You're funny." She stood on the other side of the bar gazing at the top of the counter.

"Aren't you going to eat?"

Glancing up, she said, "I already did."

"Oh. Good."

Ah, the awkward silence of the morning-after screw.

"This tastes really awesome. Thanks," I finally said, hoping it would kick start enough of a conversation to get me through breakfast.

"Oh you're welcome. I like to cook."

"Yeah?" She raised her head, but wouldn't make eye contact with me.

"Yeah. Um… I don't get to cook very often. My last roommate ate out a lot and Stephanie drinks most of her meals." I chuckled causing a slight smile to appear across her face. A couple of minutes of silence fell between us again.

I glanced around the room as I continued to eat. Something was different. "Did you clean up?"

"A little. I got up early and things were a little messy. I hope you don't mind."

"No, I don't mind. Thanks. If you're really feeling sassy I have a couple of bags of laundry that need to get done." The teasing was obvious in my voice, at least to me.

"I'll do your laundry."

"Becca, I was just joking."

"Well, I'll do it for you," she said, giving me a shy smile.

We sat in silence for the rest of the breakfast. After Becca loaded the dishwasher and cleaned the kitchen, I took her home thinking that I wouldn't see much of her after today. Little did I know she would soon become a semi-permanent fixture at my place.

Mabry

Closing my eyes, I concentrated on the way his tongue felt swirling around my stomach and then into my navel. I wanted to be turned on. I wanted it to feel sexy, but it just felt cold and wet, like a dog's nose on my stomach. Pushing those thoughts aside, I imagined that the tongue moving up my bare skin belonged to Chace Crawford. Yeah, scruffy Chace was really nice. The hard surface of the table was uncomfortable, causing me to squirm slightly. *The Tongue* must have mistook this as a response to its abilities because it started to speed up toward my chest. It pulled away briefly when it reached my bra. Immediately, it landed on the top of my breasts, licking off the sugar, right before the lemon was plucked from my mouth and replaced by a pair of cold wet lips. Letting a guy do lemon-drop body shots off of you wasn't exactly the best activity for a second year law student at Wake Forrest to take part in. Shit like this comes back to haunt you, especially if you plan on climbing the professional ladder and run for office someday. But it had been a long and stressful semester and this was a better de-stressor than banging my head.

As the sound of the chanting college crowd flooded back into my ears, a low husky voice said, "Come on, baby. Let's go somewhere alone."

"Okay," I slurred.

Grabbing my hand, he slid me off of the table and dragged me down the hall until we reached a bedroom. In one chaotic moment, clothes started flying off and around the room. He backed me over to the bed and we fell on top of it. He licked my neck while squeezing one of my breasts. Finesse was definitely not in this dude's repertoire. I felt the tip of him brush up against my inner thigh.

Shoving him away slightly, I glanced down, and said, "Hey buddy, you need to cover that up, otherwise it's not gaining access anywhere."

"Oh yeah. Sorry. I'll be right back." I rolled over on my side, facing in the opposite direction as he climbed off of me.

I had been pretty drunk. Either I passed out or had fallen asleep, because the next thing I knew, I woke up to the feel of a dick sliding into me, and the sound of a husky voice breaking through the darkness, urging me to wake up. Once my eyes adjusted to the lack of light I was able to make out the silhouette of a large muscular frame hovering over me. I lifted my hips slightly giving him permission to continue. As he moved and grunted on top of me, numbness invaded my body. The sensation of physical contact was fading for me.

When I first started having sex, the natural response of my body helped distract me from my world for just a bit. I figured it was less harmful than banging my head. I've never had a boyfriend. The guys I've been with are for the most part random. I knew their names, but over the years even that knowledge had become less important to me. This shadow looming above had me feeling nothing but fear. Was this how it got for my mom? Did she slowly start to lose all physical and mental pleasure sensations until she became completely numb to everything except the pain?

Ever since I was a little girl I had been told I was exactly like my mom. I had her azure blue eyes, chestnut brown hair, bright smile, and bubbly personality. I always loved when people said those things because I wanted to be just like her in every way, but now the thought terrified me. My mom disappeared and was replaced by a shell. Her eyes and hair were the same, but the smile and personality weren't a part of her anymore. I often wondered if she cut her wrists with the hope of feeling something, anything, before she died.

My body jostled three times before a heavy body collapsed on top and snored.

The bright sunlight streaming through the window forced me awake early the next morning. I eased out of bed, gathered my clothes, and dressed. I was hooking the last clasp on my bra when I heard a groggy cough and the clearing of a throat coming from underneath the sheets.

"Hey, where you going?" he asked.

Glancing over my shoulder I answered, "Home. Do you know where my shirt is?"

"You're hot as fuck." I had no idea how hot *fuck* was exactly, but if last night was any indication, neither did this dude.

"And my shoes… where are my shoes?"

"Don't go. Come back to bed."

"Can't." I scanned the room one more time, but didn't see my shirt or shoes. A vague memory started to come back that I took them both off before the body shots started, so they must be in the kitchen. I ran my fingers through my hair a few times before opening the bedroom door.

"I don't even know your name," he grumbled.

"I don't know yours either, so we're even."

"Will I see you again?"

"It's highly doubtful. Have a nice life." I stepped into the hallway, closing the door behind me.

Standing in my bare feet, rumpled skirt, and hot pink lace bra, I took in a deep breath, rounded my shoulders, held my chin high, and plastered a neutral expression on my face. It's the walk of shame only when you look like you're ashamed. I was a pro at disguising my feelings, so with steely, unapologetic determination, I started toward the kitchen in search of the rest of my outfit.

CHAPTER 7

THE PRESENT

Brad

I needed to change my plan of action. Telling Mabry how much I love her freaks her out too much. It always ends up with her pushing me away. So instead of telling her, I decided the best thing to do was to show her how much I love her. After getting her breakfast on Monday, I eased off a little. She was still upset that morning probably because of what happened between us at brunch. I didn't want to scare her off. Besides, actions speak louder than words.

On Tuesday, I had a large arrangement of tiger lilies delivered to her office. She found a pair of fluffy slippers waiting under her desk on Wednesday. Mabry always kicked off her heels when she was working at her desk and her feet got cold. Thursday, I left a picture on her desk that I had framed. It was of us at the Music Farm a month ago. We had gone to see the local band Marytre in concert. And then, on Friday, I left a box of Godiva chocolates with a handwritten note.

Mabry,

I know I agreed to keep this thing between us casual, but things have changed. I won't apologize for that. You're in my heart and soul now. I know you're scared, so am I. But we can do this together. We're not alone anymore. Now we have each other. I don't know what the future holds. All I know is that I need you in mine. I want to take care of you. I want to cheer you on. I want to protect you and catch you if you fall. I'll be the best man you've ever had in your life, if you'll just take a chance on me. I promise to be careful with your heart.

I love you,

Brad

It's a gray and rainy Saturday. The weather had already ruined plan A. As I put plan B together in my head, I step out of the shower, grab a towel, and walk into my bedroom. I hear Christy in the kitchen fixing breakfast. I dry off and throw on a pair of dark gray basketball shorts. I'm towel drying my hair as I walk into the living room.

"Hey, I need coffee STAT." I give my hair one more good scrub with the towel and then drape it around my shoulders. Looking up, my breath stops. Christy stands in the doorway of the kitchen, wearing boxers and a flimsy tank top, with no bra, and her blond hair gathered up into a high ponytail. But she's not the reason my lungs stop pumping oxygen. Mabry stands right next to her. The hurt in her eyes is the worst thing I've ever seen. My heart and stomach plummet. Her eyes fill with water and her bottom lip quivers. To anyone else, it would appear she's fine, but I know every nuance of her body and its reactions. She and I stand frozen, staring at each other.

"Um… look, Brad, we have company for breakfast," Christy says.

Not taking my eyes off Mabry I say, "Christy, this is Mabry. Mabry this is Christy."

"Yeah, we've done the intros, already," Christy informs.

Mabry doesn't say a word, she doesn't blink, and she doesn't take her eyes off of me. "Mabry, what are you doing here?" I ask.

The tears spill from her eyes and run slowly down her cheeks. "I don't know," she whispers.

"Look, why don't I just take my breakfast and head back to my place." Christy collects her plate and crosses the room.

"It's fine, you stay. I'm leaving," Mabry says as she rushes past me and out the door.

I look at Christy. "Go!" she commands.

I rush out the door, stopping long enough to step into my running shoes that I left on the front porch. By the time I make it down the steps to the driveway, Mabry is already at her car that's parked across the street. She struggles with her keys and umbrella. She keeps pointing the key remote at the car door, but nothing happens. Its battery must be dead. She spots me as I approach, throws her keys at the car, drops her umbrella, and takes off running. Snatching up her keys, I head after her. I'm in really good shape, working out every day, but shit, my girl is fast. I finally get close enough to be able to reach out and grab her arm. She whips around, swinging her other arm toward the side of my face. I grab it just before it makes contact and hold both arms behind her back. I look down into her eyes. The hurt is more intense and now mixed with anger.

She struggles to free herself. Grinding her teeth together, she says in a low voice, "Get your fucking hands off of me, Brad." Both of us breathe hard and fast.

"I will. But first you have to promise that you won't run."

"I'm not promising you shit."

"That wasn't what it looked like."

"How original. What's next? You were drunk? She's just a good friend? Or do I get the classic, it didn't mean anything? I shouldn't be surprised. I've had enough people warn me about you. This was a mistake."

"What?" My jaw clenches tight as all the muscles in my neck and shoulders tense.

"Coming here."

I release the grip I have on her wrists. Letting them drop, I then take one step back. I know exactly what she's referring to. People have told her I'm a player, that I lie and cheat my way through life and use women. I used to be like that, but I'm not anymore. I've worked hard to make amends for the pain I've caused and move past the mistakes I've made. I wish others would stop trying to pigeonhole me to the past.

Even with the drops of rain falling harder and continually sliding down her beautiful face, I can tell the tears haven't stopped. If anything, they've increased.

"We're not having this conversation out here. Let's go back to my place so we can talk." My tone is stern.

She takes one step toward me, places her hands on either side of my bare chest, shoving at it with all her strength. "I'm not going anywhere with you."

Since Mabry is stubborn as hell, my options are limited. Moving quickly, I dip down, scoop her up, and toss her over my shoulder. Holding her legs in place with my arm, I head back home.

Grabbing on to the waistband of my shorts, Mabry lifts herself up slightly. "Put me down, Brad!"

"No!"

"If you don't put me down right this second, I'm going to shove your pants down."

"Go ahead, Sweetness. It won't be the first time I've walked these streets naked." I continue my steady and purposeful stride back to my place.

Suddenly, I feel something sharp pierce my skin. "Ouch! Did you just bite my ass?"

"Put me down!"

"I'll put you down once we get to my place." I feel another sharp pain. "Ouch!"

"Ouch!" Mabry shouts.

"You bite my ass, I pinch yours."

We play this little game of bite n' pinch a couple of more times before she finally surrenders, letting me carry her home without any more resistance.

Mabry

If I'm to be honest with myself, the wall that I spent years building around me started to crack little by little the very first day I met Brad. I was somehow able to push him away to a certain degree, throw some spackle over the crack, and get through my day. But it didn't take much for the crack to reappear, each time weakening my wall until finally it came crashing down this week.

After Brad and I talked in my office on Monday, I saw him only in passing for the rest of the day. He didn't flirt with me, he didn't try to corner me to talk, he didn't call or text, and he didn't tell me he loved me. The breakfast told me he wanted to be friends. The lack of contact told me he was moving on. I felt empty, but I knew it was best for both of us. On Tuesday, a beautiful arrangement of tiger lilies was delivered to my office. At first, I assumed they were sent by Brad, but there was no note. I knew he was in court all day. I thought I'd at least see him before heading home, but I didn't. That night I must have picked up my phone a hundred times to call or text him, but I didn't. I just sat in my condo and missed him.

When I got to my office on Wednesday, I tossed my purse on the sofa, grabbed the files from my bag that I had been working on all night, and sat down at my desk. As usual, I kicked my heels off. Suddenly, I felt a tickling sensation run across my toes. In one quick movement I shoved away from my desk, jumped out of my chair, made a beeline to the other side of the room, and hopped on to the sofa. I paced back and forth as my imagination ran wild with what type of creature was living under my desk. I knew only one person I could call. I took my phone from my purse, sat on the back of the sofa, and sent the text.

Me: Could you please come to my office ASAP.

In less than three minutes there was a soft knock on my door as it opened. The scent of cinnamon drifted in as gorgeous and concerned eyes met my panicked expression. My anxiety calmed for a moment as I soaked in his figure. He had on a pair of charcoal gray pants, a crisp white button-down shirt, a red and gray silk tie, and polished black dress shoes. Silver cufflinks cinched his sleeves at the wrist, and his class ring from Duke and chunky watch completed the sharp look. He was a conservative lawyer, until you reached the ever present light stubble along his chiseled jawline, his finger-combed hairstyle, and piercing sapphire eyes, then you saw the sexy bad boy. Every part of my body throbbed as I thought about what the sexy bad boy had done to me when he was out of those clothes.

"Mabry, what's wrong?" he asked as he closed the door.

The sound of his deep voice brought me back to the current dilemma. "There's something big and furry under my desk. Would you go take a look, please?" I whispered.

I wasn't positive, but I thought I saw a slight smirk cross Brad's face. I reached over and picked up one of the large law books from the shelf and held it out to him.

"What the hell am I supposed to do with that? Read to it?" he asked.

"I didn't want you to approach it unarmed. It's huge."

He took the book from me. There was a moment of hesitation before he walked to my desk. With each step he took, my breathing picked up speed and my palms felt clammy. He slowly rounded the desk and crouched down to get a better look underneath, placing one hand at the edge to support himself.

"It's hard to see anything under here. It's pretty dark." He leaned forward slightly. "I don't see anything, Mabry."

"Are you sure? It was over in the right corner."

"Wait a second, what's this? SHIT!" he yelled.

Suddenly, Brad's head completely disappeared as his hand slid off the top of the desk and out of sight.

"Oh my god, Brad!" I stood on the sofa, leaning forward, trying to peer over my desk to see if I could spot him.

He jumped up, scaring the hell out of me. My eyes automatically closed, causing me to stumble back, and land sitting on the back of the sofa.

Loud laughter cut through the sound of my rapidly beating heart. When I opened my eyes Brad was leaning back on my desk clutching his stomach. "Holy hell, Sweetness, that was priceless."

"Stop laughing at me. What was under my desk?" I demanded.

"Are you sure you can handle it?" he asked, sarcastically.

I narrowed my eyes at him. He returned my look with a sexy grin as he reached behind his back. "Here's the dark menace from under the desk." In his hands he had a pair of fluffy blue slippers.

"Slippers? Those aren't mine. Why are they under my desk?"

He walked toward me and knelt down. "They are yours. I got them, so your feet won't get cold while you're working." He ran one hand up and down the back of my leg, lifting it slightly, and then placed the slipper on my foot. I shuddered when the tips of his fingers made contact with my skin. He repeated the same action on the other leg. "Man, I'm really glad you wore a skirt today," he said under his breath as he stared at my bare leg.

"Me too," I whispered, breathlessly.

He lifted his gaze to meet mine. His eyes were full of so much warmth, caring, and desire. I wanted him to join me on the sofa, so I could crawl into his lap and feel safe. "What'd you say?" he asked. Hope flashed across his face.

Clearing my throat, I answered, "Thank you. I said, thank you."

"You're welcome. I better be getting back to my office now." We gave each other a slight smile before he left.

The next day, I found a framed picture of the two of us at the Marytre concert. As I stared at it, I realized Brad wasn't just giving me gifts. He was showing me how much he loved me and wanted to take care of me. No one has wanted to do that for such a long time. The note I received on Friday completely melted my heart. I needed and wanted to be with him. The empty and lonely feeling I experience when I'm not with him is suffocating and unbearable. I decided to do what he asked and take a chance on him, on us. I'm scared, but being with him makes me feel loved, protected, and connected. I haven't felt any of those things since my mom died and I crave them. I crave him.

When I got to Brad's this morning the door was slightly open, so I went on in. The sound and smell of breakfast cooking floated through the condo. I walked to the kitchen and I felt my entire world crash down on top of me. I never noticed anything between Brad and Tina other than the usual business-type interaction. There were no flirtatious smiles or looks, so I was convinced I had misheard what she said to him the other day at the office. But there was no denying that I saw a barely dressed blonde making him breakfast as he walked out of his bedroom half naked.

As I stared at him, pain and anger took over my body. I suddenly became consumed with the need to self-harm. Beads of sweat collected across my forehead as the pace of my breathing increased. My fingers twitched. I wanted desperately to grab handfuls of hair and rip the strands out. I needed the quick fix until I was able to get home. Somehow I managed to get my legs to move and I left as quickly as I could.

Mabry, you're such an idiot. People warned you. This was just a sick game to him. Something for him to pass the time away.

After two more pinches, I give up the struggle until we reach Brad's door. He opens it, takes a step through, and I immediately latch on to the doorframe stopping him in his tracks.

"Goddammit, Mabry. Let go." His voice strains while he tries to pry my grip free by moving forward.

"There is no way in hell that I'm going back in there with her."

"She's not here. She went home. Would you just let me explain?"

"You don't owe me an explanation. We're just fuck buddies, and apparently, I'm not enough of one for you."

With one hard jerk, my fingers break free from the doorframe and I go flying through the condo and into the kitchen, where he lands me on the countertop. Placing his hands firmly on either side of my hips, he cages me in. Sapphire eyes bore into mine. Beads of water trickle down our faces and bodies, making a puddle on the floor. We stare at each other for several seconds while we catch our breath. I haven't been this close to him in a week. He looks incredibly sexy wet. The scent of cinnamon and fresh rain drifts between us. His smell is intoxicating. I'm hurt and pissed, but the pull toward him is too strong.

How am I going to get past this?

"I've missed you," he says.

"Yeah, you looked pretty lonely with your naked blonde." My voice is flat.

"She wasn't naked and she isn't *my* blonde."

Holding his gaze, I say, "You got balls, I'll give you that. You get caught with the blonde and oh, let's not forget your romantic date with Tina. Why did you do this to me?"

I pound on his chest. He doesn't budge. I pound on it harder as my sobs become uncontrollable. He grabs my wrists and pins them to my thighs.

"I was asking Tina if she thought a picnic dinner at the fucking gardens would be romantic enough. Christy is my neighbor, my *lesbian* neighbor. She was helping me figure out a plan B."

"Plan B?"

"I was going to pick you up later this afternoon and take you to Middleton Place Gardens for a candlelight picnic dinner. But since it's pouring down rain, that's not going to be possible."

I let what he just said sink in without responding.

"Do you honestly think I would tell you I love you and then fuck another woman?" His voice breaks and the pain in his eyes is crushing.

"You've been with a lot of women. I'm sure you've told some you loved them."

"I've never said those words to anyone. I've never even thought I loved anyone until you showed up."

His eyes are full of sincerity and pleading.

"I want to love you so bad," I say.

"Then love me," he whispers.

"I'm scared. There are things about me…"

"You weren't a dude at some point, were you?"

"No," I say, laughing.

"Look, the stuff people have said about me is true, but I'm not that guy anymore. If you let me into your heart, I'll spend the rest of my life proving it to you."

The electricity between us causes my body to vibrate. I close my eyes and replay his words in my head. When I open them I'm met with the warmest and most loving look I have ever seen.

Taking in a deep breath, I say, "I do love you."

His eyes look as if they double in size and then fill with tears. "Thank you. You won't be sorry," he says, choking on the words.

He places quick kisses on my forehead, moving down my temple, to my cheek. He pulls back slightly, and then brings his hands up to my face. There is a look of awe in his expression as he gazes at my lips. Leaning in, he nibbles across my bottom lip, taking his time. Gently, he sucks it into his mouth as his thumb glides over my cheek, causing my eyes to close and my lips to part. His tongue slides into my mouth, stroking mine slowly. Brad's kisses are all-consuming. His focus is so intense, as if there is nothing more important in the world to him than kissing me. Raising my hands I find his hair and tangle my fingers through it. I open my legs more and he instinctively moves between them, deepening our kiss. His arms wrap around me as my legs wrap around him. We cling to each other like two lost souls who have just found their salvation.

Brad breaks the kiss and rests his forehead against mine. "I love you so much, Mabry."

"I love you, Brad."

He picks me up and carries me through the bedroom and into the bathroom. Our eyes stay connected the entire time.

"You're shivering. I need to get you out of these wet clothes and into a hot shower," he says against my lips.

"What a coincidence. I need to get you out of *these* wet clothes and into a hot shower." I toss him a wink and a flirty smile.

I unwrap my legs and slide down his body. Brad turns the water on. As steam fills the room, we remove each other's clothes, tossing them into a pile on the floor. He follows me into the shower, wraps his arms around my waist, and pulls me back against his hard chest. His lips find their way to my neck. Melting into his body, I let him and the hot water warm me. His hands move up to cup my breasts and he massages them. Between touching, kissing, and being pressed against him, I'm having a hard time standing. I turn around in his arms and look up at him. I slowly let my tongue come out and glide across one of his nipples. He takes in a deep breath. My hand runs over each ripple of his abdomen, down his V, until I reach his hard dick. Folding my fingers around it, I slide my hand up and down. Suddenly, I feel Brad's hand on top of mine, halting my movement.

"Sweetness, we're not doing that right now," he says, his voice ragged from being aroused.

"We're not?" I whisper with disappointment, as I look down.

Brad places his index finger under my chin, tilting my head up, and says, "You just told me you love me. We're not going to have a quick fuck against a tile wall after that. I need you in my bed, so I can take my time and make love to you slow and easy."

"Oh my."

⁂

Several hours later, I'm lying naked on my stomach in Brad's bed. We've spent most of the day making love. I feel so relaxed and light, as if I'm floating above the mattress. I have never had so much sex in one day. I never wanted to until I met Brad. His lips glide down my back, placing a path of feather light kisses as they move. There's so much reverence in his movements. He's not just touching my skin. He's touching my soul. I've never felt cherished like this before. He lingers for a moment on the dimple at my lower back.

"I love every curve of your body," he says against me.

I feel the tip of his tongue slide across my skin and dip into the dimple. "Heyyy!" I say, laughing, as I turn over.

Brad's hand grabs my hip, stopping my movement. "Stay put. I'm not done worshiping your ass yet."

"But you're tickling me."

"I'm going to be spanking you, if you don't stay still."

"I think I'd like that." I wiggle my ass a little.

Brad lets out a loud growl. Vibrations run through my body and I feel the weight of his head as he plants his face on my lower back.

"Are you okay?" I ask.

"Yeah, just give me a minute. My head is swimming with visions of you being a very bad girl."

"I'm very good at being very bad, you know," I say in a low deep voice.

"This is so much better than a picnic," he says before resuming his trail of kisses.

"Mmmhmm," I purr.

Shifting to the other side, he moves up my body, his lips landing at the spot just below my ear.

"Turn over," he whispers into my ear. His warm breath flows over my neck as his hand slides up my back, causing wave after wave of shivers to run through me.

I flip over onto my back, looking up into his beautiful eyes. Raising my hand to his jaw, I run my fingers over his stubble. Holding my gaze, I feel his hand travel across my stomach and run up my torso. He brings his face to mine, placing the same feather-light kiss on my lips. I playfully nip at his upper lip before he slides his tongue in, meeting mine. Pulling back, he studies my face for several seconds.

"Why is there so much sadness in your eyes?"

His question catches me off guard. "Wow, you're not one for easing into a conversation, are you?"

"Subtlety has never been one of my strong suits."

"I'm not sure what you're talking about. I'm happy. You make me happy."

"You don't have to answer me right now, but you will answer me soon. I need to know, so I can fix it."

"I love you," I say, in part because of his patience with me, but also to try to change the subject. I know I'll need to tell Brad about my past soon. I'm scared of his reaction. I have no way of knowing if even the possibility of inheriting my mother's illness will send him running or not.

He picks up my hand, kissing the tips of my fingers, and says, "Every time you say that, it takes my breath away."

We shift our position, so that we're lying on our sides, face-to-face. "What were you like as a kid?" I ask.

"I was a handsome, charming, and intelligent young lad. Pretty much a mini-version of what you see before you now." His trademark smile appears across his face.

"You forgot modest and humble." My voice full of sarcasm.

"Yeah, that too." His smile fades and his expression turns vulnerable. "And lonely."

"Lonely? How could Mr. Charming ever be lonely?"

"I had friends I hung out with, but you know how kids are. A lot of times they want to be your friend because of your pool, the family beach house, or boat. It's hard to tell sometimes who likes you and who's in it for the stuff."

"You had your brother and both your parents."

"Yeah, Peyton and I have never been very close and you've met B and B."

"B and B?" I ask in confusion.

"My parents, The Bastard and The Bitch."

I don't laugh because even though the tone of his voice is light I can see the sadness in his eyes. "So, I take it you're not close to them either."

"It's hard to be close to people who never wanted you in the first place."

I cup the side of his face. "I'm sure that's not true."

"Well, when you overhear your parents reminiscing about driving to the clinic and how it was a mistake not to have gone through with it. Well, it paints a crystal clear picture that they didn't want me."

Tears sting my eyes and all the breath leaves my lungs. I've been around his parents enough to know they were frauds. They both put on a good act for clients, but I had experienced firsthand how cold his mother can be and what a lecherous fake his father is. Mrs. Johnson conducted my interview. She was professional in her questions, but had a condescending expression on her face the entire time. I was actually surprised to have gotten the job. On my first day, I arrived early to get settled into my office. I hadn't met Mr. Johnson at that point. He came into my office to welcome me to the firm. We shook hands, he held mine a little too long as his eyes roamed up and down my body. My creep radar went on high alert and I knew then I had to keep my distance from him.

I place a soft kiss on Brad's lips. "I feel sorry for them."

"Why?"

"Because they've missed out on knowing an amazing man."

Wrapping my arms around his neck, I pull him into my chest. As he nuzzles into me, I run my fingers through his soft hair. We stay like this, holding each other tight, and drift off to sleep.

CHAPTER 8

THE PAST

Brad

"Were you just smelling my dirty clothes?" I asked.

Becca startled and quickly dropped the pair of my jeans she had her face buried in. "I was just checking to see if they needed to be washed. I found them crumpled up on the floor in your bedroom."

"Well, let me give you a piece of advice. If they're on the floor, then chances are they need to be washed." She looked up at me with the most pitiful expression on her face, like a child who had just been reprimanded. "Look, Becca, I have a class I need to get to."

"Is it okay if I stay and do your laundry? I also thought I'd cook dinner. That is if it's okay with you."

"You know I don't expect you to always do my laundry or cook for me." I didn't expect it, but I had to admit, that part of this "relationship" was pretty good. It was almost like having Miss Sally around except I never had sex with Miss Sally. Although, hers were the first set of tits I ever noticed.

"I like doing things for you, Brad. It makes me feel useful and wanted."

"Well, as long as you enjoy it." I turned to leave.

"When will you be home?" she asked.

"Um… I'm not sure. I might go hang out with Jason for a while."

"Well, I'll be here waiting for you." There was a weird tone in her voice. I stared at her for a few seconds, trying to see if I could spot the crazy in her eyes.

Things with Becca and I were different than anything I had ever experienced. We had been doing this for a little over a month, but it was as if we had just met. I didn't know any more about her now than I did that night we met. And to be honest, I didn't want to. I didn't call her or ask her to come over. We didn't go out together on dates. I never looked for her around campus. She just showed up at places. I went to parties and hooked up with other girls, but never felt as if I was cheating on Becca. You can't cheat on a relationship that doesn't exist. I figured she would get tired of being basically my maid and disappear soon enough, but that never happened. Something was going to have to change and soon because I felt a shift in her feelings toward me.

I was making a mental note of all the things I needed to get done this week. I had to stop by Jason's place and get the notes from Ethics class and then go get my car washed. I was supposed to meet Mom in thirty minutes for dinner. She was in town for business and must have been feeling guilty about something. When she thinks she's not being a good mother, which is rare, she buys me some expensive item or meal. She'll ask a few inane questions, that I'll mindlessly answer, and then we will stare at each other for the next hour. This charade seems to soothe her guilt and at least I get a good meal out of it.

"Faster, Brad! I need it faster!" she moaned.

I was going as fast as I could. I wasn't a fucking hummingbird. She was the one who needed to hurry up. I liked Becca, okay, but she took forever to come. When we first started fucking, it was a challenge. I tried to beat my best time, but now I was over it, and ready to move on. For the past week and a half I'd been dropping hints that things were coming to an end, but she didn't seem to be picking up on any of them. It wasn't that I didn't like having her around. She ran a lot of errands for me and did my laundry every week, which really freed up my time. But I could feel she was getting too attached and thinking we were something more than we were. So this was it. One last goodbye fuck and I was out of her and here. That is, if she'd finish up already.

"I'm almost there," she yelled out.

"Becca, I have to meet my mom for dinner in like thirty minutes," I grunted.

I thrust into her hard one more time causing her to finally come unglued.

"Ooooh, Brad! I love you!" she screamed.

Shit, this was going to be awkward.

I started to climb off when her arms wrapped around my neck, stopping me.

"Don't move yet. Stay inside of me for a while." The grip she had on my neck was like a vise.

"I can't, Becca. I told you I have plans tonight."

I saw tears pool in her eyes as her grip loosened. I slid out and off of her as quickly as possible. I need to go ahead and let her know this was the end of the road for us. Tossing the condom in the trashcan, I quickly threw on my boxers and jeans. Glancing back, I saw her lying on her side, curled up in a ball, watching me. A few tears managed to roll down her cheeks. I shrugged on my shirt and buttoned it. I felt her eyes burning a hole in my back.

Regardless of what women think, it's difficult for a guy when he has to breakup with them. There were usually tears and either fury or begging. I'd rather deal with fury because it makes for a quick getaway and confirms that break-up was a good call.

The beggars were more difficult because I had to sit there and pretend to care while I listened to them whine—usually for a prolonged period of time. I'm always somewhat physically attracted to the girls I'm with, otherwise I wouldn't be fucking them. But things usually fell apart when they opened their mouths. I'd never been very interested in listening. The only exception had been Amanda Kelly. I really liked what came out of her mouth. I liked Becca, but I liked her more for her ability to get the wrinkles out of my shirts than anything else. I inhaled a deep breath before turning around. This was it, I couldn't put it off any longer.

As our eyes locked, I got a strange feeling that what I was about to do would hurt her more than it had the other girls.

I cleared my throat and said, "Becca, I think we're done."

"I know, you said you have plans and you're dressed already," she said quietly, struggling to hold her voice steady.

"I'm not talking about tonight. It's time we move on."

Slowly raising herself up onto her elbows, she blinked a couple of times in disbelief. "I don't understand."

Sweet Jesus, this girl's got a 4.0 average. Apparently, book smarts doesn't translate into real-life comprehension.

"We should start seeing other people," I said as neutrally as possible. My intention was never to be mean, but if the chick pushed me, I had no problem laying it out there.

"I don't want to see other people. What did I do wrong?"

"Nothing. In fact, you do my laundry better than our maid."

"Is it because I said I loved you?" Panic surfaced in her tone. "You don't have to say it back right now, if you don't feel it yet."

The look in her eyes was pathetic. I don't understand why girls can't just let things go. Why do they need to dig and dig for an answer or an explanation until they force a guy to hurt them? I didn't have the time or patience to deal with a beggar today. I needed to turn her into a hater, so I wouldn't be late for dinner.

"Becca, the thing is I'm never going to feel it for you."

"Why?" Her voice cracked and tears streamed down her face.

"Because, I'm just not." I glanced at my watch seeing the time ticking away as my impatience grew.

"But I've always done everything you asked me to do and I don't think I've asked a lot of you. I don't need to hear you say the words, Brad. Just don't run because I said them."

"I'm not running because you said them." Pausing for a moment, I knew what I was about to say would tear into her, but she left me no choice. "Becca, it was fun for a while, but now it's over. We were never anything more than fuck buddies, more emphasis on the fuck than buddies. I'm done and have been for a long time. Sorry, but I need to leave now or I'll be late for dinner."

Not giving her a second to respond, I grabbed my jacket, turned, and was out the door in one fluid movement.

The next day I pulled onto campus, headed to Jason's to pick up the notes from class he was lending. I parked the car and walked toward his dorm. As I rounded the corner I was met by a flurry of activity that made me stop. I recognized a lot of the faculty, staff, and students who were standing around talking. Suddenly, I felt a hand on my shoulder.

"Shit Brad, I've been trying to get in touch with you all morning," Jason said with relief in his voice.

"I've had my phone turned off since last night. I forgot to turn it back on." Mom outlawed cell phones at the dinner table. Or rather, she outlawed mine and my brother Peyton's cell phones at the dinner table. She, on the other hand, needed hers close by for business. What a hypocrite.

"I'm really sorry, man. Are you doing okay?" Jason asked.

"Yeah, I'm fine. Why wouldn't I be?"

The look on his face morphed from concern, to confusion, to shocking realization.

"You don't know?"

"Know what?" I asked.

My gaze shifted away from him toward the crowd of people standing around the ambulance that I hadn't noticed before.

"It's Becca…"

Those were the last words I heard before seeing a white sheet-covered stretcher, flanked by two paramedics coming out of the dorm across the parking lot. In one torrential downpour the sights and sounds flooded my senses. I heard crying, gasps, orders yelled, car doors slamming, and sirens.

Not looking at Jason, I asked, "What happened?"

"I'm sorry, Brad, I thought you knew. I mean I know you guys have been together for a while… I just assumed someone had already told you."

"Told me what?"

He placed his hand on my shoulder in comfort and said, "Becca killed herself last night."

"Fuck me."

The second I saw the doors to the ambulance close, I knew I had to get out of there. My pulse sped up and I started to get lightheaded. I saw Jason's mouth move, but didn't hear any words come out of it. I needed to get away from the crowd. I couldn't think clearly standing there in the middle of the parking lot. I walked to my car as quickly as possible and headed home. My place was a short ten-minute drive from campus. By the time I got there I was on the verge of hyperventilating, sweat was pouring down the back of my neck, and the sound of my heart beating filled my ears. I sat on the sofa, elbows on knees, and ran my hands through my hair a few times, hoping to calm down.

My reaction confused me. I wasn't sure why I was panicking. All I did was break up with her. I'd broken up with a ton of girls. Sure, they would be hurt and angry. Hell, a few even threw things at me, but none of them ever killed themselves. I thought back to last night and the way her eyes looked at me just before I rushed out of her room. They were haunted with loneliness and the desperate need for a connection to someone. It was a look I knew too well. After all, I saw it in the mirror every day. I had a feeling breaking up with Becca was going to impact her more than anyone else, and still, I just turned away. I abandoned her just like I had been all my life and just like my fucking parents, I kept walking.

With my face buried in my palms, my body trembled as I tried to remember if anyone saw me come out of her room last night. I wondered if the police would want to question me.

Christ, what if my parents find out.

I took in several deep breaths and tried to think rationally. I didn't cause her to do this. I had no idea she was mental. I glanced up, looking across the room at the chair that was stacked with folded laundry. Laundry that Becca had done yesterday. The panic in my chest turned into a dull ache as I thought about the times she was here, cooking and cleaning. She never asked for anything from me, not even to return the "I love you." No one had ever told me they loved me before. This young girl, who had never harmed me, was the first, and I acted as if her words were meaningless. Not being wanted by someone you love is the worst feeling in the world. It makes you feel as if your very existence is pointless. I kept telling myself that I didn't kill Becca, but unfortunately, I kept feeling like I did.

Mabry

Groggy, I shuffled into the kitchen where my roommate, Alexis, was in the middle of making coffee and humming an upbeat little tune. She and I met during our first year in law school. She'd been living here for a couple of weeks, and so far, so good. Well, except that, Alexis was a morning person, and I was definitely not. That was especially the case this morning. I had been out most of the night with my new buddy, Kevin. He was a third-year law student. We had been spending time together for a month or so, nothing serious. I didn't do serious. I did distraction and Kevin was a decent distraction. We would study together sometimes, grab a meal here and there, and have sex when the mood struck us.

Sitting down at the kitchen table, I planted my face in the palm of my hands. I was working on a raging migraine brought on, no doubt, by one too many Fireball whiskey shots last night. The sound of the coffee mug making contact with the table caused me to wince in pain.

"Rough night?" Alexis asked.

"Yeah, but I like it that way." I lowered my hands reaching for the mug of relief and gave her a smirk.

"You're such a slut, Mabry."

"I know, but you love me in spite of it all."

I closed my eyes, taking another sip of coffee. When I opened them, Alexis was sitting across from me, a serious and apprehensive look on her face.

"Can I talk to you for a minute?" she asked.

"Can it wait?"

"Not really."

"Okay, then, shoot." I took in a deep breath.

"Let me just say first, that I really like living here."

"But…?"

She shifted uncomfortably in her chair and said, "Mabry, I'm no prude, but I really don't want to hear you and Kevin screwing each other."

"What are you talking about?" I asked, surprise in my voice.

"I heard you guys last night."

"That's impossible."

"It's okay. I mean, what you do is your business. I don't look down on you because of it. I just don't want to hear it."

"Alexis, what exactly do you think you heard? Kevin wasn't even here last night. We were at his place and then I came home."

"I heard your bed squeaking and your headboard banging against the wall."

Shit.

I sat frozen, not exactly knowing how to respond. I must have been head banging. The details of last night were still a little fuzzy. Lately, there had been times that when I was with a guy the disconnect was so suffocating I would self-harm in order to feel something. Even a momentary burst of pain helped before the numbness set in. Being disconnected from other people was my preferred state, but it left me empty and wanting. I missed the feeling of being a part of something, of someone. I hadn't let anyone affect me for such a long time. It was a lonely existence, but a safe one. At times, the loneliness got to me and last night was one of those times. I needed to be more careful with Alexis living here.

"I'm sorry you heard that, but I swear, it wasn't Kevin and me. I must have been having a bad dream and was just thrashing around a lot. I'm not a fan of the sleepover. I usually go over to his place, it makes for a quick and easy getaway."

"Oh, well, I'm sorry. I just assumed," she stammered.

"It's okay."

After a few seconds of awkward silence, she stood and said, "I'm going to do some laundry. Do you have anything you need washed?"

"I have a few things tossed on the floor of my room. I'll go get them." I started to stand.

"I'll get them. You stay and finish your coffee."

As I sat there relief mixed with shame washed over me. I knew what I had been doing and I wasn't exactly proud of it, but it had become such a part of me and how I coped. I was startled out of my thoughts when I heard Alexis yell.

"Oh my god, Mabry!"

Standing, I rushed toward my room, meeting Alexis in the doorway. "What's wrong?"

"Are you okay?" she asked, panicked.

"Yeah, why?"

"There's blood on your pillow."

"I must have had a nose bleed. I get them sometimes," I said, desperately trying to act like this was no big deal.

Vibrations ran through me as panic and embarrassment flooded my body. I knew I had been feeling empty last night when I arrived home and that I banged my head a few times, but I didn't realize any damage had been done. I walked past Alexis into my room, trying to remain as calm as possible. There wasn't a huge amount of blood on the pillow, but it was definitely noticeable. I heard Alexis gasp behind me.

"Mabry! We need to get you to the hospital. There's blood on the back of your head."

"Alexis, I'm fine. I must have hit my head when I was getting into bed last night. I was pretty drunk."

"Let me take a look at it." I moved away from her as she walked toward me with her hand extended.

"No! I said I'm fine."

"Mabry, you hit your head so hard that it caused it to bleed. You need to see a doctor."

"I don't need to see anybody. It was a stupid mistake. Just mind your own business and leave me the fuck alone." I turned on my heels and quickly headed to the bathroom, slamming and locking the door behind me.

I paced the bathroom several times before turning on the shower, letting steam fill the room. That was a close call. I had never been that close to having someone discover what I did. I couldn't let anyone find out. The shame and humiliation would kill me. I stepped into the shower and let the hot water cover me. I raised my hand, touching the back of my head, and winced when I felt a sizable bump that was tender to the touch.

Fuck me. I've got to be more careful next time.

CHAPTER 9

THE PRESENT

Brad

I pull up to Mabry's place, kill the engine, and send a quick text letting her know I'm outside waiting. The past two weeks have been incredible being with her. I finally feel like I know where I belong. I want to be a better man. I want to improve every part of myself because that's what she deserves.

A few minutes later she walks out of her place wearing a pair of dark jeans, a body-hugging green T-shirt with a matching cardigan, sleeves pushed up to her elbows, and a pair of green plaid tennis shoes. Her hair is in a low side ponytail with several strands framing her face. She has on pale pink lip gloss and a little blush, her makeup simple, but perfect. She's so adorable and sexy. I've been out with girls who wear expensive clothes, a ton of makeup, and have every hair strategically in place, but none of them can hold a candle to Mabry. She doesn't need clothes to make her look gorgeous, which is good, because I prefer her sans garments as much as possible. I can't believe how lucky I am that she's let me be a part of her life.

A smile slowly creeps across her face as she walks up to me. "Hey baby," I say, flashing her *the smile*.

"What is this?" Surprise and confusion are evident in her voice. I love throwing her off balance.

"It's my Harley Davidson Softail Classic," I answer, taking off my helmet.

"Did you just get it?"

"No, it was a gift to myself for graduating law school."

"How did I not know you had a motorcycle?"

"Sweetness, I cannot reveal all the awesomeness that is me at one time. It would blow your mind if I did. Now, sway your sexy little ass over here and climb on."

As she approaches I hold out the helmet I bought for her. Her eyes light up when she says, "Oh, it's so pretty. The blue matches your eyes. Did you get it because it matches your eyes?"

"Yeah, I got it because it matches my pretty eyes," I say, teasing her. "Come here so I can put it on you."

We lock eyes as I put the helmet on her and secure the strap. I lean in and give her a soft kiss on the lips.

"You're my very own Jax Teller," she says with a sexy as hell grin.

"I love to hear you say that."

"Well, you are mine."

"Oh, most definitely, but I was referring to being compared to Jax. He's the biggest badass on TV." She narrows her eyes at me. "Let's get rolling." I hold out my hand to help her climb on behind me. She doesn't make a move; she stares straight ahead. "Mabry, is everything okay?"

"Huh?" I raise an eyebrow in her direction. "Sorry, I was just thinking about Jax's ass."

"Yeah, me too," I say, all dreamy-like. She bursts out laughing and climbs on behind me. "What? I'm secure enough in my manhood."

Her arms slip around my waist as her inner thighs hug my hips, and my entire body instinctively molds back against hers. It always catches me off guard how perfect we fit together. The energy between us is so palpable that I can feel the low steady hum of our bodies as Mabry hugs me to her. I close my eyes for a split second, taking in a deep breath. My world has shifted so dramatically since she came into my life. I feel connected and as if I now have a purpose. I'm not a drunken mistake. Raising her hand to my lips, I place a kiss in the center of her palm.

The feel of her chin presses into my shoulder as she whispers in my ear, "I love you, Brad." She always knows when I need to hear her say it.

"I love you too. Let's get this show on the road."

"Where are we going?" she asks, while I'm putting on my helmet.

"Making up for lost time," I answer.

Mabry

We wind our way through the narrow streets of downtown Charleston, passing the beautiful multicolored historic homes, the artisan market, and over the bridge on highway sixty-one headed to who knows where. As long as I'm with him, it doesn't matter what Brad has planned. The past two weeks have been heaven. I'm happy. It's been so long, I'd forgotten how it actually felt. Hell, I'd forgotten what it's like to feel anything, except pain. Since meeting Brad, the emotions I had spent years numbing had fought to escape. Each time I was with him they broke free a little more until I was no longer strong enough to keep them from surfacing. That day at his place when I finally let go and allowed myself to love him is either going to be the smartest thing I'd ever done or the dumbest.

I love, want, and need Brad in my life. But no matter how hard I try, I can't completely get rid of the gnawing fear, that if this ended, I wouldn't be strong enough to go on. Would I imitate my mom, and not be able to survive without him? I haven't self-harmed for two weeks, but the urge is still there. Not as strong, but still present for some reason. After my mom died I couldn't imagine a day when I would be happy again. Somehow I had convinced myself that by some miracle, if that day did come, the desire and need to hurt myself would vanish, but I was wrong.

We pull into the driveway of Middle Place Gardens and Inn. This is where Brad's Plan A was supposed to take place a couple of weeks ago. It's one of my favorite places in the world. I remember coming here as a child with my mom for the day. We would tour the gardens, which always had something in bloom no matter what time of year. We'd also visit the stable yards, which housed the type of animals that were used on the plantation at one time or another. But my all-time favorite part of the gardens was the joggling board, which was a long bench made out of pliable wood. The seat was springy, so a person was able to bounce up and down on it. Mom and I would sit and bounce for the longest time when we were here. No visit was complete without time spent on the joggling board.

Climbing off of the bike, I say, "We're doing Plan A."

"Plan A, modified," Brad corrects, as he walks behind the bike and unstraps a duffel bag I didn't notice before.

"What'cha got there, Jax?" His sexy lips form into a huge grin. He really loves being compared to Jax, which causes me to giggle.

"Just a few things that we'll need for our stay."

"How long are we staying?"

"All day." He strides over, stopping directly in front of me. His eyes shift from my lips to my eyes. "And all night." Leaning in, he nips at my lower lip before sliding his tongue in, giving me a quick, but deep kiss. Then he walks toward the entrance.

Quickly following behind, I inform him, "Brad, I didn't bring anything to change into."

"Got you covered, Sweetness." He pats the side of the duffel.

I reach out and grab his upper arm, turning him in my direction. "I don't have clothes."

"You can wear those jeans tomorrow. I brought you another T-shirt."

"I don't have a toothbrush."

"All taken care of," he says, grinning at me.

I move closer and say in a low voice, "I don't have a change of underwear. I'm okay with wearing the same bra, but I don't have an extra pair of panties in my purse."

He leans in, our noses almost touching. "I went to Victoria's Secret and picked you up a little something. Size small." He winks.

"How do you know what size panty I wear?"

"I may have snatched a pair or three of yours and kept them as souvenirs." I give him a pointed look. "Why are you looking at me like that? It's not like I have them on, at least not right now anyway. Come on, let's go check-in."

Our room is gorgeous with honey-colored wood floors and furniture, decorated in rich earth tones. The inn backs up to the woods filled with pines and moss-covered old oak trees. The entire back wall of floor-to-ceiling windows makes it feel as if we are in a big luxurious treehouse. It's breathtaking, secluded, and peaceful. After putting our one piece of luggage away, we head out to explore the gardens, starting with a carriage tour that travels through the lush woodlands and around the banks of the flooded rice fields. We stop and eat the picnic lunch that the inn packed for us and then leisurely stroll hand-in-hand until we come up on my favorite thing, the joggling board. It's in the same exact spot it had been in when I was a child. I climb on and a huge smile immediately breaks out across my face as I begin to bounce.

"Come bounce with me."

"You don't have to ask me twice. Bouncing with you is my favorite thing to do in the entire world," Brad says, as he straddles the bench, facing me.

"Why is it that everything out of your mouth always sounds so sexual?"

"Just lucky, I guess."

We sit in silence for a few minutes, bouncing, and taking in our beautiful surroundings. I scoot closer to him, brush my lips on his, and whisper against them, "Thank you for this."

"You're more than welcome," he whispers back.

I pull away slightly and look out at the pond. "This is my favorite place in Charleston. I used to come here a lot with my mom."

"I know."

My head jerks and I look at him in confusion. "How do you know? I don't remember talking about it."

"I saw the picture on the bookshelf in your office of you and your mom in front of the Middleton Place House. You look really happy in that picture, so I figured…"

I don't let him finish his sentence before my lips descend on his. All at once, my tongue slides into his mouth, my hands travel up his muscular arms, over his shoulders, and into his messy hair. I hear and feel a deep growl vibrate from his chest, causing me to pull him in closer. When I pull back, both of us are gasping for air.

Looking into his beautiful sapphire eyes, I feel my tears building. "No one has ever done anything this sweet for me."

"I want to spend a lifetime doing sweet things for you." He leans in and places soft kisses along my jawline to behind my ear, and whispers, "And to you." I feel his smile against my neck.

I playfully shove him away. "Leave it to you to make this tender moment sexual."

"Hey, I'm not the one shoving my tongue down throats."

"Touché."

Turning away, I straddle the bench, leaning against his toned chest, as his arms wrap around me. My eyes close as I tilt my head back and focus on the feel of Brad and the sounds of nature.

"Mabry?"

"Hmmm."

"Tell me about your mom," Brad says, his voice low.

I keep my eyes closed and force my body not to react to his words, but I can feel myself stiffen and move away from him. His hold tightens around me. He's not going to let me avoid this.

I clear my throat and ask, "What do you want to know?"

"Everything or as much as you want to tell me."

I open my eyes and look straight ahead. I've never said a word to anyone about my mom. People knew the story about how she died, but not from me. I take in a deep breath. I'm not exactly sure how much I can tell him. He deserves the entire story and the truth, but I don't know if I can give him either.

His lips lower to my ear. "It's okay, you don't have to tell me anything." The hurt in his voice causes my chest to cave in and I know I have to do this. I have to give him this.

"She was a great mom. She was fun, caring, and made sure I knew how much I was loved every day." I pause, trying to contain my tears. "She loved to sing. She couldn't carry a tune, but that never bothered her. When I was young we would play tag in the backyard. Did you ever play that?"

He tries to pull me even closer and whispers, "Yeah."

"Momma made up a song called, 'You'll Never Get Away'. It was the same line over and over. She'd start out singing it really slow and as she got closer to catching me the song would speed up." My voice strains slightly as I attempt to sing.

"Oh, oh, you'll never get away,
Never get away,
Never get away,
Never get away,
Never get away..."

"Then one day she stopped singing, and smiling, and caring about anything or anyone. She stayed in her dark room most of the day."

"Where was your dad?"

"He worked a lot. I would hear them sometimes at night in their room. He'd start out asking her nicely to take her medicine and encourage her to get some help. She would cry out and these gut-wrenching sobs filled the house. Daddy would get frustrated and angry with her and then he'd give up. I'd hear the bedroom door slam shut followed by the front door. And I was left there all alone to listen to my mom until he came back home."

"Did your dad ever do anything?"

"He let her disappear."

Tears streamed down my face and my body trembles. I feel Brad's lips touch my neck. "You don't have to tell me anymore."

"It was like that for two years before she slit her wrists. I was the one who found her."

"Fuck."

"She didn't even leave us a note. She just left me and Daddy."

"I'm so sorry, baby." Brad's voice cracks.

"People should always leave a note telling you why they did it. There's nothing worse than someone you love leaving and not telling you why. I miss her so much."

Brad's arms lock around me. Sobs take over my body, and my

heart and soul shatter. The urge to bang my head grabs me. Without thinking, I rear my head back, except instead of slamming against a cold solid surface, I make contact with a warm strong man who catches me as I fall.

CHAPTER 10

THE PAST

Brad

I was sitting in the parking lot watching as all the people filed into the campus chapel. I'd been out here for an hour, but hadn't been able to leave my car. The Hyams family, along with the university, had planned a memorial service here for faculty, staff, and students. It had been almost a week since Becca's death and I was still in shock. I hadn't left my place, not even to go to class. People who thought we were a couple just assumed it was because I was too upset by her death. I was upset, but not for the reasons they thought. Becca and I were far from being a couple. We were barely friends. The fact was, while she was alive, I never gave her much thought. I didn't even really think of her during sex. Sometimes she was a model, sometimes a movie star, and sometimes she was even Amanda. It was rare that I actually screwed Becca.

I hadn't slept since that day. Every time I closed my eyes I saw her dark green ones looking up at me, lost and alone. I'd racked my brain trying to remember if there had been any signs, but I came up empty every time. Then the realization hit me. Becca could have been wearing a huge sign that read, *I'm Committing Suicide Tuesday at 8 pm,* and I wouldn't have noticed. I didn't care about her. I treated her the exact same way I treated every girl who had ever been in my life. The reason I liked having her around was because she did my errands and didn't ask for anything. In return, I fucked her when I needed a release, simply because I was too lazy to go out and find another girl that I was actually attracted to. I had been inside of her and yet all I knew about her was that she got the wrinkles out of my shirts and made a mean pot roast. I knew a few things about the other girls I had been with, but the only reason I knew things about them was because they talked, some nonstop. Becca barely spoke and as usual, I never asked any questions. Disappointment and shame flooded me. I knew I wasn't the most caring person in the world, but I hadn't realized I was becoming one of the coldest.

The night I left her, I wanted to get away as quickly as possible all because I didn't feel like dealing with the tears that were headed my way. While I was sitting across from my mother pretending to listen as she droned on about work, my thoughts weren't on Becca, they were on the cute little blond waitress. I turned my back on her and left her alone. I'd become numb to my pain and loneliness, while Becca's pain finally consumed her. She believed her life was disposable and then threw it away. I was to blame for that. I did the same thing to her that had been done to me all my life. I treated her like she was nothing, an inconvenience, a mistake. The last few people walked up the steps to the chapel and entered. I had to go in, I owed her that much.

Getting out of the car, I felt a tingling in my hands as I adjusted my tie. My stomach quivered and my breathing accelerated while I reached into the back seat and grabbed my jacket. As I approached the door, I hesitated for a moment before finding the courage to enter. Once inside, I stood frozen, looking at the somber faces in the packed chapel. I had no clue Becca even knew this many people. The place was quiet, except for the cries up front from her mother. You could tell she was trying hard to hold them in, but they kept escaping. I found a seat just before the preacher took the podium.

He talked about what a good person and daughter Becca was. Next, the head of the Art Department got up to speak. She talked about Becca's love of art and what a great student she was. That, while at Duke, she volunteered for an art therapy program for special needs children in the area. As she spoke, I noticed that several paintings resting on easels were placed around the chapel. They were mostly abstracts. I knew Becca was an Art major, but that was all. I didn't even know she painted.

Speaker after speaker talked about a warm, sweet, shy, and giving young woman. When Stephanie spoke, she could barely hold back the tears as she remembered stories from her childhood growing up with Becca. She talked about how courageous Becca was and how she had to overcome so many obstacles in her life. I sat listening intently to every word, finally taking the time to get to know Becca Hyams.

The last two people to approach the podium were Becca's parents. My breath caught as I looked into the grief-stricken eyes of her mother and the vacant gaze of her father. I had never seen two people so broken in my entire life. I had also never seen two parents who loved their child as much as Mr. and Mrs. Hyams.

As Mr. Hyams stepped closer to the microphone his eyes were downcast. His hands shook as he clutched something that I couldn't see. Clearing his throat, he began, "My wife and I want to thank each one of you for coming here today to say goodbye to our daughter." His mouth trembled and his eyes filled with water. "It's never easy losing a loved one. I've lost both my parents, grandparents, and a few friends over the years. The pain that you feel is intense because you'll miss them. The frustration is overpowering because there's absolutely nothing you can do, except adjust to a life without them. But when you lose your child…" The tears spilled over and onto his cheeks as his chest heaved deeply. "…Just the thought of a child dying before their parent is so excruciatingly painful and devastating. I guess no human was able to get past even the thought to try and assign words to these feelings when it actually happens." He looked down at the object that he'd been tightly holding. He raised it up and out facing the mourners. It was a stone the size of his palm. Gazing at it, he continued. "Becca was always an artist. This is a present she made me for Father's Day when she was seven years old. She painted orange tiger paws all over it. We were big Clemson University fans. So much so, Becca used to say, if any of us got cut we would bleed orange." His eyes immediately shot up looking at the audience. The sudden realization of what he just said hit him. Becca had slit her wrists. A shudder visibly ran through his body. "I'm sorry," he whispered and stepped back from the podium.

Mrs. Hyams hesitated while looking out at the faces who came to remember her daughter. Slowly she stepped forward and said, "When you lose a baby a piece of your heart and your hope for the future are taken from you. The longer your child is with you, the more it hurts when you have to let them go because you have gotten to know them so much better and love them so much more. Becca was a wonderful daughter. She was generous and kind, never saying no to anyone who needed her. She gave of herself without asking for anything in return. Her father and I will always be extremely proud of the person she grew up to be. Her entire life was a struggle, but she fought hard to overcome her problems. She was a strong young woman, except for one moment, one night, when she felt she didn't have the strength to fight anymore." Her shoulders slumped forward as the sobs overtook her body. Mr. Hyams wrapped his arm around his wife and led her back to their seats.

I felt tears build behind my eyes and my chest caved in as grief and sorrow flooded into me. Becca never demanded anything from me and I couldn't give her five minutes that night. That five minutes could have saved her life. I didn't have the time or interest and now a young girl was dead in part because of me. I wanted to rewind the past month and give Becca time and my friendship. I never thought about or felt the repercussions from my actions, but Becca changed all that, not only in the way she died, but also in the way I learned she lived.

It had been a month since the memorial service. I had been living life somewhat like a hermit. I made a conscious choice that day before leaving the chapel that my life was going to be different. I couldn't bring Becca back, but I wasn't going to let her death be in vain and not learn from it. I thought changing the way I treated people, women especially, would be fairly easy. After all, I knew right from wrong. I knew there were times when I had been horrible to people, but the feeling of guilt in regard to my actions was momentary at best.

The first week back in class was the hardest. I had a lot of offers from girls who wanted to help me through the grieving process. I actually considered the first few. I wanted some relief from the guilt I felt about Becca and what better way to forget then to be crawling all over a cute girl. But I didn't do it. I realized it was a knee-jerk reaction. It's how I had coped with the pain and loneliness all my life. The fact was, the coping mechanism I depended on hadn't worked in a very long time. The girls had become nameless faces. The more notches I added to my bedpost, the more the numbness set in. I barely felt anything at this point.

I was standing at the bar waiting for my drink order. Jason had talked me into meeting him at Charlie's, a local bar and favorite of Dukies. Looking around, I noticed the usual college crowd of frat boys and sorority girls. At the end of the bar, I saw three guys from my civil law class, Tyler, Cole, and Derek. All of them were arrogant assholes who basically got into Duke because their fathers were either congressmen or judges, along with being Duke Alumni. I knew I was an arrogant asshole too, but I had the grades. I didn't need my douche bag dad to get me into a top-notch law school.

They were standing around a hot redhead who was seated at the bar. All were pretty drunk, but the girl was more so. I watched as she downed three shots in rapid succession that had been placed in front of her. Cole bent down and whispered something in the girl's ear. She nodded her head in agreement and pushed away from the bar. Cole and Derek each grabbed one of her arms and walked toward the door as Tyler paid for their drinks. I knew these guys were up to no good.

I followed Tyler as he headed out the door to join Frick and Frack, making sure to stay a few steps behind him so I wouldn't be noticed. Approaching the car, I saw Cole hovering over the girl, his hand up her skirt and his mouth covering hers as Derek watched.

"Let's move this party to a private location," Tyler announced, stopping in front of the other two guys.

Cole's hand continued to disappear farther up the girl's skirt.

"Cole, come on. Don't wear her out. Ty and I want a go at her," Derek said, popping Cole on the arm.

Cole finally pried his lips away from the girl, shoving her in Derek's direction. "Here, she's pretty tasty."

The girl collapsed into Derek's arms. "Come on, baby. Don't pass out on us yet." Propping her against the car, he grabbed one of her breasts as he kissed her neck. Tyler and Cole stood back laughing and cheering him on.

I looked away briefly and cringed. I wasn't only disgusted with what was going on in front of me, but with the fact that I had been one of these jerkoffs. I never forced a girl to do anything she didn't want to do, but I had been a part of convincing a wasted one to relax and go with the flow.

Stepping forward, I slapped Tyler on the back. "Hey dude, what's going on?" I asked.

"Bradley!" Tyler slurred.

"Brad!" Cole chimed in.

Derek still had his face buried in the girl's neck.

"Hey man, you wanna join us for a little party?" Tyler asked.

"Yeah, Brad, come on. She's all ready, willing, and able," Cole said, as he walked up to me and put his arm around my shoulders.

Shrugging out of his hold, I stepped forward toward the car and pushed Derek off the girl. "Hey, what the fuck, dude?!" he yelled.

Grabbing the girl's arm, I said, "She's completely wasted and doesn't have a clue about what's going on." I looked down at her blurry eyes. "What's your name, sweetheart?"

"Um… Tabitha, I think," she mumbled as she fell into me.

"This is bullshit. She's totally into going with us." Cole stepped in front of me, grabbed my arm, and tugged.

Looking him directly in the eyes, I said, "Get your fucking hand off of me."

"Brad, get the fuck out of here. She's ours," said Derek.

"Fellas relax," Tyler interrupted.

"No. I've spent a ton of cash on this pussy and I want what's owed to me," Cole demanded.

"Brad, why don't you just come with us and you can have your turn with her after we're done." A slimy grin crossed Tyler's face.

"I don't think you understand. She's not going with you assholes."

"When did you become so fucking high and mighty? I remember one night in particular when you had your dick in one chick while your finger was in another," Derek said.

"I've never raped a girl."

"Wait a second. No one here is talking about rape," Tyler said, panic in his voice.

Stepping up to Tyler, I got right in his face. "You listen to me. I'm taking this girl home so she can sleep off whatever you slipped in her drink. You and these other two motherfuckers are going to go back to your place. Whether you jerk off to your collection of porn or suck each other's dicks, I don't give a fuck. All I know is she won't be getting any of you douche bags off tonight. If you get in my way, I have Jessica, your longtime girlfriend on speed dial. I'm sure she'd be devastated to know her boyfriend is cheating on her. She'd probably call her daddy, the senator, who in turn would call your daddy, the judge. You wouldn't want all these daddies to know what a low-life slime you were, now would you? It would be quite the black mark on your legal career."

Tyler and I stared at each other for several seconds. I knew he didn't want to look like a pussy in front of these guys, but I also knew he needed Jessica and her father's contacts to achieve the career he wanted.

He took one step back. "Let her go, guys. She's not worth it." Cole started to protest, but Tyler's pointed look shut him up.

I grabbed Tabitha by the arm and led her back to my car. Once in the passenger's seat, her head tilted back and she passed out. Rounding the front of the car, I called Jason, told him I wasn't feeling well and was headed home. I tried several times to wake up Tabitha to ask her for her address with no success. I had no choice but to take her back to my place.

Once there, I carried her up to my condo and laid her on my bed. As I removed her shoes she sat up abruptly, latched on to the waistband of my jeans, and unzipped them.

"What the hell are you doing?" I asked.

"You're really cute," she said groggily. "I just want to thank you."

"That's okay. You don't need to thank me." I removed her hands from my crotch and placed them in her lap. She looked up at me confused for a second before falling back on the bed and passing out again.

As I stared at her, a sinking feeling took over my stomach. I knew if this had happened a few months ago, I would have let her continue. I would have used this girl just like I used Becca. I wanted to think I was better than Tyler and those dickheads, but deep down I wasn't. I was just as slimy as they were. I pulled the comforter over Tabitha, headed into the living room, and wondered if a person could truly learn from his past, leave it behind him, and change for the future.

Mabry

The chapel was at near full capacity. It made me curious because the Becca I had known was really shy and kept to herself for the most part. I wondered just how many of these people actually knew her or were they just sympathy leeches. A lot of leeches attended my mom's funeral. People who acted as if they had just lost their best friend when in reality, they couldn't have cared less. From the moment my mom got sick, no one bothered with us. None of her family or so-called friends ever came by or called to check on her. When she died, a mixture of leeches came out of the woodwork. Family members stopped by hoping to inherit some priceless heirloom while female "friends" stopped by sniffing around my dad, the grieving widower. It was disgusting. Dad and I were the only two people who honestly loved my mom and were devastated by her death.

When I heard Becca had committed suicide I was shocked, but not that surprised. The shock was from the timing of it, but the fact that she died by her own hands seemed inevitable to me. She and I were roommates at Clemson until she had to drop out midway through our senior year due to her depression. I had seen her fall into some extremely dark moods during our time at school. She'd pull herself out of them eventually, but never completely. We kept in touch through the occasional phone calls as well as emails. Once she felt able to handle the pressures of school again, she decided a fresh start was needed, so she transferred to Duke. The last email I received from her was four days before she killed herself. Her words sounded happy. She really liked her classes and had been working with special needs children. She even mentioned that she had met a guy. They had been together for a little over a month and she was deeply in love with him.

Glancing at the first few pews in the chapel, I tried to figure out which guy was Becca's boyfriend, but everyone wore the same expressionless face except for her parents. It was heartbreaking to look at them. The deep ache of loss radiated off of them. I wondered if they knew this day was coming. That it was just a matter of time before she succeeded in completely disappearing. Becca had attempted to kill herself before while we were living together. I had come back from class in the middle of the day and she was asleep. I gathered my books and headed to the library to study. An hour later, I arrived back at our room and she was still in the exact same position sleeping. I called her name a few times and nudged her, but she didn't respond. Finally, I noticed a half empty bottle of pills on her nightstand. She was rushed to the hospital and had her stomach pumped.

I was so pissed off at her for what she had done. She knew I'd be the one to find her and how much agony this would cause her parents. She had a mom and dad who would do anything to help her, but she didn't think about the effect her death would have on them. I'd give anything to have two parents who loved and adored me as much as Becca's parents did her. I wanted to be here for Mr. and Mrs. Hyams, and Wake Forrest was only an hour and half drive from Duke, so I came.

After the service, I stayed seated, waiting for the crowd of condolences to thin out. Neutral face after neutral face gave the obligatory "I'm so sorry for your loss" to the family. Just before I made my way to them, I saw him. Well, I saw the side of a chiseled jaw, speckled with stubble. Even though I didn't fully see his face, I could tell his expression was different than the others. There was true sorrow and regret in it. I thought he must have been Becca's boyfriend, but as I watched him approach and speak with her parents, it was obvious they were all strangers. I would have thought that even if they hadn't met before today, certainly they would have met before the service. I watched him interact with the Hyamses for a few seconds. Something about him held me there. He was a complete stranger, but the urge to go over, wrap my arms around him, and give comfort was undeniable. I reached back to grab my purse. By the time I turned around, *he* was already gone.

I was immediately blinded by the fluorescent lighting above, as my eyes fluttered open and frantically darted around the sterile room. The rest of my body remained frozen in the bed. I was confused, having no idea where I was, how I arrived, or why I was here. Just then the door swung open. A middle-aged man with salt-and-pepper hair and dressed in scrubs entered. He didn't say anything. I wasn't sure if he knew I was awake. I watched him flip through some papers and then look up at the machine that was beeping with my heart rate. He returned looking down at the papers in his hands as he approached my bedside. The beeping got faster with each step he took until finally he looked up and saw me looking back at him.

"Well, hello. I'm Dr. Burnett." He showed me a slight smile before glancing back at the papers.

"Where am I?" I asked.

"You're in the ER at Wake Forrest Baptist Medical Center."

"Why?" I tried to remember the events from earlier in the day, but kept drawing a blank.

An entire month had already passed since Becca's memorial service, and memories of her and my mom continued to plague me. I knew attending the service had the potential of being a major trigger for me, but I felt I could handle it and keep my emotions under control. I did okay initially, but then images flooded back, first in my dreams and then during the day. I'd find myself spacing out a lot in class. My mind wasted no time placing me back in my mom's room staring at her lifeless body. Then fast forwarding to see Becca lying in almost the same position in her bed. I'd been fighting the urge to self-harm. I knew if I kept banging my head that eventually I would cause permanent damage. I started digging and scratching my nails into my upper thighs, thinking that it was less dangerous. It worked for a little while, but didn't numb me to the pain the same way head banging did. But I knew if I banged my head only a time or two, I would slide right back into the behavior. So I fought the urge as long as possible until this week when I fell off the wagon.

The reason was nothing out of the ordinary. I was at a bar, met a guy, got drunk, screwed said guy, felt empty, went home, let the loneliness consume me, and gave in to the urge. I'd banged my head and scratched myself every day this week without even one trigger causing it. I craved the adrenaline rush that I got when my head made contact or my nails scraped across my flesh. Relief washed over me every time I saw blood rise to the surface of my skin or in that millisecond when my head bounced forward after pounding it against a solid surface.

"Ms. Darnell, are you in a relationship?" the doctor asked.

"What?"

"Do you have a boyfriend or girlfriend?"

"No."

"Have you been the victim of a recent attack?"

"No. Why are you asking me these questions and why am I in the ER?" My tone was a mixture of panic and anger.

"You were brought in by your roommate," he said.

"Why did Alexis bring me in?"

"She found you unconscious on the floor of your bathroom. Do you want to tell me what happened?"

"I didn't eat today. My blood sugar probably just dropped and I passed out." I shifted my eyes to look just over his shoulder instead of directly at him.

"You have scratches on both upper thighs, extending from the knee all the way up to the very top of your leg. You also have multiple abrasions along with bumps and bruises on the back of your head. This didn't happen because you skipped a few meals. If someone did this to you, you can tell me. It would be strictly confidential."

"No one did anything to me."

He hesitated for a moment, cleared his throat, and asked, "Mabry, do you hurt yourself?"

Chuckling slightly, I answered, "That would be insane. Why on earth would anyone physically hurt themselves?"

"Different reasons. Some people do it because the physical pain is easier to deal with than the mental or emotional pain. Some people do it to numb themselves. Some people think it's no big deal. After all, they control when and how they hurt themselves. But the natural endorphins that the brain releases when you inflict pain on yourself is addicting. Soon you have to cut or embed sharp objects deeper, burn your skin longer, or slam your head back harder to achieve the rush. You could end up causing permanent damage or worse."

Looking into his warms eyes I could tell he knew that he had discovered my secret. "Are you keeping me here for any reason?"

"You have a mild concussion, but since you don't live alone, I feel okay with discharging you." Reaching into his shirt pocket, he pulled out a business card and handed it to me. "Take this. It's the name and number of a counselor who's there to listen."

I glanced at the card and then back up at him. "Can I go now?"

119

"Sure, I'll go sign your discharge papers."

As I watched the door close behind him, panic and shame overtook me. I knew he legally couldn't tell anyone, but the fact that someone knew my secret was mortifying. I knew there was a possibility of brain damage, but I was always careful not to let things go too far, except for a few times. I read the name and phone number on the card before I began flipping it through my fingers. I didn't believe talking to this person would do any good. No amount of counseling would erase the pain of my past. It was buried in me too deeply.

CHAPTER 11

THE PRESENT

Brad

It's been a month since Mabry and I had our romantic weekend at Middleton Place Gardens. Opening up to me about her mother's suicide and the way her father basically checked out was extremely difficult for her. When she allowed me to see her pain, I knew she had let me into her heart completely. Since then, I've shared more with her about my upbringing and how my parents left me to raise myself. Mabry wasn't surprised. She picked up on how my family was from the first day she started at the firm. My parents are able to fool a lot of the people most of the time. They appear as warm and caring people who still respect each other even after years of being divorced. They are just as cold and calculating now as they've always been. Mabry saw right through their act.

We've talked a little about our past "relationships". I knew Mabry wasn't a virgin when I met her, although I wished she had been. The thought of another man's hands on her was almost too much for me to bear. Some of the females around the office had warned her to stay away from me. A few of them knew my reputation from high school. The rest I had fucked at some point during my summer internships. When I graduated from law school and came to work here at the firm, my past followed me. I had changed by then and wasn't the same asshole these women once knew, but none of them believed it. Anytime a new female joined the firm she was immediately informed to stay away from me. It never bothered me before because there hadn't been anyone I cared about until now. I told Mabry most of the stories were true a long time ago, but I'm a different person now.

I haven't opened up about Becca and how she was the catalyst that caused me to wake up, grow up, and change. I struggle back and forth about my decision to tell Mabry everything. I mean, it was in the past. I'm not that guy anymore. What's important is that I've changed. I love Mabry and I'm committed to her in every sense of the word. It's because of that commitment to her that I know I need to be honest and tell her everything. I'm sure she's wondered what caused such a dramatic change from the way I used to live my life, I just have to wait until the right time presents itself and so far it hasn't, or I haven't let it. I'm scared Mabry will leave me if she finds out I was even remotely involved with a girl's suicide since she saw the way it destroyed her own family.

Since Becca's death, I'd gone out with a couple of girls. I even tried to seriously date this one girl, Stacia. She was nice, smart, and exotic looking. All her stats looked great on paper. There was just something missing between us. Admittedly, I have been pretty gun-shy about even going out on a date since Becca. I never saw her death coming and I sure as hell can't live through another experience like that. But when Mabry walked into the conference room that first day at the firm all my apprehension and fear evaporated.

In the beginning, I thought of Becca every single day after her death, because I never wanted to forget the way in which she changed my life. Her death forced me to look at myself and how my actions affected others. Now I think about our brief encounter and how, because of it, I could possibly lose the most important thing in my life, the woman I love. I'm not sure if I'm overthinking it or not. I mean, we're in love so maybe it isn't the biggest deal, but just the thought that it might destroy us makes my voice catch in my throat, stopping the confession. I wonder if I will ever truly be able to leave the past behind.

I love any time with Mabry, but Sundays are my favorite. We don't plan anything. We just spend time together. We started switching off staying over at each other's place. Today we are at my place. It's late morning and we are still in bed, working. Being new lawyers, you never really have an entire day off. I glance up at her and smile. She's sitting with her legs crossed in front of her, reading over case studies. Her hair is piled up on top of her head, all messy. She's wearing one of my blue Duke T-shirts, loosely knotted at the waist exposing my favorite pair of her black lace boy shorts. Her face is still flushed from our early morning horizontal workout. Dark-rimmed glasses frame her beautiful eyes and she's concentrating, which means her tasty bottom lip is drawn into her mouth. I'm leaning against the headboard, my legs stretched out in front of me, crossed at the ankles, wearing a pair of faded jeans, drawing up a few contracts on my laptop. We've been in these same positions before, doing the same exact thing, and still I can't get over how perfect it feels to *be* with her.

"What are you staring at, buddy?" she asks, giving me a flirtatious smile.

"The most beautiful creature on the planet." I wink at her.

"Well, aren't we full of cheese this morning," she teases.

"That's one of the reasons why you love me so much, Sweetness. I provide you with your recommended daily dose of calcium."

"That reminds me, I'm hungry." She removes her glasses and places them on top of the files in front of her. Leaning toward me, she brushes her soft lips over mine and kisses me lightly. "Do you want anything to eat?"

A wicked grin slowly crosses my face. "Oh, you mean food? Nah, I'm not hungry for food." She narrows her eyes at me and shakes her head before climbing off of the bed. I watch as her sexy little ass sways its way out the door.

My life has never been as good as it is at this moment. When I look at Mabry I have a thousand different emotions run through me. I'm happy, content, excited, and completely at peace. I feel wanted and needed. I have a purpose now. Mabry has given me a life I never knew could exist. The raspy sultry voice of Duffy singing "Mercy" from the other room catches my attention.

As I reach the kitchen I see Mabry standing in front of the fridge, looking in. With one arm resting over the door, her hips move back and forth to the music. I cross my arms over my bare chest, lean against the doorframe, and enjoy the view. She grabs what looks to be a yogurt. Closing the fridge, she absentmindedly starts singing as she dances over to the drawer and pulls out a spoon. She still doesn't notice me staring at her. I can't help but think that her singing and dancing in the kitchen is a trait she inherited from her mom. She gets into her performance a little more, using the spoon as her microphone. My smile grows so big it makes my face hurt. Closing her eyes, Mabry hits a high note and spins around toward me. Her eyes shoot open and she startles seeing me there.

"Dammit! You scared me," she yells.

"Please don't stop. This is the best floor show I've ever seen."

"Dance with me."

"Oh no, Sweetness. This is all you."

She places the yogurt on the counter and seductively saunters toward me. "I know you have to be a great dancer."

"Yeah? How do you know?" I ask.

She unfolds my arms from my chest, tugging me to the center of the kitchen. "Because, I've seen and felt your hip action."

She guides my arms around her waist and then wraps hers around my neck. Our hips connect and our foreheads rest on each other's as our bodies slowly move together.

"See, it's all in the hips," she whispers against my lips.

I glide my hand up her torso all the way to one of her tits and my thumb automatically starts circling her already hard nipple. Our breathing becomes heavier. With my other hand, I push on the small of her back, pressing our hips closer together. I feel her fingers slide up the back of my head into my hair. I move my hand from her back down to cup her ass as I bend her back slightly, slipping my tongue into her partially open mouth. We straighten up and I back her toward the corner of the counter. Both our tongues stay firmly planted in the other's mouths. I reposition both my hands and grab the hem of her T-shirt, breaking the kiss long enough to slip it up and over her head.

Starting at her neck, I nibble my way down until I'm on my knees in front of her, bringing me face-to-face with her tits. Mabry's fingers stay tangled in my hair as she pushes my lips harder against her body. Sliding my tongue out, I run it roughly across her nipple before taking it into my mouth and sucking hard. She loves it when I do this. My lips begin traveling down her stomach and circle her pierced navel, as my fingers hook around the top of her panties. The panties slowly slide down her legs, my mouth following in their path with slow open-mouth kisses, until I reach between her thighs. I linger there for several seconds flicking her clit with my tongue. A loud gasp escapes Mabry and I feel her knees buckle against my chest. I lean her towards the counter for support, coaxing her to lift her legs, so that I can remove her panties, tossing them to the side. I run both hands up along the back of her legs and to her ass, burying my face deeper between her thighs. Her hips begin to rock back and forth as she attempts to ride my tongue.

I slide my tongue out and kiss the inside of her upper thigh. "Fuck, I never get tired of tasting you," I say against her skin. A loud moan rumbles from her chest as her fingers dig into my hair deeper.

I stand, lifting her up onto the counter, position her hips at the edge while pressing her back to the wall.

"You consume me, baby," she says breathlessly.

My lips glide up her chest, her neck, across her jaw until they reach her lips. "I adore you, Mabry," I tell her just as breathless.

Unbuttoning my jeans, she pushes them down using her legs. She wraps herself around my hips and pulls me in as close as possible. Burying my face in her neck, I place my hands on either side of her hips, holding her still as I thrust into her. My breathing comes out in short quick spurts, my grip intensifies, and the air shifts between us. Beads of sweat pop up on our skin as my movements speed up. Mabry braces herself against my shoulders. I lift my head and look into her beautiful azure blue eyes and for the first time all I see in them is love. The sadness that had been a permanent fixture is gone. I make a vow right then to myself that I would spend the rest of my life making sure the sadness doesn't return. She's taken over every part of me, my heart, my mind, my soul, and my body. It's as if our souls have fused together and I know she's the one I've been waiting for my entire life. My dick begins throbbing intensely as Mabry squeezes perfectly around it. Our bodies are so in sync with one another's, it's overwhelming. We continue to lock eyes as our bodies shake uncontrollably. She feels it just as intensely as I do. Our connection is mind-blowing, causing tears to trickle down both our faces.

Trying to catch my breath, I rest my forehead against hers and ask, "Do you think it's possible to love someone before you've met them? Because I think I've loved you my entire life."

"I know it is because I've been waiting for you my entire life."

Mabry

"Soooo, things with you and Hottie McGee are getting pretty serious?" Sylvie asks.

"Hottie McGee?"

"Don't toy with me, woman. You know who I'm talking about."

Between work and Brad I've missed the monthly book club brunches a couple of times and haven't talked to Sylvie in a while. She insisted we meet tonight for drinks, dinner, and a little girl talk.

"Yeah, things are really good," I say with some hesitation in my voice.

Sylvie looks at me trying to read my expression. "You don't sound very convincing. What's bugging you? Spill."

"You're going to think I'm *nuts*." The word comes out of my mouth before my brain has a chance to think. Sylvie doesn't know I self-harm, but she knows how terrified I am to become like my mom and that it's one of the main reasons why I've never let anyone into my life. She also knows that certain words like "nuts, crazy, and insane" hit a nerve with me. "You remember when we were kids and we'd dream about what it would be like to have a boyfriend?"

"Yeah, mine was going to be Justin Timberlake," she says wistfully.

"The boy would be hot, sweet, would do anything for us, and tell us how incredible and beautiful we were. But then when we got older and actually started dating we found out they're not like that. They're loud, obnoxious, self-centered, smelly creatures who think the ability to burp and fart at the same time is a talent to be admired."

"To be fair, doing those two things simultaneously does take a bit of bodily control and an innate sense of timing," she says with a hint of sarcasm in her voice.

"Brad is the dream."

A huge smile forms on her face as she reaches her hand across the table, placing it on top of mine. "That's wonderful, Mabry. I'm beyond thrilled. You deserve the dream." I cast my eyes down. "You believe that, right? You deserve to be happy and have someone special in your life."

Looking up at her, I feel tears collecting behind my eyes. "When he looks at me everything horrible in my life disappears. For the first time I can see a future and I'm not alone in it." She squeezes my hand and I see her eyes filling as well. "But then something triggers the realization that those horrible things aren't gone. I'll never be free of them."

Sylvie squeezes my hand harder, looks me directly in the eyes, her expression stern. "You listen to me. You are not your mother, Mabry. You have got to stop letting her death dictate your life."

"Depression runs in families, Sylvie, and I've had episodes," I whisper, my voice trembling.

"You had a mother who was sick and for whatever reason that day she lost sight of what was important. Your father buried his head in the sand and allowed her to slip away. The two people in your life who were supposed to love, protect, and cherish you let you down. I'd have episodes too if that shit happened to me. I know depression can be inherited, but it's not guaranteed, sweetie. You need to talk with a professional and figure out exactly what you're afraid of, living or dying. If you run from one then you're headed straight towards the other. Since your mom died I think you've been at a standstill, not knowing which direction to go in."

I know logically Sylvie's right, but when fear possesses you most of your life, logic falls by the wayside. I've never been to counseling to help deal with my mom's death or my father abandoning me emotionally. I dealt with my problems by self-harming, sleeping with nameless guys, and medicating myself with either alcohol or drugs. I guess that really can't be considered as "dealing" with my problems. I've never faced any of my issues. I never had a reason or desire to, until now.

My plan after dinner was to head home and put in a couple of hours of work, but somehow I find myself sitting in my car outside of Brad's place. I'm watching him through his window. The boy needs to invest in either blinds or drapes. He's sitting on the sofa working on his laptop, as usual. He has on the blue Duke T-shirt that I love to wear because it smells like him. I was the last to wear it. I wonder if he's got it on because it now smells like me. The sleeves hit right in the middle of his upper arm muscle. Those arms are so sexy especially when they strain against the material when he folds them over his chest or around my body. His baseball cap is in its familiar backward position on top of his head with a little of his chunky dirty-blond hair sticking out at the opening above the adjustable strap. His ever present stubble runs across his defined jawline that I love running my teeth up and down. Just a half hour ago, I was falling apart, allowing my fears to take control. Now, seeing Brad for a few minutes somehow melts all of my doubts away, and I can see my future with him. I pick up my phone and send a quick text.

Me: Hey sexy beast.

I watch as a big bright smile appears on his face and reaches all the way to his eyes.

Brad: SWEETNESS!!! I miss u.

Me: I miss u 2. U look mighty sexy when u work.

Brad: Where r u?

Me: In ur driveway.

Brad: What'cha doin' out there?

Me: Swoonin' & droolin' over u.

He looks toward the window and waves. Holding up his index

finger, he indicates for me to wait a second. He places his laptop on the coffee table. My phone chirps with a text.

Brad: Turn on 95 SX.

I find the radio station on my phone and click the live stream. "Wild Ones" by Flo Rida fills the car. I look up and see Brad through the window, doing his best Channing Tatum impression from *Magic Mike*. As he dances, his hips rock smoothly back and forth at first. He grabs the hem of his shirt and slowly pulls it up and over his head. Somehow he manages to keep his baseball cap in place. Arms raised high in the air, the hip-gyrating speeds up as he approaches the window. Laughter bursts from me involuntarily.

I love him so much.

A heel groove followed by a deep grind to the floor are next. He throws a little "Sprinkler" move in before disappearing from sight. Just when I think the show's over he crosses in front of the window performing the classic "Moon Walk", ending with grabbing his baseball cap and tossing it to the side.

I get out of my car, run up to his front door, and knock. He fills me with so much joy and peace that I feel as if I'm going to explode with emotion. The door swings open. My eyes immediately zero in on his gorgeous upper body and I sigh deeply.

"Hey," he says, slightly out of breath.

"Hey," I say, holding up a dollar bill.

Looking at it, he narrows his eyes and says, "A dollar? Baby, I left my heart out on that dance floor."

"A dollar plus this…" I lean in, pressing my lips to his. I glide the tip of my tongue across his bottom lip before sliding it in. Brad's chest vibrates with a deep growl. I pull back and we stare at each other.

His hand comes up, cupping the side of my face. "Yum, appletini," he says, grinning. "You had a good time with Sylvie?" His thumb runs over my cheek.

"Yeah, I did." I pause briefly, then ask, "Do you ever get scared?"

"Of what?"

"This thing between us? It's intense. It feels like more than love. I just don't know what the word is or even if there's a word for it." I turn my head and look away.

He touches my chin with the tip of his index finger, guiding my gaze back to him. "No, I've never been scared of it. It's always felt like the most natural thing in the world."

"What if something happens?" I whisper.

"Mabry, there's nothing in this universe that could happen to keep me from you. I don't know how *not* to love you."

I fling my arms around his neck and hold on tightly. Brad's strong arms encircle my waist.

"I love you so completely," I whisper into his ear.

My feet lift off the ground slightly as he carries me in to his place, closing the door behind us. I want to be the best person I can be for Brad. Sylvie is right. It's time I start dealing with my problems. I've been standing still with no clear direction toward life or death. I don't want to be like my mother or father. I want a life and I want it with Brad.

CHAPTER 12

THE PAST

Brad

"Shit." I started to turn around and leave before she noticed me. I thought I was pretty clear on the phone that I wanted to meet her alone. I should have known better. Some things never change. I took in a deep breath and braced myself for the assault before walking to the table.

"Sorry I'm late. The traffic was horrible," I apologized.

"That's okay," she said, smiling up at me nervously.

Cold blue eyes bored into me as I slid into the booth. Clearing my throat, I said, "I was expecting it to be just the two of us."

"If you thought for one second that I would let her come and meet with you alone, then you're a dumber Smurffucker than I gave you credit for," he bit out between gritted teeth.

"What the hell did you think I was going to do to her, throw her across the table and screw her brains out?"

In a split second his arm reached out and grabbed a fistful of my shirt, pulling me toward the table. "Tweet, go get in the car."

"Noah, please," she said in a low voice as she placed her hand on Stewart's upper arm. I felt his grip loosen immediately. "What do you want, Brad?"

"I want to talk with you alone."

The two of them exchanged looks. "He just wants to talk," she told him softly.

"I'll be right around the corner at the library. Text me when you're done and I'll come get you," he said.

"I will." His eyes scanned her face just before he leaned in and brushed his lips across hers. "I love you," she whispered.

"I love you too," he said.

I usually looked away from such nauseating displays of PDA, but this time my gaze was frozen on these two. I had never seen honest-to-god true love before.

Reluctantly, Stewart got up to leave. "It's always such a pleasure to see you," I said, sarcasm dripping from my words.

"Smurffucker, go fuck yourself." He glanced back at Amanda one more time before walking away.

"Wow, he *really* hates me," I announced.

"He doesn't hate you."

"Yeah, he hates me."

"Yeah, pretty much," she agreed.

"Um... does he know that I *have* actually screwed your brains out on a table?"

"No." Her body stiffened as she leaned back, shaking her head and huffing out a breath of annoyance.

"So I'm like your dirty little secret," I said, unable to keep the smirk off my face.

"Listen, you and I are ancient history."

"It wasn't really that long ago."

She leaned toward me and said in a low irritated voice, "He's never asked and I've never offered the info, but I'm sure he figured out that we did *things*. Now if you don't tell me in the next five seconds why you wanted to meet, I'm out of here."

Just then the waitress arrived at the table and took our drink orders. This wasn't going exactly how I imagined it would. I'm pissing Amanda off more than anything else. Changing the way I acted toward girls was harder than I thought, especially with the one I liked. The old Brad never cared if a girl had a boyfriend. If I was attracted to her, I'd go after her. My feeling was, if her boyfriend was satisfying her then I wouldn't have a chance.

I always had a chance.

It was so natural for me to flirt with Amanda and fall back into our banter. I missed that. I missed her. But she wasn't mine and I needed to show her and her relationship with Mr. Fucking Perfect some respect. I kept my gaze focused on my hands that were fidgeting with my napkin as I tried to organize my thoughts, what I wanted to say, and how I wanted to say it. The waitress returned to our table. I watched intensely as she placed the coasters on the table, then two straws, and finally our drinks.

I looked up and past Amanda. Then I took one quick glance at her, to test the waters on how receptive she'd be to my attempt at sincerity. "I'm sorry. I shouldn't have said any of that stuff," I admitted. "How are you?"

"I'm fine. Why did you want to meet, Brad?" she asked again, her voice flat and guarded.

"I've been fine too, thanks." She didn't respond.

Stop being a Smurffucker, Brad.

I shifted in my seat and cleared my throat. "I wanted to say how sorry I was for everything that happened between us."

"Why?"

"Why what?"

"Why are you apologizing to me now?" Confusion and curiosity were written across her face.

I swallowed the lump in my dry throat. "Because I wanted you to know that the time we were together was the best time of my life." I took a large gulp of my drink.

"I don't understand. How could you say that and still bet on how long it would take to screw me?"

"Amanda, I was a ball-less prick. I still am in many ways, but I'm trying to change. I never wanted to be that guy; I just fell into it somehow. The bet was disgusting, but you have to believe me when I tell you that whenever I was with you, even on that day, had nothing to do with a bet."

"Then why did you go through with it?" I could see tears forming in her eyes. The ache in my stomach hit me hard seeing how what I had done still affected her so much.

"I wanted you to be my girl and I knew you couldn't be. You'd never look at me the way you looked at Noah. I held off having sex with you as long as I could because I wanted to keep you in my life. I knew once we had done it and you found out about the bet, we'd be over."

"That's bullshit. You didn't have to tell those guys."

"Yeah, well, that's where the ball-less prick part of my personality comes in. I wanted you so much, but I had to get out before I fell further. I didn't trust myself to stay away from you, so I needed you to hate me. That's why I went through with the bet. I know that day went from you *giving* me a part of yourself to me *taking* it away from you." As I remembered back to that day in my bedroom and the look on her face right before I left, I felt my throat burn and close up. "You were the only person I had ever cared about and I went ahead and humiliated you anyway. I'm so sorry I did that to you." My voice was unsteady.

"That night I showed up at your door and that entire summer… Why didn't you turn me away? Why did you let me keep coming back?"

"I missed you like crazy. You needed to pretend I was Noah that summer and I needed to pretend you were mine. I acted like an ass because you still needed to hate me. You had to be the one to walk away because I knew I couldn't."

Sitting back, she stared at me trying to figure out if I was being sincere. She let my words roll around in her head and watched the emotions on my face. "Why, after all this time are you suddenly struck with a guilty conscience about what happened?"

"I told you, I'm trying to change. I'm trying to grow up and be a better person. Besides, I always felt guilty."

She hesitated before she said, "Thank you for apologizing." I exhaled a deep sigh of relief at her words. "You weren't entirely to blame for what took place."

"No, I take full responsibility. The bet was…"

"Oh, the bet was totally a douche bag move on your part. I was referring to the entire summer. I could have walked away, but I didn't. I think it's safe to say we used each other equally."

Amanda had been through a lot since the last time I saw her and it had changed her. There was a peace and contentment that radiated off of her now and obviously a tremendous ability to forgive, even a Smurffucker like me.

"You and Stewart seem good."

"We're very good." There was a shift in her expression. Her face glowed with happiness at just the mention of his name. She was finally by his side, where she belonged.

"I'm glad. He's one lucky son of a bitch," I said, sending a grin her way that quickly disappeared as I thought how much I missed having her as my girl, even though it was pretend.

Somehow she read my expression. "Thank you. You'll find what Noah and I have someday, you know."

"Eh, maybe." I paused for a few seconds and then asked, "Everything else with you going well?"

"Yeah, life is pretty perfect." She smiled.

"When I've interned at my father's firm, I'd see your sister at the courthouse sometimes. I always asked her about you."

"Yeah, she told me. I knew there was more to you than what you let people see." She sent me a wink.

"Gotta keep the intrigue alive. The ladies love the mystery." I winked back at her and she chuckled. I took a long look at her gorgeous face and teal eyes. If I found someone half as great as this girl, I too would be a lucky son of a bitch.

"Well, I guess I better go and meet up with Noah. We have dinner plans."

I threw some money on the table and we both stood.

"Thanks for meeting me today," I said.

"I'm glad I came."

I leaned in, placed a soft kiss on her cheek and whispered, "Have a fantastic life, Beautiful. You deserve it."

We stared at each other for a few minutes with a mixture of regret and sorrow, but also forgiveness. We realized because of our circumstances we may not be the best of friends, but we definitely knew we were no longer enemies.

Mabry

I stood out in front of my house for the first time in two years. My dad and I rarely spoke anymore. At least when I was still living at home we would exchange the occasional, "How are you?" or "See ya later". But since I had left for college I almost never came home, he never visited me at school, and neither of us took the time to call each other. It was as if there had been a huge colossal argument between us and we both took a vow of silence. I knew why I had stopped talking to him, but I never understood why he stopped talking to me.

The minute my mom died, my dad stopped being my dad. It was confusing because when mom was alive, he was a good dad. I was closer to her, but he still took part in my life. I looked up to him and respected him. As a little girl, I knew he would be there for me whenever I needed him. I felt his protectiveness naturally. The last time he shielded me from the ugliness that life could throw at me was the night Mom killed herself, when he pushed me out of the room. I've thought about that moment for years and wondered now if he was trying to protect me or get me out of the way so he could be alone with the love of his life.

After Dr. Burnett released me from the hospital, I took a break from self-harming. The concussion diagnosis scared me enough to force down my urges for a little while. Memories of my mom and Becca still occupied my thoughts the majority of the time. I lost count of how many times I replayed Becca's memorial service in my head. The look on her parents' faces, the words used to describe her, the hurt that was so striking in the face of the boy who I assumed to be the one she loved. I wondered how he was handling things. I remembered the pull I felt toward him. Whenever I thought about him and Becca I felt a wave of jealousy. She had someone to love, who loved her, and would miss her. That day I wanted to hold him and feel that love, even though it wasn't directed toward me. Part of me wanted someone in my life, but then I would think of my mom and the way she devastated my dad. She not only left me, but took him with her. I've experienced dark moods and even though I've not had suicidal thoughts, the possibility is there. I couldn't fall in love. If it were to happen and the darkness overtook me, I would be destroying two lives.

I knew I needed to get the self-harm under control. The concussion was a close call. I thought maybe if I understood what happened to my parents it would help me with the anger I felt toward both of them. After all, I was all grown-up now and able to comprehend the situation better. I never contacted the counselor on the card the doctor gave me. I didn't feel like trudging through my entire history with a stranger who would more than likely give me quick simplified answers and stupid self-help exercises. I figured I'd try to get some answers from my dad.

I took in a deep breath and started up the steps. As I got closer to the door, I felt a tingling in my arms and legs, as my body temperature rose, and my insides quivered. This reaction was ridiculous. I was just going to ask my dad a few simple questions. Questions that had plagued me for years. He owed me this. Turning the doorknob, I took one more deep breath, before pushing the door open. The place looked exactly the same and I was immediately transported back to feeling like the sad little girl who almost suffocated in this house. I heard the TV playing in the family room. I put my suitcase down and headed in that direction. When I caught sight of my dad sitting in his recliner, I gasped. He looked so old and pathetic. I cleared my throat.

Twisting in his chair, he looked over at me, his expression slack. "Mabry?"

"Hey, Dad." The title stuck in my throat. I hadn't said that word or thought of him as my father in a long time, so the term felt foreign coming out of my mouth.

He pointed the remote at the TV, turning it off, and then looked at me for several seconds as if he didn't recognize me. "I didn't know you were coming here today."

I huffed out a breath, unable to hide my annoyance. "I left you a message last week, letting you know I was coming for a visit. Didn't you get it?"

He looked confused. "That was last week? I'm sorry. I lose track of time."

"Damn, you'd think a father would be a little more excited about his daughter coming for a visit, who hadn't been home in two years."

"I am excited. The days kind of run together sometimes. You just surprised me."

I slid over a stack of newspapers, making room on the sofa, and sat across from him. "So, how have you been?" I asked, looking at the piles of mail, clothes, and takeout boxes strewn about the room. It doesn't look like he's cleaned this place since the last time I was here.

"Well, things are okay."

"Things don't look okay. When was the last time this place was cleaned?"

"I know. I'm not much of a housekeeper."

"You should hire a maid to come in a few times a week."

"Yeah, I will."

I thought my memories of the aftermath of Mom's death were pretty vivid, but being back here and seeing my dad, they appeared in HD. I wanted to fire off the questions I've been wanting answers to and then get the hell out of there, but I knew now wasn't the time. He still seemed in shock to see me back here.

"I'll go put my things up and then make dinner."

"I don't really have much food in the house. We could order out if you want."

Standing, I said, "Sounds fine." He gave me a weak smile before I headed down the hall.

The stale smell hit me as I stepped into my room. In fact, the entire house had a terrible musty odor. I wondered when the last time a window was opened to allow fresh air in. My room was exactly how it was two years ago, which was exactly how it was the day my mom died. The house was like a fucking time capsule. As I walked around looking at my past, resentment and anger kept building with each minute. I hated how weak and pathetic my dad was. I hated that he had let the house deteriorate like this. I hated that his existence was still in the past. Standing in front of my dresser, I caught the reflection of my bedroom door in the mirror. The first door I hid behind, shutting the world out. The first door I sought relief from. The first door that gave me my first lumps, bumps, and bruises. Maybe my dad wasn't the only one living in the past.

The next morning I woke up early and removed the piles from the family room. I dusted, mopped, and did several loads of laundry all while my dad sat and either watched the TV or read the newspaper. Occasionally, I caught him staring at me. The look in his eyes was strange, as if he still couldn't believe I was there.

I sat at the kitchen table sorting through a ton of unopened mail. "Dad, did you know you have past due notices?"

"I'll get to it tomorrow, Mabry. Don't worry about them."

"Well, do you have the money to pay your bills?"

"Yes," he said flatly, never looking up from his newspaper.

"Then you need to pay the bills on time. You can set up automatic draft so they'll come out of your account."

"Maybe I should do that. I have a hard time remembering those kinds of things. Your mother used to take care of all that, you know." He said it as if she had just died a few weeks ago instead of eleven years ago. I resented the fact that he was still using her death as an excuse to avoid his responsibilities.

"You can't keep using that as an excuse."

He finally looked up from his paper. "I'm not using it as an excuse. It's a fact. She handled all of the bills."

"She's been gone for eleven years, Dad." Annoyance flowed through my tone.

"What does that have to do with anything?"

"You act as if she just died."

"Some days it feels that way. I miss her so much," he said in a low voice.

"Then why did you let her do it?" I asked under my breath. My tone matching the lack of emotion in my face.

"What?" He slowly lowered the newspaper.

Looking up and directly into his eyes, I repeated, "Why did you let her do it?"

"Do what?"

"Kill herself, Dad."

His expression shifted from sad to offended. "Why would you ask something so horrible?"

"Why won't you answer me?"

"Because there is no answer. I adored your mother. I would never do anything to hurt her."

I stood and walked toward him, stopping a few feet away. "You never did anything to save her either."

"Mabry, that's enough. Why are you being so cruel to me?" His voice was shaky.

"You knew she was sick for a long time and you didn't do anything. You let her slip away." Years of pent-up anger and resentment were rising to the surface. My legs felt weak and were barely holding me up. I reached out and placed my hand on the back of the sofa to steady myself. I was determined not to move. I wanted answers. I needed answers. "Just tell me why you never forced her to go to the doctor or take her medicine."

"You can't force a person to do something they don't want to do." The sadness returned to his eyes.

His words slapped me in the face. I slowly walked to the sofa and sat. I was always angry at my mom for leaving me, but over the years I had come to believe that she had no control over herself. That she was lost so deep in the darkness that she couldn't distinguish a right decision from a wrong one. I believed she wanted to stay with us, with me, but needed a hand to reach out and guide her back to us.

"Why did she want to leave us?" My bottom lip quivered as I tried to hold back my tears. I looked at my dad, my eyes pleading with him to answer, *She didn't have a choice. Her actions were out of her control.*

"She was just tired," he said flatly.

"She wasn't tired of being my mom." Tears were streaming down my face.

"She was just tired of *being*, sweetheart, so she finally made the choice that day to stop."

She made the choice.

My chest caved in as all the air rushed out of my lungs when I heard those words. Sobs were escaping me at a rapid pace while my heart and soul shattered.

She made the decision to leave me. She didn't want to be my mom anymore.

My eyes were so blurry from my tears I didn't see my dad approach and sit beside me. I flinched when I felt his hand on my shoulder.

"I'm so sorry, Mabry. She did love you, but she just couldn't pretend to be happy any longer." His voice trailed off, whispering the last few words.

Wiping my eyes, I took a couple of deep breaths, trying to compose myself, and asked, "Did you blame me? Is that why you just left me alone?"

We stared at each other for several seconds. The look in his eyes answered my question.

"It was hard to be there for you because you're just like her, and I missed her so much. I still do. Even now it hurts. You have her blue eyes, soft chestnut hair, and creamy pale skin. You're so beautiful." He raised a trembling hand, cupping the side of my face, and gently ran his thumb back and forth over my cheek.

The air in the room changed and so did the look in his eyes. I could tell he no longer saw his daughter sitting in front of him. He was looking at the love of his life. A chill ran through me when he shifted his position. His hand slid to the back of my neck. Leaning toward me slightly, he pulled me in closer as he tilted his head. I jerked away from him and jumped up. My breathing was shallow and erratic. I felt like I was going to be sick.

"I've got to get out of here," I blurted out.

I ran down the hallway to my room, quickly threw my things in my suitcase, and headed for the front door. Before leaving I looked back and saw my father still on the sofa, sobbing into his hands. Tears gushed out of me as I realized that any hope I might have had to someday get him back was gone.

CHAPTER 13

THE PRESENT

Brad

I'm sitting in front of her as she leans back on my desk, proofing a letter for me, her dark rimmed glasses perched on her adorable little nose. Her hair is pulled up into a messy bun, exposing that spot right at the nape of her neck that drives her crazy when I run my tongue over it. As usual her makeup is light and natural, except today she's wearing a deep red lipstick, making her lips look extra pouty. She raises the pen she's holding and slips the tip of it into her mouth. My dick immediately twitches. My eyes roam down her body admiring the way her light gray dress glides over every curve so smoothly. I wonder if she's even wearing panties. I shift uncomfortably in my chair. Looking down I recognize the sexy black heels with the strap around the ankle. They were draped over my shoulders and digging into my back a couple of nights ago when I had Mabry on the edge of the dining room table, my face buried between her thighs. I look back up, trying to control the urge to shove her dress up and have a repeat performance of that night. My eyes stop at the wide black leather belt around her waist. *Fuck me.* We've used that on occasion too. No matter what part of her body my eyes land on, my dick reacts. I know she feels my gaze because her nipples are hard and straining against the material of her dress. I take in a deep breath and let it out quickly.

"You sure you wouldn't be more comfortable sitting on my lap?" I smirk up at her.

The corners of her mouth curl into a sexy grin. The pen she's holding is aimed in my direction. "We agreed. No funny business at work."

I run my hand up her thigh and feel the shiver that moves through her body.

Sweet baby Jesus! I think I feel a garter.

"Sweetness, the business I'm thinking about engaging in would definitely not be funny. I hope it wouldn't be anyway." I ease out of my chair, inching my way up her body as I say, "That'd be quite a blow to my ego if you were to laugh as I bring you to the ultimate height of ecstasy." I flash her *the smile* as I cock my eyebrow.

We're face-to-face now. My hands planted firmly on either side of her hips, caging her in. Her chest rises and falls a little faster than normal as she looks directly at me. My lips skim down the side of her face heading toward her mouth, and I nibble lightly at the corners. She's so caught up in the moment, I'm able to take the letter from her and toss it on my desk.

Moving my mouth to her ear, I whisper, "Let's play hot secretary and bossy naughty boss."

Her body shakes as the most beautiful sound in the world flows out of her mouth. "It's amazing how you can get me hot and make me laugh at the same time."

"I'm a full-service love machine, Sweetness. I can make you laugh, moan, scream, and beg for more." I kiss a path along her jaw and down her neck.

"So this hot secretary and bossy naughty boss... Who gets to be the boss?" she asks in a low sexy voice.

"You'll always be the boss of me," I say against her neck.

"Okay." It comes out like a sigh as she tilts her head to the side, exposing more of her neck to me. She allows me to linger a few seconds before shoving me back. The look in her eyes is smoldering, intense, and makes me completely hard. "Well, Bradley, I was not pleased with the report you turned in to me." She places her hands on the desk, leaning back on them for support.

"I apologize for my incompetency, Ms. Darnell. Maybe this will please you." I take a step toward her.

She quickly extends her leg, planting the sharp heel of her shoe on the lower half of my chest. "I'll be the one to tell *you* what pleases me."

A huge grin crosses my face.

"Now, do as you're told or I'll report you for being insubordinate."

"You're the best girlfriend ever."

She pushes her heel gently into my chest. "Get serious or I'll be forced to slap that hot as fuck grin off your face." She tries to keep the stern look, but a slight smirk sneaks across her lips.

"Yes ma'am." A smile starts to play on my face but I quickly make it disappear.

Lowering her leg, she instructs. "Pay attention, I'm going to tell you exactly what I want you to do." She peers at me over her glasses. "Do you need to write this down?"

"I got it."

"Excuse me?" she asks, flirty sarcasm flowing through her words.

"I mean, no ma'am. I'll pay attention and remember everything you tell me."

She removes her glasses and places them on the desk. "Good to hear that, Bradley. The first thing I'll want you to do is get on your knees in front of me and run your nose up my leg to my inner thigh while your hands shove my dress over my hips."

My breathing picks up and every hair on my body rises. "Yes ma'am."

"Then I want your tongue to flick me down there," she says, glancing down. "I like it fast and hard."

I take in a big gulp of air. "I can do fast and hard."

"Next, I'll have you to peel my dress off. You'll then drag your tongue up to my tits and suck them hard. I basically want everything hard, Bradley. Do you think you can be hard with me?"

"I'm already hard."

She smiles and says, "I can see that. You know just the thought of you inside of me is making me wetter than I've ever been before."

"Mabry..." My entire body vibrates with tension. I can feel tiny beads of sweat on my forehead and my breathing sounds as if I've sprinted around the building several times.

"No, no, no..." she says in a sing-songy way.

"Ms. Darnell, as I'm getting harder so is the ability to stand here and not attack you."

"Just one more thing. After you sufficiently tongue fuck me, you'll bend me over this desk..." She stands, turns, and bends over the desk in front of me. "...you'll properly fuck me. Pounding into me hard, fast, and continuously."

I make my way to her immediately. When she stands, her back meets my chest, surprising her. My hands glue themselves to her tits, massaging and pinching as I suck that special spot at the nape of her neck. Her hands grab my hips, pulling them to her as she grinds her ass against my dick.

"Brad, we can't do this now. We need to stop," she moans breathlessly.

My lips move to just below her ear. "Shhh, Ms. Darnell, I'm working on a raise."

A cute giggle escapes her. My hands move down to the bottom of her dress. Hooking my fingers under the hem, I slide it up. Suddenly there is a loud knock on my door, jolting both of us out of the moment. Mabry spins around to face me. She runs her palms down her dress, and then up around her hair, tucking in any stray pieces. I try to calm my perfectly good, but wasted hard on. I'm combing my fingers through my hair while Mabry's putting her glasses back on, just as the door opens and my brother Peyton sticks his head in.

"You're supposed to wait until somebody says come in," I growl at him in frustration.

"Now, what or who could you be *doing* that would be inappropriate for me to see? Oh, hi ya, Mabry."

"Peyton, you're such a dick..." I say.

Mabry places her hand on my chest, stopping me from laying further into my brother. She keeps eye contact with me as she stands and says, "I need to get going. I'm meeting Sylvie."

"Again? You two had a girl's night just a couple of days ago."

"She's having guy trouble. Since I found the most perfect Mr. Perfect in the world, she wants some pointers," she says in a low voice, not wanting Peyton to hear.

"Well, lookie who's full of cheese today." I grin, then lean in, kissing her on the forehead, and whisper, "Can I come by tonight?"

"Yes, please. I'll text you when I'm home." Her face lights up with a gorgeous smile before she turns and walks toward the door.

"Mabry," Peyton says, standing up straight as she approaches.

"Peyton," Mabry says, walking out.

Peyton doesn't hide his admiring glare of Mabry as she passes him. "Mmmm, that's one fine piece of..."

"What the fuck do you want?" I ask, cutting him off.

"Dad wants us in his office now."

"For what?"

"Don't know, bro, but he looks pissed."

"He always looks pissed," I point out.

"Yeah, well, he looks exceptionally pissed today."

The air is stifling in my father's office or maybe it just feels that way to me. He's sitting behind his massive desk, his face partially hidden in shadow with his chin resting on his laced fingers. He doesn't make a move or a sound to greet Peyton and me as we enter. Both of us know instinctively to sit in front of his desk in silence until he's ready to speak. As the seconds tick by, I occupy my mind with thoughts of being with Mabry and finding out if she is, in fact, wearing a garter.

"I'm glad you're smiling now because you won't be in a few minutes."

"What?" I ask, jolted out of my Mabry haze by the deep baritone of my father's voice. I glance over at a chuckling Peyton.

My father's cold piercing eyes fixate on me. He's already being condescending with just one look. "Do you know a Rebecca Hyams?" he asks in a stern accusatory tone.

The answer "no" is on the tip of my tongue because at first the name didn't ring a bell. I always knew her as Becca. Once it sank in, so did my chest and stomach.

"I knew her at Duke." My answer sounds slightly defensive.

"Did you fuck her?" He says it so bluntly it catches me off guard.

"Damn, way to get to the point, Dad," Peyton remarks.

The best way to handle my father is to answer his questions as straightforward as possible using the minimal amount of words. "Yes."

"Were you dating? Was it a relationship?"

"No. We were together just a handful of times. I didn't even know her that well." A pang of guilt shot through me. Every word that comes out of my mouth is true, but it feels as if I'm belittling Becca's impact on my life somehow.

"So, no "I love you's" ever passed between the two of you?" he asks, continuing the interrogation.

I hesitate, remembering the night Becca told me she loved me. "No. Why are you asking me about Becca?" Instead of just coming right out with the information, he's goading me. I'm getting irritated with his little game of twenty questions.

"She committed suicide while at Duke, but I'm sure you knew that already." He leans back in his leather chair.

"What's that got to do with Brad?" Peyton chimes in.

"When was the last time you saw her, Bradley?"

"I guess during my second year in law school, so about two years ago."

"Specifically, when was the last time you laid eyes on her?" He's in full lawyer mode now.

I'm getting more and more uncomfortable with each question, but I suppress the urge to shift in my seat. Staying still and grounded shows strength and confidence. Moving about and fidgeting shows your opponent that your nerves are surfacing. This has been drilled into my head by my father since before I entered law school. My eyes are pointed directly at him, but I'm looking over his shoulder at the row of law books that line his bookshelves. I didn't want to answer "specifically" when I saw her last.

"That night," I whisper.

"Excuse me?"

My glare moves to meet his. Clearing my throat, I repeat my answer, "That night. I saw her the night she committed suicide."

"Fuuuck." I hear Peyton mutter.

"Now you answer my question. Why are you asking me about Becca?"

Leaning forward, he shuffles through some papers in front of him, picks up one, and tosses it across the desk toward me. I glance down at the document. "Because her parents are bringing a wrongful death lawsuit against you, *Son.*"

I immediately look up at him when I hear the venomous sound that comes from his mouth when he calls me "son".

"I don't understand," I say, slightly dazed.

"Well, it's pretty simple. They claim you were directly responsible for the death of their daughter."

All the air leaves my lungs. I had worked hard to get past the guilt I felt regarding my connection with Becca's death, but it all came rushing back with that one sentence. My past is about to meet my present.

Mabry.

"How is that possible?" Peyton asks. "She committed suicide. She decided to take her own life. This is total bullshit."

"They don't even know me. How can they think I had anything to do with her death?"

"Apparently there's a letter that implicates you as being the major cause of her distressed mental state which caused her to take her own life." He spouts out the information as if I'm a client. A client he can't stand to represent.

"Brad, listen, this shit isn't going to make it to court," Peyton says.

I stare straight ahead in silence. I have so many thoughts and feelings whirling around inside of me, but I block them all out. There's only one thing I'm able to focus on.

Mabry.

"Peyton's right. This won't make it to court. The docket is so backed up it would take years. Besides, this is a frivolous suit. No judge in his right mind would even take the time to consider hearing it. My guess is they want money, plain and simple. They see a cash cow and are ready to pounce," my father explains.

"How much?" I ask.

"One point two million."

A whistle shoots from Peyton's mouth.

"Fuck, I don't have that kind of money."

"No, but the firm and I do." My father's eyes burn into me. His words are full of sarcasm.

"It's been two years. Why now?"

Mabry.

"They claim they've been too overwhelmed with grief to take action until now. I think it's taken them this long to find a lawyer who would take the case."

"Who's their lawyer," Peyton inquires.

"Tennyson McGuire."

Fuck me.

"Shit, he's good," Peyton says.

"Not only that, he's hungry. He knows this suit will garner him attention even if he's able to squeeze just a dime out of us. Most likely, they'll want to deal. They'll come down some on the amount and drop the case if we go ahead and pay up. They know we don't want this to get out and have the family name and reputation of the firm dragged through the mud. I'll have Tina set up the meeting." He turns toward his computer and clicks away at something.

Peyton and I look at each other, wondering if we are free to go. We both hesitate for a moment before standing.

"Peyton, let me speak to your brother alone, please," my father says abruptly, never looking at us.

Peyton glances over at me before exiting.

"Sit down, Bradley," he commands. He swivels his chair in my direction and leans back. His expression flat. "Did you have anything to do with this girl's death?"

I'm not sure how to answer his question. Technically, no, I didn't do anything besides break up with Becca. I had no knowledge then of her mental status or that she was going to kill herself. But I've always felt partially responsible, and apparently I am since Becca mentions me in her letter.

Mabry.

"I broke up with her that night."

"Goddammit!" His eyes blaze as he clamps down on his jaw. He sits there for a moment, jaw clenched so tight causing muscle in his neck to twitch. He's considering his next verbal assault.

I need to get out of here and be alone, so I can think straight. I decide to swallow my pride. "I'm sorry."

"This is one expensive fuck, Bradley. I hope this teaches you to be more discriminating and to stop putting your dick into every hole that walks by."

"You mean like you, *Dad?*" I sneer.

"Oh, here we go. The blame game. My personal life never interfered with raising you. I provided well for both you and your brother. You had everything you needed growing up."

"Except a father." I bolt out of the chair and head to my office, never looking back at him.

Back in my office I continuously pace the floor. I can't stop thinking about Mabry. Running my hands up my face and through my hair, I feel my heart pounding hard against my chest. I loosen my tie, trying to stop the choking sensation in my throat. I walk to the window and brace my hands on either side of the frame. Looking out, I'm able to see the Charleston Harbor. Watching the waves, I try to calm my breathing and think clearly. I keep telling myself that I have no idea what her reaction will be when I tell her about Becca, but the gnawing sensation I feel deep in the pit of my stomach tells me everything is about to break.

Please God, don't let me lose her over this.

My phone chirps with a text. I pull it from my pocket and look down at a picture of Mabry's legs, her stilettos and her sheer black stockings hooked to a black garter.

Mabry: Hey sexy beast. I'm waiting 4 u.

I consider making up an excuse not to go over, but know I have to talk to her before she hears this from anyone else. I'm afraid that once the sun comes up tomorrow the office rumor mill will be in full swing. Letting out a deep sigh, I reluctantly type out a response and hit send.

Brad: *B right there. I love u.*

As I head over to Mabry's, I try to mentally prepare for my past to collide with my present, and pray that my future with her doesn't become a casualty.

Mabry

I hated lying to Brad tonight about where I was going after work. I'm just not ready to tell him I'm seeing a counselor. I'm not sure why, exactly. Maybe it's because I didn't want him to view me as weak. I've always thought going to any type of counseling was a sign of weakness. It probably comes from the fact that my dad never took me after my mom's death. I had convinced myself that I just had to suck it up and get over it by myself. Of course, at the time I was fine with that. I didn't want to talk about it to anyone. Looking back now, I can see how irresponsible and thoughtless it was of him. I wonder how different our lives and relationship would have been if he had sought help for both of us back then.

A bell chimes as I enter the counseling office of Jennifer Clark. The waiting room is decorated in calming brown, green, and cream hues. An overstuffed sofa is against one wall, flanked by two small end tables, with matching chairs facing it. A stack of out dated magazines on meditation and self-help are spread across the coffee table between the sofa and chairs. The lighting is dim, with just a few lamps in use. The sound of synthesized angel harps floats out of a boom-box and mixes with the trickling of water from a small fountain in the corner of the room. The room reeks of jasmine and has several green plants sitting around. It's like a New Age purgatory.

I take a seat and scan through one of the magazines, needing to keep my hands and mind occupied. I sit alone for several minutes struggling with whether or not to stay or leave. Being here makes me uncomfortable despite the clichéd calming elements. I'm afraid of what questions she's going to ask me, my answers to them, and what they'll reveal about me. I'm afraid I've inherited more from my mother than just my looks and the counselor will finally be the person to voice what I'm terrified of, a future of becoming just like Mom. When I hear the music of Yanni play, I decide this isn't for me. Tossing the meditation mag on the table, I stand, but then I hear the sound of a door opening down the short hallway leading to the back of the office. My hand reaches for the doorknob, but before I'm able to make my escape, a woman takes a few steps in my direction.

"Mabry Darnell?" she asks.

I cringe just before turning to face her, knowing I now have to go through with the appointment. "Yes, I'm Mabry Darnell."

"Hi, I'm Jennifer Clark." She extends her hand and we shake.

"Here's the paperwork I filled out online." I hand over my insurance info and the questionnaire regarding my history.

"Thank you. You can go on back. I'll be right with you. It's the last door on your right." I simply nod and head down the hall to her office.

Once inside, I take a seat in the chair by the door. Then I get up and move to the sofa by the window. Then I move back to the chair. Finally, deciding the sofa is where I want to be, I drum my fingers on the wooden armrest. Just when I'm about to bolt, the woman enters, closing the door behind her.

Shit.

"How are things with you today?" she asks, taking the seat across from me.

The question catches me off guard. If things were okay I wouldn't

156

be sitting in a counselor's office. I give her a weak smile and simply answer, "Okay."

The room is quiet as her eyes roam over my questionnaire. I dart my eyes around the room, trying not to look at her expression, wondering if she's thinking what a nut case I am based on my answers.

"So, Mabry, I see this is the first time you've been to see a counselor."

"Yes." My answer comes out quick as if she startled me. "Sorry, I'm a little nervous."

"I can tell. We'll start off easy." She gives me a warm smile. "Why have you decided that now is the right time to seek counseling?"

"I have some things in my past that are effecting my present. I constantly push people away and I don't want to anymore."

"Why do you think you keep people at a distance?"

"I'm terrified of getting hurt," I answer in a low voice.

"It's interesting you use the word 'terrified.' That's a pretty intense word, more than scared or afraid," she points out. "Is that why you've not had any long-lasting relationships?"

"I haven't had any relationships except for my best friend, Sylvie, and even that I hold at a distance." I feel a pang of guilt when I admit that. Sylvie has been a good friend to me and the fact that I haven't let her completely in makes me feel ashamed.

"I see on your form, though, that you are in a relationship now. What's his name?" The look in her eyes is caring.

"Brad." I can't help the smile that appears on my face. Just saying his name calms me down.

"Well, obviously, you didn't push Brad away."

"I tried to."

"Why didn't you succeed?" she asks.

"Brad's different and I'm different with him. I wasn't looking for anything serious, I never have, but it was always serious with him. From the moment we met, he made me feel things and I hadn't felt anything in a long time. I caved in to those feelings and then craved them. At first, I tried to be with him, detach from it, and then go about my life."

"Compartmentalizing your emotions, without them spilling over into the rest of your life, is a very difficult thing to do, especially for us women. We're very emotional creatures."

"I've always been able to do it before with other people," I say.

"Well, you say Brad's different." She tosses my words back at me with a smile. "What is it about him that caused you to stop pushing?"

"He makes me truly happy. I'm not talking the superficial "happy," like when you get a promotion at work or buy a fabulous pair of shoes. True happiness is when you feel contentment and joy deep in your soul, no matter what problems are swirling around outside of you. People underestimate that feeling. It's such a simple short word, but it holds so much depth and power. When it's been absent from your life for so long you forget just how precious a gift it really is."

The rest of the session with Jennifer flew by. We discussed more about Brad and me, as well as my past encounters with men. I was surprised how much easier it got to talk to her once we started. Even though we didn't touch on the subject of my parents or my self-harm, I feel the weight I've been carrying around start to ease up. For the first time since my mom's death, I feel hopeful about my future. I finally believe it will be possible to have one with Brad.

I rush back to my place excited to let him know he can head on over. I'm in such a good mood I decide to have a little fun. I could tell earlier, when his hand ran up my thigh and by the look in his eyes, that he was wondering if I had a garter on under my dress. I position myself on the sofa, twisting and turning my body in order to get the garter down to the stilettos in the shot. As I type out a short text, I can feel the heat and tingles build just thinking about his sexy smile when he reads it.

Me: Hey sexy beast. I'm waiting 4 u.

Brad: B right there. I love u.

I'm a little surprised and disappointed that he didn't respond with one of his cheesy or sexy comebacks. Brad was pretty pissed that his brother interrupted us. The dynamic between the two of them is interesting. Being an only child I didn't know if it was typical sibling rivalry or not. In front of others, the brothers would joke and act like I assume brothers acted, but behind the scenes I had noticed contentious looks pass between them. Brad didn't talk about his family very much. I knew the issues with his parents. But the only thing he ever told me about Peyton was that they have never been close. I hope things with his brother didn't get out of hand after I left.

CHAPTER 14

THE PAST

Brad

I was standing by the window in the conference room waiting for the meeting to start. As I listened to Matt, another first year-lawyer, tell me about some girl he met last night, I felt a vibration start in my chest and quickly spread through my entire body. Initially I ignored it. Maybe the coffee I was drinking went down the wrong way. Another vibration shot through me a second after the first one subsided. I looked at Matt to see if he noticed anything strange happening to me. Obviously he didn't, because he continued to mindlessly talk. My eyes swung around the room, coming to an abrupt halt on an azure blue gaze.

Damn.

Things were pulsing and throbbing on me that hadn't pulsed or throbbed in a long time and I was still glued to the eyes. Finally, I forced myself to take the rest of her in. The view just got better and better. All the parts were there and they were aligned in a spectacular fashion. I had to talk to her before the meeting.

"Good luck with that, Matt," I said, not hearing anything that had come out of his mouth since she walked in.

I was halfway across the room when I was stopped by a hand attaching itself to my upper arm. "Hey Brad."

"Hey Mia."

"You want to grab a couple of seats before the meeting starts?" I'd known Mia for a year. She and I interned together at the firm last summer. She's been trying to get into my pants ever since our first week. She was beautiful, but like with every other woman, nothing in me stirred enough to want to act on her interest.

"We're probably going to be sitting for a good while, so I'll wait until just before it starts." I took a step toward my azure blue target, but Mia still had a firm grip on my arm.

"So did you hear about Robinson? He got caught cheating on the bar and ..."

Her voice disappeared as I watched Peyton saunter up to azure blue with a big grin on his face.

Fuck.

What the hell is he doing? She was my vibration. Heat crawled across my skin as my chest tightened. What was wrong with me? I didn't even know her name. All I knew was that she was the first female who ever elicited this much of a reaction out of me.

"Sorry, Mia." I tugged my arm away from her claws. "I need to talk to Peyton before things start up."

I made it over to azure blue and Peyton in three quick strides. Her eyes shifted from him to me before I reached them.

Slapping Peyton on the back a little harder than probably necessary, I said, "Mornin', brother." Azure blue gave me a slight smile.

After recovering from my slight assault, he looked at me annoyed. "Mornin'."

My eyes were once again glued to hers as I asked Peyton, "Aren't you going to introduce us?"

"Sorry, I was still trying to recover from having the wind knocked out of me. Mabry Darnell, this is my "little" brother, Brad."

Double entendre, motherfucker.

I flashed her *the smile* before I turned to him. "You might want to get that checked out. I mean, if that little tap knocked the air out you," I looked back at Mabry, "you might be having trouble with oxygen flow, which causes your appendages to stop working and your stamina to be nonexistent."

I flashed *the smile* and cocked an eyebrow in her direction. She laughed and then the most beautiful smile I had ever seen appeared across her plump lips. I swallowed hard.

"What the fuck are you talking about, Brad? My appendages and stamina are in top-notch condition," Peyton said in a low voice.

"Mia is looking for you," I told him as I stayed focused on Mabry.

"Oh really, well, if you'll excuse me then. Mabry, I'll catch up with you later," he announced before walking away.

Mabry and I took each other in for a few more seconds.

"Hi," I said with a grin.

"Hi," she said returning my grin.

"I'm Brad."

She narrowed her eyes at me and a slight giggle left her. "I know."

"Yeah? How do you know my name?" I stood there, chest all puffed out, feeling pretty cocky that this gorgeous woman who makes every part of my body hum had obviously asked around about me, wanting to know my name.

"Um… your brother just introduced us like five seconds ago," she said, a little sarcasm seeping into her tone.

Fuuuuck meeee!

Not my smoothest moment.

Over the next month, Mabry and I ended up working a lot of cases together. Our personalities and work styles complemented each other. She challenged me intellectually, pushing me to delve deeper into research, look at things from a different perspective before making decisions. I valued and cared about her opinion of not only my work, but of me. The two of us were in my office working late on the Peterson case. We were sitting on the floor between the sofa and coffee table eating the takeout we had ordered. My sleeves were rolled up to my elbows and her hair was piled up on top of her head. My tie and her shoes were off. Being with her was so natural as if we had been together for years. I've asked her out pretty much every day since our first meeting and she's continuously turned me down, but I was tenacious and didn't give up easily. Besides, I knew she liked me just as much as I liked her. There was no way the pull and connection between us could be one-sided. She was telling me about law school while she spread the containers of food out in front of us. I could watch her talk all day.

"...I had a 4.0 GPA and since I interned every summer during school, when I told Mr. Dukes I was coming back to Charleston he told me about his college buddy, your dad. He put in a good word for me and here I am."

"That was the best decision my father has ever made," I said grabbing a set of chopsticks. I glanced up at her and saw a light pink blush speckle her cheeks. "You're a great lawyer, Mabry." She shrugged her shoulders dismissively. Playfully, I poked her with one end of my chopsticks, causing her to look at me. "Hey, I mean it. You're better than most of the junior associates here."

"Thank you," she said, giving me a shy smile.

"Aaaand…?"

Her beautiful eyes looked off to the side as she sucked in her lower lip, then they darted back to me. "Thank you *very much?*"

Shaking my head I said, "You're supposed to say, 'Thank you very much, Brad. That means the world coming from someone as brilliant, gorgeous and hot as you are.'"

"Sorry, I need practice. I'm not real good at ass kissing."

"Well, I'd be more than happy to let you practice on my ass." I threw a smirk and a wink at her.

A breath caught in her throat as she darted her eyes away again and nervously rummaged through the takeout bag. I loved tipping her off balance. She was so cute that way.

She huffed, blowing her bangs up and off her forehead. "They didn't include any forks," she said, slightly annoyed.

Swallowing a piece of my sesame chicken, I said, "Use the chopsticks."

Scrunching up her eyebrows she looked at the two sticks as if a person would need to be a rocket scientist to figure out how to use them. She tentatively picked them up and peeled the paper away that they were wrapped in. I continued to eat while watching her out of the corner of my eye as she tried to position the chopsticks correctly between her fingers and attempted to pick up a piece of chicken. I felt her eyes on me, watching as I popped another piece in my mouth and then picked up some rice and vegetables with ease. She attempted using the prehistoric eating tools a couple of more times without success. She was stubborn and determined to master them herself.

Unable to keep the smile off my face and the laughter out of my voice, I turned to her and asked, "Mabry, you've never used chopsticks before, have you?" Sarcasm flowed through each word.

She narrowed her eyes at me. "Smartass."

"I'm a smartass with a belly full of Chinese," I said patting my stomach. "It's delicious too. Gimme." I extended my hand, flexing my fingers for her to hand over the chopsticks. She looked back and forth between my hand and the sticks before finally slapping them into my palm. "Turn around."

"Turn around?" she asked confused.

"Yes, so your back is to me."

"What are you going to do?" She sounded alarmed.

"I'm going to show you how to feed yourself. Just trust me and turn around." She did and I moved in closer to her.

I took the chopsticks and positioned them while keeping her hand covered with mine, so I could guide its movement. I felt a wisp of her hair tickle my cheek. As we picked up a small piece of food, I inhaled quietly. God, she smelled incredible, like vanilla and ginger. The ginger could have been from the food, but mixed with Mabry it was the best smell I had ever experienced. My eyes closed while I breathed in a little more of her. I caught an unobstructed view of the very top of her tits and my hand went slack. I felt Mabry jerk around and then yelp.

"Ugh, I think a snow pea went down my bra," she said snapping me out of my haze.

"What?"

"Snow pea. In. My. Bra."

Lucky snow pea.

She unbuttoned her top button, shoving her hand into the front of the bra. My eyes couldn't help but stare. More of her tits appeared, and she giggled a little as she fished out the snow pea. I was also treated to a glimpse of her bra. Her *black* bra. Black is my favorite color for bras, panties, garters, any lingerie really. It can look classy or slutty, it's quite versatile.

"I'm sorry. Let me help you." I grabbed for a napkin, which brought our lips within an inch of each other's. My gaze alternated between her eyes and lips. Her tits were noticeably moving up and down as her breathing increased.

"Brad…," she whispered.

"Mabry…" My voice was low.

"This is a bad idea."

"It's a *very* bad idea." I took in a big gulp of air.

"Office hooks-ups never end well." Her voice was breathy and sultry.

"So, I'll quit." I grinned.

"Sure, you'll quit your father's firm," she said, sarcastically, a hint of a smile across her face.

"So you quit."

Giggling she said, "Not gonna happen, buddy. It's just that… I'm not in a serious relationshipy place right now."

"Me neither." My skin was burning up and I felt lightheaded being this close to her. Her lips were within reach and already slightly open. "Mabry, you're going to have to stop talking, because I gotta get in there."

Leaning in, I tilted my head slightly, and sucked gently on her bottom lip. I cupped the side of her face, running my thumb across her soft cheek. A whisper of a moan drifted out of her, causing me to deepen the kiss. As my tongue slipped in between her lips, she gently sucked on it, guiding it completely into her mouth. I ran my hand down her arm as her fingers slid through my hair. Grabbing her hips, I pulled her onto my lap. One hand rested on her hip as the other traveled up her thigh, across her other hip, and to her lower back. Mabry had my head in a vice grip, pulling me as far as possible into her mouth. I had never felt a kiss like this before. Then it dawned on me. I had never felt a kiss. This kiss with Mabry was deep and slow, but my body's reaction was frenzied. Everything inside of me accelerated. My heart beat revved up, my lungs pumped hard, and the vibrations that started in my stomach catapulted to the surface of my skin. I kept trying to go deeper, wanting more of her. This wasn't just a kiss—it was a life-altering experience.

Needing to take a breath, we pulled back slightly and rested our foreheads against each other's, our lips staying connected. "Wow," Mabry gasped.

"That was amazing. Better than I had dreamed about," I said, the words coming out in spurts between breaths.

"You've dreamed about me?"

"Since the first time I saw you, Sweetness."

"Brad, I don't think…"

I sucked on her bottom lip, stopping her from continuing. Releasing it, I said, against her lips, "Mabry, you talk too much."

A slow sexy grin appeared across her face. Long sleek fingers tangled up into my hair again before her tongue swirled back in my mouth. I don't know how long we sat there kissing and touching each other. I wasn't aware of anything else when Mabry was in my arms. All I knew was that I could kiss her forever.

Once Mabry and I were able to pry our lips apart for more than five minutes, we headed to my place. My lips landed on hers the second we walked in the front door, and I continued consuming them as I backed her into the bedroom. I guided her toward my bed, turned, and sat down, allowing her to move in between my legs. Our lips and tongues never stopped devouring each other's as our hands tried to decide where to touch. My palms slid down the contours of her toned body until they landed on her firm little ass. Clutching it, I crushed her against me as her fingers ran aggressively through my hair. Apparently, Mabry and I had two speeds so far, zero and off the charts. I needed to slow things down. I wanted to savor every moment with her.

I made myself pull away and said, "Back up a few steps." Her eyebrows knitted together with confusion. "Trust me?"

"Yes," she said, trying to catch her breath.

"Then do as I say." I grinned at her.

Keeping eye contact, she stepped back, stopping about three feet away. My eyes roamed up and down her body while she waited for my next command. She wore a snug white button-up shirt and a dark burgundy pencil skirt with matching patent leather four-inch heels. The air in the room felt thick and hot, almost to the point of suffocating. My chest felt heavy as oxygen pumped in and out of my lungs. Beads of sweat formed at the back of my neck as my temperature skyrocketed. The need to touch her was overwhelming, but I didn't want this to end quickly. I dug my tingling fingers into my thighs, forcing them to stay put. I was so hard I was about to explode and she was still fully dressed.

I cleared my throat, trying to get my vocal cords to work. Looking her in the eye, I said with a gravelly voice, "First unbutton your shirt but don't take it off."

Her eyes stayed focused on mine as she worked each button slowly. I couldn't help the smile that appeared across my face when the second button was freed, revealing the black bra with white polka dots. I had only gotten a quick look earlier and didn't see the polka dots. I liked it. It wasn't the typical lacey bra. It was different and unique, like Mabry. She stood there silent, waiting for my next command.

"Turn around and face the other way." She did it without hesitation. "Take your skirt off. When you slide it down I want you to bend all the way over. Oh, keep the heels on."

My heart pounded hard against my chest wall as each of the zipper's teeth were released. Slowly she pushed the skirt over her hips until it pooled at her feet. Matching black and white cotton boy shorts covered her just enough, allowing the bottom curve of her ass to peek out from under the material. I inhaled a deep breath and let it out as slowly as possible. I needed a minute to pull myself together before I came like a pubescent teen jerking off to his first Playboy centerfold.

"Step out of your skirt, Mabry, and then face me."

It looked like her knees buckled slightly as she turned around. The heavy rise and fall of her chest caused her shirt to fall away exposing more of her beautiful body. I soaked all of it in, from her toned legs all the way to her smoldering eyes, and everything in between. My fingers and dick twitched. I needed to touch her now.

"Come over here and sit on my face," I commanded, giving her *the smile*.

"No."

I was so mesmerized by Mabry that I didn't hear her answer, then I realized she wasn't moving. "Did you hear me?"

"Yes, I heard you and my response was no," she said defiantly.

"Excuse me?"

"It's my turn now."

A boxer-dropping grin spread across her plump well-kissed lips as she walked toward me. When she got closer the light in the room hit her stomach, causing a quick flicker of sparkle to ricochet off of her.

Fuck me hard! Her bellybutton was pierced.

She was standing so close in front of me I could feel her warm breath float over my face.

"Get up and go stand over there," she demanded, tilting her head towards where she'd been standing.

I raised my hands, unable to keep myself from touching her any longer. She took a step back as I was about to grab her. "No touchy feely until I've had my turn," she informed, her gaze moving from my crotch up to my eyes.

Our eyes stayed connected as I moved my hands away from her, surrendering to her command. I stood and then laced my fingers behind my head, while walking over to my designated spot, and said excitedly, "Yes ma'am."

Mabry

Brad and I switched places. My eyes ran up and down his body as he stood there, hands resting on his narrow hips, waiting to hear what my orders were going to be. I had been turned on before, at least at one time my body had naturally responded to the touch of a male hand on it, but for the past couple of years even that had dulled. Looking at Brad fully clothed had me hotter than any other guy I had been with or fantasized about. The reaction he elicited from me was scary, overwhelming, and uncontrollable. My mouth watered just thinking about what was under those tailored clothes he wore.

My panties were already saturated. Before I embarrassed myself by leaving a big wet spot on his bed, I leaned back on my hands, draped one leg over my knee, and shifted my position. Plus, it caused the shirt to fall completely away from my body, giving Brad a clear view of my bra, panties, and piercing. The look in his eyes when he noticed the small diamond almost brought me to my knees. It looked as if he was about to pounce on me.

Swinging my leg back and forth, I cocked my head to one side and said, "Take your shirt off."

He pushed the material up a little higher than necessary, making sure I got a good look at his abs as he untucked his shirt. The glimpse of tanned skin and ripples caused my legs to squeeze together tightly. He unbuttoned his shirt halfway down, pulling it up and over his head, then tossed it to the side. I drew in a ragged breath as my entire body clenched. The sight of his naked torso was almost too much for my senses to bear. Every part of me was pulsating so hard and fast, I thought I was going to implode. My hair plastered itself to my forehead as small beads of sweat rose to the surface of my blazing skin.

My gaze scanned every deep indentation, smooth slope, and defined curve of his muscles. His arms and chest looked strong and solid, but also warm and protective. I got the strange sense that if they were surrounding me all my pain would disappear. Noticing him smirking, I realized I hadn't said anything for several minutes.

"Sweetness, we need to move this along. I've almost come five times since we got in here."

My Brad haze slowly drifted away as I whispered, "Sorry." I sat up, straightened my shoulders, and tried to get back into the playful power struggle we had going on.

This was just some adult fun, Mabry. Stress reliever. You can't do serious.

"Shoes, socks, pants, boxers, all of it off," I commanded.

In my experience, penises, in general, were not attractive. In fact, I had spent the majority of my sex life avoiding looking directly at them, but the one in front of me was gorgeous and fully erect. My mind was completely blank as I continued to be mesmerized by it and by him. Before my brain registered what was happening, I felt a strong arm wrapped around my waist, lifting my body up slightly, and laying it back onto the mattress. Looking up, I stared into intense sapphire eyes as Brad hovered over me, his hands on either side of my head. Swooping down, his lips captured mine as his tongue barged into my mouth. I ran my nails roughly down his back, causing a deep moan to vibrate from his chest. My fingers twirled into his messy hair, and I pushed on the back of his head, wanting to get him as far into my mouth as possible. It was as if we were both trying to crawl inside each other. This was starting to feel like more than sex to me. It was intimate, and vulnerable. Two things I didn't and couldn't do.

Tugging on his hair, I pulled his lips from mine. "I want to ride you," I said breathlessly as I pushed on his shoulders.

Brad fell backward while I climbed on, straddling him. The

second I shrugged out of my shirt, he sat up, attacking my neck with his lips. Closing my eyes, I allowed my head to fall back, exposing more skin for his magic mouth to consume. His hard dick was between us, moving up and down my stomach as his hips rocked. My body vibrated from the growl that came from him when his dick glided over my pierced naval. His large hands swept around to my back, unclasped my bra, and pulled it off. Wrapping my arms around his head, I leaned into his ear and whispered, "Suck my tits hard."

His lips surrounded my pointed nipple, sucking so hard I thought I was going to come unglued. The pain was exquisite. I yanked him away and directed him toward the other, wanting the same treatment.

Suddenly, Brad pulled away, his breaths coming out in short quick spurts. Resting his forehead against mine, he said, "I want to lick, suck, and fuck every part of you all at the same time."

"Yeah?" My quick breaths matched his.

"I need to get a condom on and get inside of you."

"Where are they?" I asked.

He placed his hands on my waist, lifted me up, and placed me on the bed in one fluid movement. Reaching over to his nightstand he grabbed a condom and ripped it open.

Holding out my hand, I asked, "Can I put it on you?"

"You sure?"

I nodded my head.

Brad laid back on the bed as I rolled the condom on. He was so hard it felt as if he could explode at any minute. I went to climb on top of him, but he grabbed my shoulders, stopping me. Pushing me back onto the bed, he crawled over me and pinned my hands above my head. His gaze traveled between my eyes and lips, finally settling on my eyes. "You're so beautiful, Mabry," he whispered.

"So are you." His dick fit perfectly between my thighs as he grinded against me. "I thought I was going to ride you."

"Not the first time, Sweetness. I want every part of our bodies touching. I need to feel your legs wrapped around me and your tits rubbing against my chest. I want to be able to look into your eyes and watch you come."

"Okay," I whispered. It was the only word that my mind and mouth were able to produce.

Brad kissed my lips and then moved down, landing in the crook of my neck. "I'm going to rip your panties off, baby. If I don't get my dick inside of you soon I'm going to go insane." My hips automatically pressed into his at the same time I cringed slightly when I heard him use the word *insane.*

Releasing my hands, he kissed down my body, the tip of his tongue making several brief appearances. He climbed off the bed and stood looking at me with desire, longing, and awe evident in his eyes. My body screamed with sensation. Shivers ran through me at the same time heat prickled my skin. I felt the blood pump through my veins as the ache between my legs grew.

His fingers hooked the waistband of my panties. "Lift up your hips."

I did as he said and I felt the cotton slide down my legs. I was completely exposed but felt safe. Brad's warm hands ran the length of my legs a few times before lifting my right ankle and placing my foot on his lower chest. His hands caressed my calf and then slid to unbuckle my shoe. After slipping my Mary Jane off he placed a light kiss on the top of my foot and gently placed it back on the bed. He treated my left leg the exact same way except instead of placing it back down, he trailed his lips along my inner calf, up to my thigh, stopping at my center. His tongue alternated between fast and slow flicks of my clit, causing my hips to gyrate. A loud long moan escaped from me and I felt him smile against me.

I had never allowed any guy to take this much time with me. Usually when I hooked up it was quick and detached with the sole purpose of numbing my pain. Unfortunately, over the past couple of years all it managed to do was numb my physical sensation. I couldn't remember the last time I was actually focused and mentally present during the act of sex until now.

His tongue slipped deep inside of me and glided across all the right places. My hands fisted the sheets as my knees tightened around his head. The movement of his tongue increased, causing my hips to buck off the bed. Brad's large hands grabbed my hips, trying to still me as he continued to drive deeper inside. My loud moans quickly turned into screams as Brad's lips vibrated with his deep low growls filling the air. All coherent thought becomes nonexistent. The only thing that existed was the feeling of what was being done to me. It's all pure sensory. My muscles tense as a mass of convulsions overwhelm my body. Wave after wave of sensation crashes over me until all of me feels like I'm plugged into a lightning bolt and I explode.

My body was drenched in sweat and trembling as my head continued to swim. I thought I'd experienced orgasms before, but they weren't anywhere near the mind-blowing experience I had just had.

Damn, that was just his tongue.

I felt soft lips nibble up the center of my body, between my breasts, along my collarbone, and to my ear. A gruff voice whispered, "You okay, Sweetness?"

"I'm more than okay. That was… Wow!"

A deep chuckle tickled my neck. Lowering onto his elbows, he positioned himself over me. He felt perfect between my legs. His lips skimmed across my jaw to my mouth where he gently traced the outline of my lips with the tip of his tongue. My eyes fluttered shut as I concentrated on the way our bodies complemented each other.

"Open your gorgeous eyes, Mabry," he whispered as his hips slowly rocked against me.

My eyes opened and all the air in my body immediately escaped. In the past I never wanted to look guys in the eye during sex. They never seemed to care one way or the other. Brad held my gaze and for the first time I couldn't look away. I didn't want to. I raised my hand to his face, letting the back of it softly stroke his cheek. The way he looked at me was as if he could see straight into my soul. Like he knew all my secrets and understood all my pain. I felt the tip of him slide into me. I braced myself, knowing from experience I would need to get used to the unfamiliar feel of him inside of me since this was our first time. The strange discomfort of someone new never came. It felt like we had been together and that we belonged together.

He continued to slide smoothly into me as his mouth alternated between kissing my lips and along my neck. I found myself searching for his eyes whenever they left mine, even briefly. Something I didn't understand was passing between us. It was more than just being sexually compatible. There was a deeper connection happening. I had an innate sense that he would take care of me and protect me. What terrified me was that I felt like I wanted him to.

"This feels incredible. I could live inside of you forever," he gritted out as the rocking increased.

"I love the way you feel in me," I moaned between breaths.

What the hell did I just say?

His steady hip motion morphed into quick sharp thrusts as he continued to inch his way inside of me. My legs curled around him and tightened. He looked into my eyes one last time, showing me that this felt different to him as well. His breathing became heavier as his face moved to the crook of my neck. Harder, faster thrusts took over as he continued to bury himself deeper. My calves slid from his lower back all the way down to his toned ass. I felt every one of his muscles flex under my legs as his hips slammed against me. My body trembled and tightened. His rhythm faltered as he lifted his head, returning his gaze back to me.

"Let go, Sweetness. I got you," he breathed out.

His thrusting became frantic as he relentlessly pounded into me. An intense wave of pleasure invaded my body, letting me know I was about to have another mind-blowing orgasm. As I unraveled, I searched Brad's eyes, wanting him to see how he affected me. Just as I reached my peak, I felt his dick pulse inside of me. Another wave crashed over my body. We clung to each other as our bodies shook and went rigid, signaling our release.

Strong arms wrapped completely around my waist. Still inside me, Brad rolled us over, landing me on top of his chest. His hand stroked up and down my back as he placed a gentle kiss on the top of my head.

"Sweetness, that was...," Brad breathed out. The deep and rapid movement of his chest made me feel as if I were on an amusement park ride.

"I know." I smiled against his chest at the nickname he had given me the first week we met. I started to climb off of him, but his arm tightened, holding me in place.

"Stay. I don't want this to end," he whispered. I closed my eyes, nuzzling deeper into his warm safe chest.

Three hours and a large jug of Gatorade later, we were still in Brad's bed. I lay across the bed on my side, propped up by my elbow, wearing one of his T-shirts. Brad was on his back with his head resting against my thighs, the sheet stopping just below his hips. I mindlessly ran my fingers through his soft dirty-blond hair. This was the first time I'd ever lingered after sex. Usually, I was out the door the second the guy was out of me. Piercing sapphire eyes looked up, catching my attention. I knew it wasn't the best time to do this, but I felt like we needed to establish a few ground rules. We had to keep things in perspective and be clear on what we were doing.

"I think we should set a few rules," I said, timidly.

"I'd like you to rule me." I narrowed my eyes at him. "Okay, sorry. Um... rule number one, we're *definitely* doing this again." His sexy grin made another appearance.

I tugged playfully on his hair. "I mean it."

"Okay, what rules?" he asked.

"We don't need to go on dates. That's not what this is."

"Can we still hang out?"

I thought for a second. "Sure."

"Good. What else?"

"I'm not looking for a commitment. Like I told you before, I'm not in a relationshipy place right now."

"Gotcha, no relationshipy." He was trying to be serious, but there was a mischievous look in his eyes mixed with desire.

"We should keep this quiet. No need for anyone to know what we're doing," I stated.

"My lips are sealed, except when they're gliding over your body." He sent me a wink.

I swallowed hard. "No sleepovers. It's too…"

"Relationshipy?" he asked.

"Yeah."

"Sweetness, *sleep* is the last thing I plan on doing *over* you."

"I'm serious, Brad," I said sternly. "If you can't agree and follow these rules then we can't continue."

Brad sat up as I swung my legs over the side of the bed and stood. Grabbing my wrist, he pulled me back down to sit facing him. He leaned in, placed a soft kiss on my lips, and said, "Mabry, I'll agree to whatever you need as long as I can be near you, with you, in you, over you, and under you." He placed another soft kiss on my lips and rested his forehead against mine. "Just don't stop."

"Stop what?" I asked.

"Being a part of my life."

A shiver ran through me when I heard his answer. "I won't," I whispered.

I didn't want to leave, but I knew I had to. I was already playing with fire where Brad was concerned. I had to maintain some type of distance. Tonight was more intense than I imagined it would be.

I kissed him one more time and said, "I better go."

His hand snaked around the back of my neck and he pulled me close. Pressing his lips to mine he coaxed my mouth to open and slid his tongue in. He slowly stroked every inch of my tongue, leaving me breathless and dizzy.

Pulling away, he whispered against my lips, "You sure? We could always start those rules tomorrow. Morning sex is awesome."

"I think it's best if we start enforcing them immediately. It's too much of a slippery slope if we give in right at the beginning."

"I like when we slip all over each other's slopes." He nipped playfully at my bottom lip.

Smiling, I explained, "We need to keep things in perspective and remember what this is."

He gave me a weak smile before falling backward onto the bed. As I walked toward the bathroom, I heard an exasperated mumble from him. "Fucking rules."

CHAPTER 15

Here I Am
by
Rebecca Hyams

I'm not sure who'll look for me.
I'm not sure who'll find me
I'm not sure who'll miss me.
I'm not sure who'll care.
That I'm no longer here or anywhere.

Mom and Dad, I'm sorry that I've caused so much pain in your lives. I know what I'm about to do will hurt you, but at least your pain will end as time goes by. It needs to end, everything does. It's better this way for all of us. Now you'll be able to rest and not worry about me. You have both been wonderful parents, so don't think this is your fault. I'm the screw up and always have been. I've tried really hard to be normal, but it never felt right. I was able to pretend for a while, but it's exhausting being something you're not. I'm sorry I can't pretend anymore. I love you both.

Brad, I haven't smiled a lot in my life, but I did when I was with you. Doing things for you gave me purpose. I loved taking care of you. I loved you. When you truly love someone you don't put conditions on it. You just do it. You didn't have to tell me you loved me, but why did you have to be so mean about it? Why did you have to say you'd NEVER love me? Never is such a long time. Maybe someday you would have loved me. Why didn't you love me? I needed you to love me. When you walked out of my door everything went with you- my breath, my heart, and my strength. I'm too weak to fight off the darkness. It's been an hour since you left me, and the darkness is consuming and suffocating.

The first time I remember sinking it was like tripping. By the time my brain registered what happened, I was already down, but I could still see the light. I got back up and continued on. I was bruised, but not completely beaten.

The second time, I remember sinking it felt like someone had pushed me down. It was forceful and abrupt. The light had dimmed. I tried to get up, but the struggle was too hard, so I pretended to stand and move forward.

I don't have to remember my third time sinking, because it's happening right now. I feel like I have a boulder tied around my neck and have been tossed into the black and muddy water. It sucks you in and doesn't let go. Brad, I needed you to grab my hand and pull me from the muddy water. You left me to sink until I could no longer see the light and allowed the darkness to invade me completely.

There's no point in staying here. I have no purpose and I'm tired of pretending I do.

Becca

CHAPTER 16

PAST AND PRESENT COLLIDE

Brad

I stand in front of her door, hesitating. I have a key, but I don't use it. My stomach has been queasy ever since leaving my father's office. Riding over here I kept telling myself that Mabry and I love each other too much for this to be that big of an issue, but I can't stop the feeling of dread that has taken me over. The loss of her mother to suicide is still fresh in Mabry's heart even though it's been years. The fact is, I'm terrified that she's going to think I had something to do with Becca's death. Hell, there's still a part of me that feels like I did have something to do with it. Logically, a person knows what his actual part is in any given situation. Feelings aren't logical though. They just *are*. They haunt you, give you nightmares, and hold you responsible. Until logic and feelings sync up, you're never really completely free of any involvement.

I take in a deep breath and knock. I wait for the door to open, but instead I hear the muffled voice of Mabry.

"Brad, is that you?" she yells.

"Yes."

"I can't come to the door, just use your key."

I slide the key into the lock and turn the doorknob. The place is dark except for one small lamp in the corner. Mabry's place has an open floor plan. You can see the entire living space except for the bedrooms and bathrooms from the front door. I glance into the kitchen to see if she's in there, but it's empty.

"I'm in here, baby." I hear coming from the direction of her bedroom.

I head down the hall, my body feeling a mixture of dread and excitement. Standing in the doorway, I peer in. The room is glowing with candles. Once my eyes adjust, I see the most beautiful and heart stopping-sight. Mabry is lying on her stomach across the bed, propped up on her elbows, facing the door.

"Hey, sexy beast," she says in a sultry and playful voice.

"Hey, Sweetness. Did you forget to pay your electric bill?" I ask, walking toward the bed.

Her hair is loose and it falls over her creamy shoulder as she cocks her head to the side, giving me a wicked grin. Pushing up onto her knees, she meets me at the edge of the bed. She's wearing a black teddy with lace running across her nipples and down the middle of her body. The sides are transparent allowing me a clear view of her gorgeous curves. My eyes zero in on her phenomenal tits, pushed up high and exposed except for the nipples. My mouth waters just thinking about sucking on them. My eyes roam farther down, spotting the garter clamped onto black hose, leading to black stilettos. Pictures of Mabry bending over my desk from earlier flash through my mind. I temporarily forget what I need to tell her as the queasiness in my stomach is replaced with the fire of excitement. My skin heats up as azure blue eyes sparkle in the candlelight while traveling up and down my body. My dick isn't just twitching, it's convulsing.

"Wamfu," I breathe out.

"Wamfu?" She scrunches up her face in confusion.

"My brain couldn't decide whether to say 'wow, damn, or fuck,' so it came out 'wamfu.'"

Smiling, she says, "I like wamfu."

Grabbing my tie, she tugs me to her mouth. She places small quick licks across my bottom lip with her tongue before slipping it into play with mine. I slide the tips of my fingers under the garter, grazing her soft skin. I can already feel my hips start to rock toward her. My hands move up, touching the sides of her face. I take the kiss as deep as humanly possible, focusing intensely on the feel of her tongue, her lips, her skin, and her body pressing against mine. I breathe in the scent of vanilla. I tighten my hold on her as I get lost in the moans escaping from her.

She backs away from the kiss, needing to take a breath, and says on my lips, "I'm glad you still have on your tie, Bradley."

She's picking up where we left off with hot secretary and naughty boss. So fucking adorable.

This is not what you came here for, Brad. You need to focus. You need to tell her about Becca.

Each part of my body is on high alert right now. It's taking every ounce of strength I have not to throw her down on the bed and rip that lace off of her.

"I'll need to use that tie to secure your hands to my headboard. I can't have them getting in the way while I suck your…"

I grab her shoulders and push her back abruptly. "Mabry, I need to talk to you."

She blinks several times before realizing that I'm serious. I understand her confusion and shock. I've never stopped us, no matter where we are or who's around. Mabry's always taken on the role of the sex patrol. As long as we are out of sight from prying eyes, I'm good to go. I see the second she becomes self-conscious of her appearance and wants to cover up, thinking I'm not turned on. She's got to know I'm turned on. Every inch of me is hard and tense. The corners of her mouth turn down as her brows knit together. Climbing off the bed, she shrugs on her little black robe that barely covers her ass. When she turns toward me, her eyes are full of concern and she's biting her lower lip. I know instantly that I'm going to have to ask her to change into actual clothes. I'm not going to be able to concentrate with her looking so *Mabry*.

Rubbing the back of my neck, my eyes shut tight, I ask, "Could you change into something less… incredible?"

When I open my eyes, I see that her lip has been freed and the corners of her mouth are curled up slightly.

"Sure, I'll be right back."

We simultaneously turn away from each other. Mabry heads toward her closet as I head into the living room. I walk around the place flipping on light after light. I need to see her face clearly in order to gauge the effect my words are having on her. I pace the floor a few times before the clearing of her throat causes me to turn and face her. She's wearing a pair of brown yoga pants, an oversized beige T-shirt that falls off of one shoulder, and she's barefoot. Most of her hair is pinned up, but several pieces sit loose around her face. Mabry changing didn't have the desired effect on me I was hoping for. She's still sexy as hell and it's killing me.

She sits on the sofa, hugging her knees to her chest. "What is it, Brad? You're making me nervous," she says, her tone cautious.

I take a few steps toward her, running my hand through my hair, and try to find the right words. "I'm not really sure how to start this." I dart my eyes away from her.

I didn't like talking about my past because I was ashamed of it, especially this particular event. Mabry knew in general the type of person I was back then. She knew I slept around, but we both agreed not to discuss the specifics of any relationship or encounter either of us had with others. There was no point in that. We're different people.

We belong to each other now. I like the person I am with Mabry. I didn't want her to hear the disgusting things I had done. I head to the sofa, sitting away from her, and face straight ahead.

I'm looking down at a spot on the floor, my voice low, when I start. "You know the type of person I used to be. There was this girl during my second year of law school. It was never anything even remotely serious. I've never been serious with anyone except you."

I risk a glance at her. Her eyebrows are scrunched together tightly and the look in her eyes is right on the fence between concern and fear. I need to say it already.

"She committed suicide a little over a month after I met her. I didn't know she had any mental problems. I barely knew her."

It's slight, but I can see Mabry's body tense and go rigid. The look in her eyes tells me that she's trying to decide on what her first question needs to be.

"Why are you telling me this now?" she asks.

"The reason Peyton barged in on us was because my father wanted to see me. Apparently, the girl's parents have filed a wrongful death lawsuit against me for one point two million."

Her eyes dart quickly to mine. "Holy fuck," she says, the shock clearly evident in her voice.

"I know."

"You realize it won't make it to court. No judge will take the time to hear a case like this."

"My father thinks they're looking for a cash cow. He's setting up a meeting with their lawyer as soon as possible to negotiate a settlement."

Her back straightens as she shakes her head. "Negotiate a settlement?" she asks in disbelief. The tension in my body relaxes somewhat as she shifts into lawyer mode. "Why would your father want to even bother with considering a settlement? This is a frivolous lawsuit."

"He doesn't want his name or the firm's reputation tarnished with the negative publicity."

"What evidence could there possibly be that would implicate you and what lawyer would even bother with a case like this?"

"Apparently, she left a note and Sir Douche is the lawyer," I inform.

A look of surprise crosses her face. "I can't believe Ten would take on a case like this. It doesn't sound like him."

I grind my teeth hearing his name. Rubbing my palms over my thighs, I try to keep my hands from forming into fists. I don't like that her words imply that she knows Sir Douche that well. I refocus my thoughts on the fact that Mabry's not freaking out about this. Instead, she's ready to support and defend me. As long as I have that, nothing else matters. Hopefully, an agreement can be reached at the meeting with the Hyams and I can leave Becca in the past. The touch of Mabry's hand on my arm breaks me from my thoughts.

"I'm sorry, Sweetness. What did you just ask me?"

"What was the girl's name?"

"Becca." I see out the corner of my eye Mabry's head jerk completely in my direction.

"Becca what?" she asks, hesitantly.

"Becca Hyams," I say, looking at her.

Her eyes grow in size and her expression morphs into something unreadable. "It was you." Her voice has a dazed tone to it. "You were the boy at the memorial service. I saw you there."

My entire body twists toward her. "You were at Becca's service? Why?"

"We were roommates at Clemson for almost four years. She tried to kill herself at school. Once she felt strong enough, she wanted a fresh start. That's why she was at Duke."

"Fuck. I never even knew where she was from. She just said upstate."

Lowering her legs, Mabry asks, "You had over a month-long relationship with her and never got the basic information?" There's an accusatory tone in her voice all of a sudden.

"Stuff like that didn't interest me back then," I say as I look into her eyes.

"She was in love with you," she says, her voice so low it's almost a whisper.

"Did you talk to her about me?"

"I got an email from Becca a few days before she killed herself. She said she'd met someone and was totally in love with him." I wince at her words, especially the last few. "Did you have any feelings for her?" Her voice is low and soft as she fidgets with the bottom of her shirt, bracing herself for my answer.

I hesitate for several seconds. I don't want to come off as a complete asshole and tell her I barely thought about her friend during that time. "I felt sorry for her when we first met."

Mabry huffs out an annoyed laugh. "So it was a pity fuck?"

"I don't know what it was. I was a completely different person then. I did shitty things all the time to people. Becca was no different."

"Do you have other ex-lovers that have killed themselves?" she bit out, sarcastic anger flowing through her words.

Defensiveness shoots through me. I jump up from the sofa, walking halfway across the room before turning toward her. I stand there, hands resting on my hips while I look down at the floor for a few seconds. I don't want to sound angry and have this escalate into an argument. "I don't know what you want me to say, Mabry. I fucked women until I got tired and bored with them. I didn't stick around long enough to get to know them or give a shit about them. I had no idea Becca would do something like that. I wish I had. Maybe she'd still be alive."

Her eyes soften the longer we stare at each other. "I'm sorry. I shouldn't have said that. We've both done things in the past we aren't proud of. It's just that she was my friend. When was the last time you saw her?"

I swallow hard before answering. "I saw her earlier that night."

"The night she killed herself?"

"Yes," I whisper. I watch as the tears build up in Mabry's eyes. I know what she wants to ask me, but can't bring herself to. "Mabry, I didn't have anything to do with Becca's death." I can hear the pleading in my voice.

"I know," she whispers.

Walking to me, she wraps her arms around my waist and hugs me to her. My arms immediately encircle her body as I bury my face in the crook of her neck. A deep sigh escapes from me and a wave of relief takes over.

"You're not going to leave me?" I sound so pathetic.

She pulls away from me and rests our foreheads together. "No, I'm here, baby. I love you."

Mabry is the first person to ever be in my corner without having ulterior motives. My parents have always been more interested in protecting their name and reputation, I rarely show up on Peyton's radar, and as for "friends", it's always depended on what was in it for them. I hear a rush of breath escape as I tighten my arms around her. I'm completely at ease at this moment, knowing the most important person in my life is by my side.

Mabry

Pregnant. I thought Brad was about to tell me he just found out he had gotten a girl pregnant back during law school. I never thought the name Becca Hyams would come spilling out of his mouth. We're lying in bed, me on my back, leaning against the headboard with Brad's arms curling securely around me as his head nuzzles deep into my chest. He's asleep while I gently run my fingers through his hair. We've been in this position for the past forty-five minutes. Our night of hot sex was put on hold for obvious reasons. Brad needs comfort and reassurance that I'm not going to leave him. I'll never forget the look of fear in his eyes when he told me the news. I've seen a lot of looks in those gorgeous sapphire eyes—confidence, cockiness, flirtatiousness, determination, hurt, and pain—but never fear.

He told me the details about his relationship with Becca. Well, most of them. I didn't need a blow-by-blow description about the two of them having sex. I'm having a hard enough time trying to keep my own imagination from running away with thoughts of his hands and lips all over her and vice versa. Exhaustion set in and we both decided to call it a night. He stripped down to his boxers, I slipped out of my yoga pants, and we climbed into bed.

Becca Hyams had become a distant memory for me over the past couple of years. As the memories have faded, so have the triggering effects of her death. God, Duke is such a big school. It's hard to believe that out of all the female students, Brad picks the one who was completely unstable, and my friend.

I'm trying hard to focus on external things like the pressure of his body as it presses into mine with each breath he takes in or how soft his hair feels on my fingertips, but it's a struggle. My mind is all over the place. It flits back and forth between the past and the present. I look down at him, only able to see one side of his face, just like the day of Becca's memorial service. I remember the pull I felt toward him, wanting to comfort him just like I'm doing now. Neutral expressions covered almost everyone's face that day, except for Mr. and Mrs. Hyams, Stephanie, and Brad. Even though I didn't know who he was that day, I remember sensing the sorrow and regret that radiated off of him. His words tonight didn't match my memory of him. Basically,

Becca had been just another girl, like all the other girls. Nothing serious. No emotional attachment. Nothing. But how was I, a complete stranger at that time, able to feel the strong sadness that he had? He wasn't at the service just as a courtesy. He needed to be there. I didn't ask him details about the last time he saw Becca. I'm not sure why. Maybe, I'm scared of the answer.

Becca left a note.

The Hyams I knew were not vindictive or opportunistic people. They wouldn't do something like this without good reason. There's obviously something in the note that has prompted them strongly enough that they blame Brad. My thoughts keep coming up with possible scenarios. Becca either read more into their relationship or Brad is downplaying it. What exactly had he said to her that night when he broke things off with her? Was she in a fragile state and he just walked out on her? By his own admission, he was a heartless prick back then. My mind drifts further back. I wonder if my mom acted differently the day she took her life. Was she more depressed or more agitated? Did my dad have a feeling that morning as he went to work that my mom wouldn't be alive when he got home? She had been sick for so long.

I feel the slight pressure on the back of my head and realize I absentmindedly have been lightly tapping my head against the headboard. A prickling sensation takes over my skin as heat spreads over me. Suddenly, my chest is heavy and having Brad glued to it is suffocating me. I need to move. I need air.

I try to pry his arms from around me, not wanting to wake him. I manage to set one arm free and then wiggle out from under him. Brad stirs a little and I feel his arms tighten once more around me.

"Brad." I push on his shoulders, needing him to roll off of me. He doesn't respond. "Brad," I say a little louder. He's still holding on. "Brad!" I shout at the same time I shove him off of me.

"What? Is anything wrong?" he says, groggily.

Swinging my legs over the side of the bed, I sit there, my chin to my chest, trying to breathe. I flinch when I feel a hand touch my shoulder.

"Mabry, are you okay?" Brad asks, concern lacing his tone.

I raise my hand indicating I need a minute. "I'm fine. I must have been having a nightmare." I lie.

"I'm sorry. Do you want to talk about it?"

"No." The word bursts from my mouth.

I bolt up off of the bed when I feel his arms wrap around me again. I head toward the bathroom. "I just need a glass of water and a second," I say over my shoulder just before closing the bathroom door.

Leaning against the door, I inhale a couple of deep breaths. Heat pricks at my skin like a thousand tiny needles being pushed into me all at once. I want to bang my head so badly. The urge has never completely left me, but the intensity of it has lessened to the point that I've been able to control it. I feel my throat closing and I gasp for air. I haven't hurt myself since Brad and I became an official couple. My legs are restless and twitch as my arms tingle. I try to steady my now ragged breathing, but my chest is so tight I can't take in enough oxygen. I look at my reflection in the mirror, trying to will myself to go back to bed. But, as I hide in my bathroom, my body instinctively goes into self-harm mode. I feel my heels push against the tile floor and my nails dig into my palms. I close my eyes, taking in another deep breath, and hold it. Forcefully, I push off from the door and head to the sink. I grab a washcloth and drench it in cold water. Covering my face with the cloth, I keep reminding myself that Brad is only a few feet away and could hear me if I give in to the urge. I push the wet cold into my face harder, hoping it will take the edge off, as I fight the pull of my addiction.

CHAPTER 17

Brad

Before my eyes even open, I turn on my side and reach for her. All I feel is a cold pillow and empty sheets. By the time she came back to bed last night, I had fallen asleep and didn't feel any movement when she climbed in next to me. Since we've been an official couple, I've started each day with her scent of vanilla and her warm soft body pressed against mine. I hate waking up without her next to me. I let one second tick by before I jump out of bed and go searching for her.

I find Mabry in the kitchen standing at the counter with her back to me. She's already dressed for work in a pair of black pants that wrap around her hot little ass perfectly and a matching black jacket that stops just above the aforementioned hot little ass. I feel the front of my boxers move. Mabry's ass is calling me, demanding me, really, to fondle it. I glance quickly at the clock on the stove to see if I have enough time to answer the call. Who am I kidding, there's always time for a morning grope. I walk up behind her and press my chest to her back. Her hair is done up into a ponytail giving me clear access to that nape, so I place a soft kiss on it. Planting my face in her neck, I inhale as my hands run up and down her ass, squeezing gently along the way.

"Mornin', Sweetness," I say, my lips grazing her skin.

Her body jerks when my hands land on her. She pulls the mug of coffee she's drinking away from her mouth. "Brad...," she says, sounding a little annoyed. "You shouldn't sneak up on someone like that. I'm holding something hot."

"So am I." I smile against her neck and squeeze her ass a little harder.

She shrugs her shoulders and steps away from me, walking to the counter opposite from where I stand. Facing me, she leans back, and just before taking another sip of her coffee, says, "We don't have time for nonsense this morning. We'll be late."

I pop a K-cup in the Keurig and flip it on. Mimicking Mabry's stance, I lean against the counter, crossing my arms over my chest, and say, "You. Me. Naked. Hands, lips, and various other body parts sliding all over each other. That makes a whole lotta sense to me."

She tries to force the corners of her mouth to remain neutral, but they manage to quirk up just a little.

We stand in silence finishing our coffee. Quiet mornings aren't unusual for the two of us. Mabry's not a morning person, at least as far as talking goes. She does enjoy certain activities when she first wakes up that help get her blood flowing. Usually. Something feels off to me as we drink our coffee. I notice she doesn't look at me for very long before her eyes dart to somewhere else in the room.

"Everything okay, Sweetness?" I ask.

"Mmmhmm." Her eyes making quick contact with mine.

"Then why won't you look at me?" My question causes her gaze to shoot directly to mine. "That's the first good look I've gotten of those gorgeous azure blues today."

Without commenting, she walks to the sink, rinses out her mug, and heads out of the room. "I'm going to leave for the office now."

"You don't want to ride in together?"

"There's a few things I need to catch up on."

I grab her upper arm as she passes by me. "Don't do this, Mabry."

"I'm not doing anything. I have work…" She still doesn't look at me.

"Fuck that. You're shutting me out and I want to know why. Last night you seemed okay with things."

"I didn't sleep well last night. I'm just tired. Plus, I think I'm PMS'ing."

PMS, the mortal enemy of all mankind.

Her hand covers mine as she tilts up on her toes and places a soft kiss on my lips. "I'll see you in a little bit," she says warmly.

"I love you," I tell her.

"I love you too." She gives me a weak smile before heading out of the room.

c♋ఌ

"So McGuire is taking his time getting us a copy of the suicide note," my father says. "You need to tell me absolutely everything about your relationship with this girl. I want as few surprises as possible when we meet with them."

I'm sitting in my father's office trying to prepare for our meeting with Becca's parents, but the only thing on my mind is Mabry. I've barely seen her today. She's been in her office since I arrived at work. I've checked on her a couple of times. Each time, she gives me the same weak smile that she gave me earlier today and then directs her attention back to either a law book or her computer monitor. She's shutting me out and I don't know why. Last night she said she wouldn't leave. I can't figure out what could have changed overnight.

"Bradley." I hear a sharp angry voice say.

"What?"

"Would you get your head out of your ass for five minutes and focus on this mess you've gotten us into?" my father bites out.

"Sorry, what was the question?"

He huffs out a breath of impatience as he glares at me. "Details. I need details on the type of relationship you had with this girl."

"We met at a party and she went home with me."

"Willingly?" he asks.

I sneer at him and answer, "Yes, willingly. I've never forced a girl to do anything she didn't want to do."

"I have to ask these questions, Bradley. You're my client now, not my son."

I try to stifle the laugh before it bursts from me, but I'm not successful. He removes his glasses and places them in front of him. Leaning back in his chair, he takes a moment to compose himself. I can see his anger teetering on the verge of boiling over.

"Is there something you want to get off of your chest, Bradley?" he asks, his tone cold and all business. I hate the way he says my name. There's so much spite and contempt in his voice. He waits a few seconds for me to respond. When I don't, he continues. "I'm trying to help you and protect your future. Despite what you think, I do care."

I know I shouldn't do it, but I'm like Pavlov's fucking dog. When my father starts his sincere "I care about you son" bullshit, my inner smartass takes over.

Twisting my body in the chair, I look over each shoulder before landing my eyes back on him. "Who are you talking to?"

"Why do you always have to be such a prick?"

"Like father like son, I guess," I say, my voice and expression flat.

He holds my stare briefly, then lowers his chin toward his chest and shakes his head, grumbling something inaudible. Looking up at me, he asks, "Do you want me to handle this situation or not?"

"Yes I do, but let's cut the bullshit. You're handling this case because of you and the firm, not because you give a shit about me or my future. You want details? I met her at a party. We fucked occasionally over the course of a month. She cleaned my condo, did my laundry, and cooked. We never hung out. We never went on a date. I didn't know a damn thing about her other than her name. The night she killed herself she told me she loved me while I was fucking her. I broke it off, left, and went to meet Mom for dinner. Next day I found out she killed herself. The end."

"And you never did anything to lead her on, to make her think you had feelings for her, or that the two of you had a future together?" He fired off the question like I was under cross examination.

"No."

"You're positive?"

"Yes," I say, keeping my answers clipped.

"Never got so caught up in the fuck that you blurted out something that she could have misinterpreted as strong feelings?"

"I've never gotten that caught up in the moment."

Only with Mabry.

"Did you buy her gifts?" he asks.

"No. I told you the extent of the relationship. I feel like we're just going around in circles." My patience has run out.

"Well, I'm sorry if I'm taking up too much of your precious time. I'm trying to save us one point two million dollars is all. From what you've told me and her psychiatric history, I think I can make a good case that the girl was completely psychotic and delusional. Not only is there a chance we won't have to pay a dime, we might just make a few dollars if I bring a counter lawsuit against them for defamation of character."

I look at him in shock. I know his goal is always to win at whatever cost, but to put Becca's parents through any more heartache is ruthless.

"Why would you do that? Don't you think her parents have been through enough?"

Looking at me as if I've grown another head, he says, "Sometimes people need to be taught a lesson. They can't go around and lay blame on others just because they don't want to admit they failed. These two people obviously failed as parents, otherwise their only child would still be alive." He turns back to his computer.

"And you think you and Mom succeeded as parents?"

He doesn't look at me when he answers. "You and your brother are alive and well. Both of you are educated, employed, and have comfortable futures ahead of you. So to answer your question…" His cold stern glare is aimed directly at me now. "Yes, I believe your mother and I have been successful parents."

"Do you care if I'm happy?" I ask.

Outwardly, I don't reveal any emotion in my voice or my expression. Inwardly, my chest tightens and my breathing almost comes to a complete stop as I wait for his answer. The hair on my arms rises and a prickling sensation covers my skin while the seconds tick by, my question just lying out there with no response. Logically, I can guarantee what his answer will be. After being around my father all these years, the evidence points to the fact that he couldn't care less about whether or not I'm happy. My fingers grip the end of the wooden armrest as I brace myself for his cold words.

"What kind of a question is that?" he snaps.

"The kind I'd like an answer to."

"I don't have the time or interest in engaging in this nonsense with you today. I have all the information I need. We're done here." He turns his attention back to the computer.

The fact that he evades my question is all the answer I need. The natural reaction I feel to my father's words never ceases to amaze and confuse me. I despise this man and have never had any respect for him, so why do I care even a little bit how he feels about me? I don't want to care, but I can't deny the innate need in me to have his approval and even his love.

"Becca may not have been happy, but her parents wanted her to be. I saw how much they cared about her at the memorial service. That makes them successful parents in my book."

His eyes shoot to mine. "What the hell is wrong with you, Bradley? Aren't you just a little bit pissed that these people are trying to hold you partially responsible for the death of this girl?"

"No, I'm not pissed at them. I think they're still trying to make sense of the senseless and need something tangible to latch on to. She wasn't psychotic or delusional. She was just a young girl who struggled with depression. Don't drag Becca's name and her parents through the mud. None of them deserve that."

We stare at each other for a few seconds, neither of us saying another word. I leave my father's office and walk straight to Mabry's. I hesitate before knocking. I know something is going on with her and I'm trying to give her space, but I need to be near her right now.

"Come in." Just the sound of her voice gives me comfort.

I open the door, walk in, and close it behind me. I can tell by her expression that she already knows what I need from her, but since things have been off between us today I feel I should ask. "Can I hold you for a few minutes, please?"

Without saying anything, she gets up and walks to me. Taking my hand, she leads me to the front of her desk. I sit and she positions herself between my legs, wrapping her arms securely around my neck. I nuzzle my face in the crook of her neck as my arms snake around her waist. I let the scent and feel of her soak into me. The tension in my body fades away, replaced by a calmness and peace. All I want to do is pick her up and carry her away from here. I want to go someplace where we can start over with a clean slate. I just want to be done with my past and move forward with the love of my life.

I'm not sure how long we've been in each other's arms when I feel Mabry pull away. I keep a firm hold on her, not letting her step away from me. Looking into her eyes, I see the sadness that I thought

I had gotten rid of.

"Talk to me, Mabry," I say, a plea in my tone.

"About what?"

"Something's different. When we went to bed last night you seemed okay and then this morning… I feel you pulling away from me now and I don't understand what changed overnight." I swallow hard trying to hold my emotions in check.

"I don't mean to. It's weird knowing that you and Becca were together and how she felt about you. I just need some time alone to sort it out in my head."

"Will I see you tonight?" I ask, but I already know the answer.

Shaking her head, she says, "I'm going to work late and then I think it's best if I spend the night at my place alone."

I bring our foreheads together and whisper, "I'm sorry, Mabry. If I had known you were going to be in my future, I would have been a better man in my past."

Her eyes close and she steps away. "I need to get back to work, Brad."

I'm scared to leave, so I hesitate for as long as possible before it starts to look pathetic. With each step toward the door, I can feel the hollow gnawing of loneliness take over my body. It's a familiar feeling. It used to be the norm for me. I had been able to numb myself, building up a manageable tolerance to the pain in order to get through my day. When I met Mabry, I finally got relief from the persistent emptiness. I didn't realize how intense and debilitating my pain was until I got a break from it. As it seeps back in, I pray that whatever change occurred last night to cause Mabry to shut down reverses itself, because I won't be able to tolerate being without her.

Mabry

The second I hear the door click shut tears roll down my face. It took every ounce of strength for me to step away from Brad, but I had to do it. I need some distance right now. When he's in front of me, looking so vulnerable and hurt, my resistance is nonexistent. I knew he had come from his father's office. They're meeting with the Hyams in a few weeks. Mr. Johnson is an extremely detailed lawyer and an over preparer. He doesn't like surprises. I'm sure he had Brad tell him every detail of his relationship with Becca twenty times over. When he first told me about Becca I was shocked, but then my focus narrowed in on the fear in his eyes. He was so afraid I'd leave him. All I wanted to do was make him feel better. Later, though, when he was asleep and things were quiet, my mind went on a wild rampage. The images and questions are still swirling around in my head.

Brad and Becca, naked and tangled together.

Brad walking out on her.

Becca lying dead in her room.

What was she feeling right before the blade slid across her wrists?

Did my mom kill herself right after my dad left for work that day?

Did Dad leave that day knowing how deep Mom's pain was?

What's in Becca's note?

Each time a thought flits across my mind, the craving to self-harm increases. Last night I was able to control myself and not succumb to the urge, but I came close to banging my head against the edge of the counter in the bathroom. If Brad hadn't been there I knew I would have gone through with it. Even now, my hand is slowly creeping up into my hair ready to yank at the first strand it reaches. Before last night, whenever I looked at Brad I felt free from the pain of my past, but now the view is different. I see him and feel all the pain rushing back.

I need to know what's in that note. I grab my cellphone, scroll through the numbers, and press send before I have time to talk myself out of it. He picks up on the second ring.

"Well, hello there, Bright Eyes."

"Hey Ten. How are you?" I ask, trying not to sound like I'm up to something.

"I'm fantastic, especially now hearing your voice," he answers smugly.

I haven't spoken to Ten since our date. He's called a few times and left voicemails. I always meant to call him back and explain that a personal relationship was not going to happen between us, but I never got around to it for some reason. I can tell by his tone that he suspects I need something and plans on playing the guilt card to get what he wants before I get what I need.

"So, listen, I'm sorry I haven't returned your calls. I've been crazy swamped here." It's not a complete lie. Work has taken up a lot of my time. Work and Brad.

"Oh, is that what's kept you from me? I thought it might have something to do with Johnson," he says.

"No, just busy. Listen, Ten, would you be able to meet with me tonight? I need to talk with you."

"I always have time for you, Mabry."

"Great. Um… could we meet at Boone's around 8:30?" I ask.

"Boone's at 8:30 sounds perfect. You want to give me a little heads-up as to our topic of conversation?"

"Well, what would be the fun in that?" I cringe because it sounds flirty and I don't want to give Ten the wrong impression, but asking him to tell me what's in that note is highly unethical. If I don't play the game just a little I won't get the information I need.

"True and I wouldn't want to miss out on any fun with you." I knew he meant to return the flirtatiousness, but his words just sounded smarmy.

"So, 8:30 at Boone's. See you then," I say, ready to end the conversation.

"See you then. Oh and Mabry."

"Yes."

"Maybe you'll let me escort you home tonight."

"I'll see you later." I hang up before he has a chance to respond.

At 8 o'clock, I grab my jacket, purse, and briefcase and head toward the elevators. I notice the light in Brad's office is still on. The floor is deserted except for the two of us. I feel the pull in his direction as usual, but I ignore it. Brad's office is directly in line with the elevators. I force myself to keep my eyes pointed straight ahead. I reach my target and push the button. As I stand there waiting, it dawns on me that I forgot to tell Tina to move my Thursday meeting with the Murphys to Friday. I walk to her desk to leave a note, keeping my gaze down, in order not to catch a glimpse of him. While placing the note on her desk I hear the sound of the elevator arriving. When I turn, I inadvertently look up and see him.

He's in profile, sitting at his desk, leaning far back in the chair, while looking at his computer. The sleeves of his royal blue dress shirt are rolled up, exposing his toned forearms. I love how protected I feel when those arms are wrapped around me. Raising his hand, he runs his fingers back and forth through his hair a few times. It's in complete disarray when he's done, but sexy as hell. Looking at his chiseled profile, I think back to the first time I saw him a few years ago at the memorial service. Loneliness radiated off of him then just like it does now. Before I realize it, I'm standing in the doorway of his office, forcing myself not to go over and hug him. A slow grin spreads across his face.

"What are you grinning about?" I ask.

Keeping his eyes on the monitor, he says, "The fact that you're standing at my door." He turns to face me. "I've missed you today."

Looking into his warm eyes and hearing his sexy low voice wrap around those sweet words causes my insides to melt. I know I need to leave right now or I'll end up in his lap, clinging to him.

"Don't work too hard, okay," I tell him.

The grin falls from his face. "I won't."

"I'll see you in the morning."

He gets up and rounds his desk heading toward me. "I'll walk you to your car."

Taking a step back, I shake my head and say, "No, that's fine. I'll be okay. Have a good night, Brad." I turn and head in the opposite direction before his words stop me.

"I love you, Mabry."

Facing him, I say, "I love you too. That's not ever going to change."

"But other things have changed." The fear is back in his eyes.

"It's only been one day. I just need a little time."

"Okay. Will you at least text me when you get home, so I know you're safe?"

"Yeah." My throat stings, as I try to hold on to the tears and my stomach twists in knots from the guilt I feel, not letting on who I'm about to see.

I walk as quickly as I can to the awaiting open elevator and step inside. When I turn around to press the button my eyes meet a sapphire gaze that's frozen on me.

Downtown Charleston is a beautiful place. It's an eclectic mix of historic homes, well-preserved architecture, and distinguished restaurants, living side-by-side with small local artisan shops and casual bars. Even though Boone's is only a couple of blocks away from the firm on King Street, certainly within walking distance, I decide to drive. I figure having my car handy will make for a quick getaway once my meeting with Ten is over. I park my car and head inside.

Boone's has a rustic artsy/sports bar feel to it. Local artists' paintings and flat screen TVs cover the old brick walls. Industrial modern lighting fixtures jut down from the exposed ceiling beams. There are three levels. The upper two levels are designated mostly to either live music or watching whatever games happen to be playing on the multiple large flat screen TVs. The lower level is set up more like a restaurant with dark wood tables and chairs and an open kitchen. The atmosphere is casual and relaxed. It's still a little early for the barflies to have taken over, but there is a small dinner crowd.

As I walk in, I spot Ten immediately. He's seated at one of the tables in the corner. A huge smile appears across his face as he raises and tips his beer toward me. Approaching the table, I feel my insides quiver.

I shouldn't be doing this.

My legs feel like lead with each step I take.

I feel like I'm betraying Brad.

My breathing is shallow as I try to take in as much oxygen as possible. I'm scared to find out what's in the note, but my need to know pushes me forward. As I make it to the table, Ten stands to greet me.

"Hey Bright Eyes," he says, his smile getting even larger if that's possible.

The nickname unnerves me. We're not that familiar with each other for him to be calling me that and this is not a social meeting. I bite my tongue and keep my thoughts to myself. I don't want to piss him off. I want him as willing as possible so I can find out what Becca wrote about Brad.

He pulls out my chair and I slide in to it. "Hey. Have you been waiting long?" I ask.

As he pushes my chair closer to the table, he says, "I'd wait forever for you, Bright Eyes."

He's such a Sir Douche.

A slight smile crosses my face, thinking about the nickname Brad gave him.

Ten sits across from me and signals for the waitress. His eyes travel down to my chest and then back up to my eyes. "You look beautiful."

"You're such a liar. I've had the same makeup on and have been in these clothes for the past twelve hours."

"Well, I'll have to see what I can do to rectify that," he says with a smirk.

I feel his eyes on me again and it makes me shift uncomfortably in my chair. Thankfully the waitress arrives for our drink order.

"Hey folks. What can I get you?" she asks, cheerfully.

"I'll have a Firefly Mojito," I answer.

"And for the gentleman?" She gives Ten a flirty smile.

"I'll have another Holy City Pluff Mud Porter. Thanks." He returns her flirty smile before she leaves. Turning his attention to me, he says, "I was kind of surprised to hear from you. Happy and excited, but surprised."

"I apologize again for not returning your calls. It's just been nuts at the office."

"I bet, especially with the lawsuit Junior's got hanging over his head," he says nonchalantly.

The waitress arrives with our drinks before I have a chance to respond.

"Can I get you folks an appetizer?" she asks while placing my drink in front of me.

I shake my head at Ten. "No, this will be all for now. Thanks," he answers.

We sit in silence for a few seconds, both taking sips of our drinks. He knows I have an ulterior motive in asking him to meet with me. He continues to drink his beer, waiting for me to start talking.

"So, the lawsuit... I hear you're the lead on it." My eyes dart back and forth from him to my mojito. He remains silent. "That's pretty impressive to be given a case this big already. You've only been with Clarkson and Ross for a little over a year, right?"

"What can I say? When you're good, you're good. You should come join us. We're always looking for talented lawyers. With your assets, you could go far at the firm."

I give him a weak smile and take another sip of my drink. This is harder than I thought. I really should have planned out what I was going to say. "Do you really think you'll be able to win the case?"

Eyeing me suspiciously, he takes a long draw of his beer. "You know as well as I do that this won't go to trial. There will be a settlement made. The only question is how much of one."

"What if the Johnsons don't settle?"

"They'll settle. The old man cares too much about his reputation to let Junior's wandering dick get in the way."

"I hear there's a note."

"I think we should probably change the subject." He reaches over and runs the tips of his fingers over my hand. "You know, Mabry, you and I would be great together."

My eyes glance down at his touch and immediately back up to meet his dark brown eyes. "I know you can't tell me exactly what's in the note. But is there a strong implication that he was directly responsible for her death? Are you *that* confident in your case?" I ask, shifting into lawyer mode.

"Did they send you here?" He removes his hand.

"No. No one knows I'm here. I'm not part of the case, Ten."

"The note is pretty clear about her reasons for killing herself. That coupled with your boy's past activities leads me and my firm to believe we're in for a hefty payday."

"Past activities?" There's hesitancy in my voice.

"Brad's been a busy boy," he says, sarcastically.

"He admits to having been a player. We all make mistakes when we're young."

"Mistakes, yes, but he was calculating."

"What are you talking about?"

"It seems in high school Brad and some friends had an ongoing betting game. It started off innocent enough, I guess. They'd bet on which one would be the first to feel up a girl or get a blowjob. As the boys got older, the bets and the stakes got bigger. The most charming was snatching of the V card. Their intended targets got picked each semester. The fellas would say and do whatever they needed to in order to get the girl to give it up. When she did, they'd further humiliate her by having the other two assholes appear out of nowhere and pay up right in front of her. He and his friends continued this activity through undergrad school. He's also, pardon my French, fucked the majority of the females working at your firm. Hell, he screwed one of his father's assistants in the old man's own office."

"How do you know all this?"

"Hell hath no fury like a woman scorned and one who holds a grudge. I heard about his reputation. It was simply a matter of looking up girls he went to school with and finding the ones who wanted to talk. As for the work encounters… Kristina, his father's old assistant, we work together. I knew she interned at The Johnson firm. All it took was one expensive dinner, a few drinks, and a little flirting for her to spill the beans."

I sit in silence, keeping my expression as neutral as possible. I don't need Ten to see that what he just told me is ripping my insides apart. I knew about Brad's past, but only in general terms. He and I never discussed details. Even the office gossip was nonspecific. I was just told he was a player and it'd be in my best interest to keep my distance from him. The person Ten's describing isn't my version of Brad. I'm having information overload. The Brad I love is sweet, kind, and generous. The Brad Ten is telling me about is cold, heartless, and selfish. Did he use and then humiliate Becca? Is that what drove her to finally succeed in taking her own life? My appearance continues to remain steady and undisturbed while inside my entire world breaks apart. Which Brad is the real one?

I see Ten's mouth moving, but I don't hear what he's saying. I grab my purse and rummage through it for my wallet.

"I got this. Are you okay?" he asks.

Shoving my chair back, I stand and say, "I'm not feeling well. I have to go."

I don't wait for him to respond. I leave as quickly as possible.

Hold it together, Mabry.

I get into my car and try to focus on every movement.

Concentrate on the physical actions, Mabry.

My place is only a fifteen-minute drive away, but it feels like it's taking me hours to get there. Once I make it home, I run up my steps, fling the front door open, and slam it closed. Tears pour from my eyes. My breathing is rapid and I feel my body tremble uncontrollably. I try to will it to stop, but it doesn't listen.

"…they'd further humiliate her…"

I feel the roughness of the wooden door against my back as I slide down it.

"The note is pretty clear about her reasons for killing herself."

I kick my shoes off and dig my heels into the floor, my nails already piercing the skin of my palms.

"Mabry, I met a guy and I'm completely in love with him."

My entire body tenses as it braces for the blow. My head wants to bounce forward from the first strike, but I force it to stay in place against the hard surface. The pain starts in the center of my head and quickly spreads out to cover my entire skull.

"Mabry. I fucked women until I got tired and bored with them. Becca was no different."

I lean forward and thrust my head and shoulders back with greater force than the first time. My entire body jolts on impact.

"I'm sorry, Mabry. If I had known you were going to be in my future, I would have been a better man in my past."

Closing my eyes tight, I lean over as far as possible, trying to get as much leverage and momentum to strike for the third time. Pain shatters through me. I slam my head back again, and again, and again, trying desperately to knock the thoughts and memories out of my head, but they just keep flooding in.

"Mabry, you know I love you more than anything else in this world, right?"

"Sure. I love you too, Mom."

"She was just tired of being, sweetheart, so she finally made the choice that day to stop."

I continue to throw my head back, the impact becoming weaker with my exhaustion.

"The note is pretty clear about her reasons for killing herself."

I open my eyes to blurry vision. I'm not sure if it's from the sobs or the blows to my head. I blink several times hoping to clear it up. My head swims on my first attempt at getting to my feet. I manage to stand on the second try and stumble to my sofa. I lie down and instinctively curl into a ball as I allow the sobs to take over my body and the darkness to consume my mind before drifting off into unconsciousness.

CHAPTER 18

Brad

I can't decide if I'm more worried or pissed off right now. I didn't hear from Mabry last night. I was at the office until 11 p.m. Work kept me busy, but that's not the reason I stayed. The idea of falling asleep and waking up alone caused my throat as well as my muscles to tighten. I shake my head, remembering a time when getting the girl to leave before the sun came up was my main goal in life. My goal is to never begin a day or end a night without Mabry by my side.

My phone stayed quiet, although I checked it every five minutes just in case her name flashed across the screen. I wanted her to ask me to come over, so we could talk about what's going on, but she didn't even respond to the handful of texts I sent. I decided to drive by her place on my way home. As I got closer, my chest ached seeing her car parked in the driveway and the lights on inside of her condo. In the back of my mind, I was hoping she had been out with Sylvie and wasn't home yet. Obviously, she just didn't want to see or talk to me.

Now I'm sitting at my desk pretending to work while keeping one eye on my door. I've purposely left it open, so that I can spot Mabry the second she steps off of the elevator. It's a little after 8 a.m. and

211

she's not here yet, which is unusual. I've only known her to be late one other time since starting the firm. She's always the first one here and the last to leave.

I get up, walk over to my door, and glance at Mabry's closed office, wondering if somehow she snuck in here without me seeing her. I head to Tina's desk. "Hey, Tina, has Mabry come in yet?"

"Not that I know of. I can buzz her if you like," she offers.

"That'd be great. Thanks."

Picking up the phone, Tina punches in Mabry's extension. The ding of the elevator grabs my attention. As the doors pull apart, I see Mabry make her way through them even before they fully open. She quickly heads to her office without acknowledging or looking at the two of us. The action pisses me off, but I can't deny the relief I feel seeing her. I give Tina a slight smile and follow after Mabry.

By the time I reach her office the door is already closed. I knock but don't wait for an invitation before heading in. I click the door and eye Mabry sitting behind her desk, her head in her hands. I want to be pissed off at her and demand answers as to why she didn't respond to my texts last night, but my anger melts away the longer I look at her. It's obvious she's not feeling well, and all I want to do is take care of her.

"Mabry." Concern is evident in my voice. She doesn't respond. "Mabry."

Her head pops up and she looks at me with glassy eyes. "Hi, I didn't hear you come in."

"Are you okay?"

Walking closer, I round the desk, heading toward her. She shakes her head as her hand rises, stopping me.

"I'm tired and have a splitting headache." Her face lands back in her palms.

"Have you taken anything for the headache?"

"I took some Tylenol before I left my place, but it's not helping," she mumbles.

I debate whether or not to ask about last night now or wait to see if the pills take effect. It doesn't take long before my impatience wins out.

Keeping the concern in my tone, I ask, "Why didn't you call or text me last night?"

Looking up with confusion, she answers, "What?"

"Last night, I didn't hear from you. You promised to let me know you got home safe."

"Oh, yeah. Sorry." She massages her temples with the tips of her fingers.

I wait for a few seconds, thinking there'll be more to her answer, but she just continues to massage in silence.

"That's it?" I ask, a definite bite in my voice.

"I must have fallen asleep."

"You drive the twenty minutes home, walk in the door, and immediately fall asleep? Do you have fucking narcolepsy?" Sounding more and more pissed.

Mabry looks up at me, obviously annoyed. "What's your problem? So I forgot to text you."

"Bullshit," I spit out.

"I'm not doing this right now. I have work to do." She turns her attention to her computer and flips it on.

"Please forgive me for being such an asshole. I just wanted to make sure the woman I love was safe."

I head toward the door. Reaching out, I grab the doorknob, but Mabry's words prevent me from twisting it.

"Brad, I'm sorry for last night and for just now. I'm irritable," she says, her voice soft.

I don't want to fight with Mabry. All I want to do is hold her until she feels better. Trying to lighten the mood, I give her a flirty response,

"You can make it up to me tonight."

Her answer comes quick. "I probably should go home and try to catch up on some sleep."

I let my forehead fall against the door as my stomach sinks hearing her answer. "Yeah, okay." My words are clipped and abrupt as I jerk the door open and walk out.

I fight every impulse to turn around, barge back in, and force her to talk to me. But I've learned from experience that when Mabry is pushed, her instinct to bolt shifts into high gear. I take several deep breaths, trying to calm down as I head into my office, slamming the door behind me.

Over the course of the next two days, Mabry becomes more withdrawn from me. Whenever I suggest spending time together she repeats the excuse, "I'm tired and need some time alone." My patience is completely spent at this point. I can't concentrate on anything and my muscles and nerves are so tightly wound up, that the slightest annoyance sets me off. I've barked at anyone who has come within a five-mile radius of me for the past couple of days. I knew something had to give when I made Mrs. Stevenson cry. She's the older lady who owns a local sandwich shop that we order lunch from once a week. I walk in the lounge as she was setting up our order. She smiles at me, says hello, and then it happens. I completely flip out.

"I'm sorry, Mr. Brad, but the real estate firm downstairs cleaned me out of Cape Cod chips today. I have Doritos, though," she says apologetically.

Looking at the petite, gray-haired, sweet grandmotherly lady who speaks in the softest voice, I shout, "Who the fuck eats goddamn Doritos with a fucking turkey provolone sandwich covered in fucking honey mustard sauce?"

The shock on her face is quickly replaced by trembling lips and tears. It's not until she lifts her glasses to wipe the tears away that I realize what I've done. I apologize and give her a hundred bucks, hoping no saliva will make it onto my sandwich the next time we order from her. Peyton witnesses the entire exchange. After calming Mrs. Stevenson down and walking her to the elevator, he shows up in my office, informing me that the two of us are either getting drunk, laid, or both tonight. Since my lay-ee isn't having anything to do with me at the moment, getting drunk is my only option.

I take another swig of my beer as I watch a few sailboats float by in the Charleston Harbor and then disappear from sight under the Cooper River Bridge. I'm sitting on one of the small sofas that line the outside area of The Rooftop Bar at Vendue Inn. The sun is fading and it's peaceful right now. Peyton and I ducked out of the office a little earlier than usual in order to beat the crowd. He's sitting across from me, playing with his phone, as my thoughts fluctuate from nothingness to Mabry. I wish she was sitting next to me, our fingers laced together, while the lights of the city flicker on. I'm trying hard to give her what time she needs, but I'm so lonely without her, I'm not sure how much longer I can hold out before I break.

"Dude, have you seen this app called Nipple?" Peyton's eyes are fixated on his phone screen.

My brother giggling like a school girl catches my attention. "What?"

"It's an app of an animated nipple that you play with. The entire screen is just one big nipple. You can rub it, pinch it, and make it jiggle."

"Why would you want to play with a cartoon nipple?" I ask, astounded by his stupidity.

Looking up at me in confusion, he answers, "Because there are occasions when you need some nipplage time and the real thing isn't within reach." Holding up the phone, he turns the screen toward me and smiles proudly. "Nipple in your pocket is always ready, willing, and perky for ya."

I stare at him, thinking there is no way we share the same DNA. "You're an idiot."

"What's your deal lately, little bro? I mean, I know the lawsuit shit has been stressful, but from what Dad says, your lethal dick might actually earn us some money," Peyton says, chuckling.

I take a swig of my beer as I narrow my eyes at him before commenting. "A young girl died, man."

"I know. People die every day. She's in a better place now." He raises his glass and an arrogant eyebrow in a pathetic attempt to pay honor to Becca. Peyton and my father are a lot alike. Both dickheads. "So, tell me, how's sweet cheeks in bed?"

"Who?" I ask, already pissed. I know exactly who he's referring to.

Peyton and I are only four years apart. We had some of the same friends growing up, we both played baseball and went to the same parties. I followed after him at Duke, and we work together, but we are almost strangers to each other. We don't have brotherly heart-to-heart talks about life and love. When Mabry and I first started sleeping together, we kept things quiet. Once we became an official couple, we didn't hide from curious eyes. We've never made some big announcement, but people know we're together.

He motions to the waitress to bring us another round and says, "Don't get all alpha male. I'm not challenging you to a pissing contest. Just curious. I won't make my move until you give me the all-clear signal."

My fingers grip the bottle of beer so tightly that for a moment I think it's going to shatter in my hand. "Stay away from Mabry."

A slimy smile crosses his face. "She's that good, huh?"

"I swear to god, Peyton, if you say one more thing about Mabry I will fuck you up."

"Don't blow your load, man. I get it. Sweet cheeks's pussy is off limits." He shoots me a toothy grin. "Happy? Besides, the second string just walked in."

I follow his gaze across the room and see Mia standing at the entrance. She spots us and heads our way.

"Hey guys." She picks up the pillow next to me and plops down in its place without being invited. I glance at her, annoyed by how close she is.

"Mia, thank God you showed up. I needed something hot and sexy to look at," Peyton says.

"Brad's pretty hot and sexy." She sends a flirtatious smile my way as she reaches over and touches my forearm.

"But not my type," Peyton jokes.

Thankfully, the waitress arrives with our drinks, giving me an excuse to move my arm away. I'm hoping Mia is here to meet with some friends and will move on, but she orders a drink and stays planted in her seat.

"I gotta go take a piss," Peyton announces. Leaning forward, he takes Mia's hand, raises it to his lips, and places a quick kiss on the top of it. "I shall return momentarily." He throws her a wink before heading toward the restroom.

Mia and I sit in awkward silence for what feels like forever. "So, did you come here to meet someone?" I ask.

"Yes," she says as her hand lands on my thigh.

Grabbing her wrist, I push it off of me. "What are you doing? You know I'm with Mabry."

"I've never known you to be with anyone exclusively." I see her hand creep back toward me and I shift away from her reach.

"Well, I am now."

"That's okay. I know how to be discrete," she says in a low voice.

"Why would you want to bother, knowing nothing would ever come of it?"

"Because you're the hottest guy I've ever seen and I've heard stories. I'd like to see if they're true." Cocking her head to the side, she bites her bottom lip as she gazes at me.

All it would take is one word and Mia would do anything I asked her to do to me. It's a powerful feeling knowing you have that kind of control over someone. I feel so out of control with Mabry. I miss the contact of soft skin, hearing the breathless moans, and the feel of being inside of her. My eyes roam up and down Mia's face. Everything is there, big dark brown eyes, high cheekbones, straight nose, and full lips. I stare at her trapped bottom lip. When Mabry does this, it's mindless and natural. Mia's action is staged and purposeful. I move up to her eyes that are telling me what I already know. *Say the word and I'll be down on my knees or open them up for you, Brad.* But I love azure blues even when they're sad and won't look at me. Mia's trying hard to be sexy for me. Mabry just *is* sexy for me.

I take one long draw of my beer before standing. "Tell Peyton I'll see him tomorrow."

Looking up at me with surprised dark brown eyes and pouty lips, she says, "All you have to do is tell me what you like and I'll do it."

A slight smirk appears on my face. "I'd like you to leave me alone."

I have every intention of going home, but somehow I veer off course and end up in front of Mabry's place, leaning against my car. I type out a quick text.

Me: Hey, I'm outside.

Her response takes a few seconds.

Mabry: What r u doing out there?

Me: Missing you.

Several minutes pass before the front door opens and she walks out onto the porch. Her hair is pulled up into a high ponytail with most of it having already fallen loose around her face. She's wearing a pair of long dark gray pajama pants, fuzzy dark gray socks with pink and white polka dots, and my blue Duke T-shirt. I tore my place up the other night looking for that shirt. I needed to feel close to her in any way I could and I knew it still had her scent on it.

God, I'm pathetic.

I stay put, take her in, and smile. She's the most beautiful and precious thing in the world to me. I feel her slipping through my fingers and I haven't got a clue how to stop it from happening. I've never cared if someone stayed in my life, or how they looked at me, or what they thought of me until Mabry. This is unchartered waters for me.

I walk to the steps, stopping at the bottom.

"Hey," I whisper.

"Hey," she says softly. The tone in her voice is warm and sweet, but there's so much sadness in her eyes.

We stare at each other, frozen. No words pass between us, but we see each other's pain and confusion. The moonlight is reflecting off the water building in her eyes, making them sparkle. There's been a noticeable shift in the way she sees me.

Wrapping her arms around herself, she looks away and asks, "Why are you here, Brad?"

I clear my throat and answer, "I needed to see your beautiful face. Lately, I've only been able to catch a glimpse of it as you whiz by me at the office."

One nervous hand runs over her messy hair slowly. "I'm a sight."

"You're gorgeous."

This is the closest we've been in days. I can hear the sound of my own breathing as it gets heavier and more labored. I clench my hands, trying to stop the twitching of my fingers. I want to touch her so badly. Heat spreads across my body as the ability to control myself disappears. Before she registers what's happening, I run up the steps, grab the sides of her face, and crash my lips into hers. The kiss is aggressive, intense, and unapologetic. Moans fill the air as our tongues frantically stroke each other's mouths. I need to be closer to her. She clutches my forearms for balance as I walk her backward until the wall stops us. I push my body against hers, grinding my hips relentlessly. Her body seamlessly molds to mine. I feel the bottom of my shirt slide out of my pants and up my stomach as Mabry's hands curl around it. Her fingertips graze my side, causing a deep growl to escape my chest. I want back inside of her in every way—her heart, her soul, and her body. Suddenly, I feel her stiffen and her palms push on my chest, causing the kiss to break. She tries to move away from me, but I keep my hands firmly in place on either side of her face.

Gasping for air she says, "I'm sorry. I can't. Not right now." Tears stream down her cheeks, soaking my hands.

I lean in and whisper on her lips, "Come back to me, Mabry."

"I'm trying." We stare for several seconds, neither of us wanting to disconnect. Mabry makes the first move, angling her head away from me, causing my hands to fall.

I take a step back. "Try harder," I say, attempting to make my voice sound strong and commanding, but instead it comes out shaky and weak.

Nodding her head, she whispers, "I will."

"I love you so much, Mabry."

Her head turns in my direction, but her eyes aren't looking at me. "I don't know why."

"Because it's what I was born to do, Sweetness."

I linger a few more minutes, memorizing the way she looks,

before heading back to my car. She's still standing on the porch watching me as I pull out of the driveway. While Mabry disappears from sight, the overwhelming fear of not getting past this attacks my thoughts, and I feel the physical reaction take over. I pull into the deserted parking lot of a nearby office building and shut off the car. All at once my shoulders slump forward, my chin drops to my chest, the pit of my stomach bottoms out, and I'm free-falling. Pressure pushes against my throat, my eyes, my chest, and my resolve as the sobs quietly seep out of me. I can't go back to that existence I had before Mabry came into my life. Losing her is not an option. We're in this together and right now she needs me to hold on and be strong for both of us. I can't change the past, but I'm going to fight like hell to ensure I have a future with her.

Mabry

The tips of my fingers automatically draw back the second they make contact with the area, as I gently massage the shampoo into my scalp. The designated target on the back of my head has endured a lot of abuse this week. I'm completely out of control, no longer able to fight the need to self-harm. I thought a few days of distance from Brad would clear my head, but just the opposite is happening. Memories, doubts, and fears hold my attention more than career obligations or anything else now. My mind is always cloudy and I can't concentrate for long. Tina found me in the firm's library the other day. She had been looking for me because a client of mine had been waiting in my office for more than fifteen minutes. I was just sitting in there staring off into space. I can't even remember what I was thinking about.

I carefully rinse the shampoo out of my hair, grab a towel, and gently wrap it around my head. Stepping out of the shower, I lose my balance, my foot skidding across the tile floor causing me to stumble backward. Luckily, I catch hold of the towel rack, stopping my fall. I steady myself and step out of the shower. Toweling off, I glance at the large clock on the wall in my bedroom. I have to be at the firm's weekly breakfast meeting in twenty minutes.

Fuck, I'm not going to make it there in time.

I feel a surge of anxiety rip through my body. I quickly finish drying my hair and sweep it into a bun. I rush through my makeup routine, putting on only lip gloss, blush, and mascara. As I dash toward my closet, I grab underwear from the dresser. Trying to multitask, I attempt to step into my panties while walking and end up losing my balance for the second time this morning. Toppling forward into the closet, I catch myself on the wall before I fall flat on my face. Once inside, my eyes dart back and forth across my clothes as I clasp my bra.

I always pick out this shit the night before. Why didn't I pick out something last night? Brad, that's why. Focus, Mabry. Don't think about him right now.

The sounds of my heavy breathing and the scraping of hangers along the rod as I frantically shove outfit after outfit past me fill the air. Finally, I decide on my sleeveless navy blue pencil dress and throw it on. I snag a pair of nude heels and a cardigan before sprinting around the living room to gather my phone, purse, bag, and my travel mug of coffee. I mentally check off items on my list while scanning the room one more time, making sure I have everything I need for the day before heading out the door.

The second the elevator doors open I make a beeline for my office, toss my things on the desk, and head toward the conference room. I pause outside the door and attempt to calm myself down before entering. Easing the door open, I step inside. I try to be as quiet as possible, not wanting to draw any attention. Maybe no one will notice that I'm late.

Keeping my gaze down, I sneak over to one of the chairs against the wall. I'm almost there when his deep harsh voice causes my eyes to shoot up, meeting his.

"Well, Miss Darnell, so nice of you to finally join us," Mr. Johnson says, sarcastically.

All eyes at the conference table aim in my direction. Embarrassment rushes through me. "I'm sorry. I got stuck in traffic."

A snide smirk crosses his face. "Yes, and the dog ate my homework."

A wave of chuckles makes its way around the table, stopping abruptly when it reaches Brad. His expression is stern with annoyance at the snickering, but he looks at me with soft concerned eyes. I feel the tears building up as I slide into the chair. My emotions are so raw right now that the slightest reprimand stings.

"I always feel every screw-up is an opportunity to learn something. Today, Miss Darnell is your screw-up teaching tool," Mr. Johnson states.

I hear another round of chuckles, only this time they're being muffled by the sound of my rapidly increasing pulse.

"Stop it," Brad snaps, looking at his father.

Ignoring him, Mr. Johnson continues. "This is for all you newbies. If you are even three seconds late to court you may as well not even go in. It's disrespectful and arrogant. It says to the judge that your time is more valuable than his. This also goes for being late when meeting a client." His blue eyes bore into me, pinning me to the seat. "I believe you kept Mr. Sanders waiting the other day, is that correct, Miss Darnell?"

"Leave her alone, now," Brad growls, clenching his jaw.

"Yes, Sir." My voice is weak and I can feel the slightest tremble in my chin. I need to get out of here before I fall apart.

"I suggest you get your act together, Miss Darnell, or rethink your career choice."

"That's enough!" Brad shouts, roughly pushing away from the table.

"I guess we've covered everything we needed to this morning. Meeting is adjourned." His father gives me one last smug look before standing.

I stay in my seat while everyone files out of the room, leaving me, Brad, and his father alone.

Brad approaches his father, almost getting right in his face. "What the fuck is wrong with you?"

"Don't you dare speak to me that way, especially here, I won't tolerate it." Mr. Johnson gathers his notes.

"Oh, but you can speak any way you want, to whomever you want?" Brad accuses.

"May I remind you whose name is on the door?"

"You didn't have to humiliate her like that."

"A little humiliation never hurt anybody. It builds character." As he heads toward the door, Mr. Johnson stops next to me and warns, "Two strikes, Mabry. One more and you're out of here." He glances back at Brad and then gives me a smirk before exiting the room.

Brad comes over and squats in front of me. "Are you okay?" he asks, raising his hand and tucking a piece of loose hair behind my ear.

"He's right," I say, my voice low.

"He's an asshole." His hand runs down the length of my arm, landing on top of mine.

"He's still right, though. I've been letting too many personal things get in the way of my job." I glance at him. The pain in his eyes is heartbreaking.

"It's been a rough week. How about we order takeout tonight and rent a movie? We can just relax and spend time together. Put everything aside for one night," he says as his thumb mindlessly runs over my hand.

I want to forget the past week ever happened. When I look at Brad I want to see a future instead of a past, but my mind won't let me. The longer I look at him the more my thoughts snowball.

Girls targeted, humiliated, and tossed aside.

Becca used, discarded, and dead.

Dad letting Momma slip into darkness and then away.

Dad abandoning me.

Brad playing me.

I don't want to end up like my mom and Becca.

I'm so tired of hurting. I want to be numb again.

"I can't."

"Can't or won't?" A flash of anger shoots across his face as his thumb comes to an abrupt halt and he stands.

Brad runs both hands roughly through his hair as he walks to the conference table. Resting his hands on his hips, he doesn't face me. I start to leave when his plea causes me to stop.

"Please tell me what to do to make things better." The trembling in his voice pierces my heart.

I swallow hard and answer, "I wish I knew."

I robotically move through the rest of the day, trying hard to concentrate on the tasks at hand. Mr. Johnson doesn't make idle threats. He meant it earlier when he said I had one more chance. Even though I'm one of the best new lawyers here, he doesn't tolerate mistakes. I know something has to change. I've worked too hard to get where I'm at for my career to get derailed simply because my mind is cloudy.

"You seem very distracted today," Jennifer says.

I simply give her a weak smile. My session started five minutes ago and other than the obligatory "hellos and how are yous" I've been quiet.

"Do you think it's possible to forget about the past and change into a completely different person?" I ask.

"I definitely think a person can change. I think you can move on from your past, but I'm not sure it's a good idea to forget about it, completely. The past keeps us grounded. It teaches us to be mindful about mistakes and destructive patterns that hopefully we won't repeat. But it also shows us that nothing is permanent. No matter how bad we think a situation is right now, it's only transient."

I sit in silence for a few minutes thinking about her words.

"Mabry, I know this is only our second time together. It can be uncomfortable and awkward especially when you've never been to counseling before. But I can't help you unless you open up and tell me what's going on."

"I feel like I'm fading into the past." My voice is so low it's almost a whisper.

"Can you tell me why you feel this way?"

"I found out some things about Brad's past. When I look at him now, I see reminders of my pain and fear." Tears trickle down my cheeks. "I keep trying to get numb, but I can't. The feelings won't leave me alone," I say, sounding as if I'm in a trance.

A warm hand covers mine as a tissue appears in front of me. I glance up at Jennifer's sympathetic expression. "It will take time to work through this, but don't be afraid of feelings, Mabry. Feelings, even the bad ones, let you know you're alive. When they go away, that's when you should be afraid."

"I'm becoming paralyzed by them."

"Sometimes we have to step back from a situation in order to gain some perspective, to regroup. That way you are better able to decide what's best for you. You deserve to be happy, Mabry. Don't let ghosts from the past rob you of that."

I leave Jennifer's office just as confused as when I arrived. I try to think clearly about what she said, but the same continuous loop of thoughts that have been playing in my head for the past week keep forcing themselves in. I'm caught between the light and the dark. I can see myself hanging from a cliff. My fingers digging deep into the grass, dirt, and rocks, trying to stay above ground while my legs dangle aimlessly over the edge. The harder I hold on, the stronger gravity tugs at my legs. Then little by little the blades of grass break, the grains of dirt shift, and the rocks roll away until I'm free-falling. Glimpses of my mother's life flash across my mind.

"She was just tired of being, so she finally made the choice that day to stop."

"…you're just like her."

I'm in my car sitting in front of his place staring at the front door. Out the corner of my eye, I see the screen of my phone light up with a text.

Brad: *Hope ur having a good nite. I love u.*

I close my eyes as my head falls back against the headrest. I wince at the tenderness and quickly straighten back up. I don't have the time to "work through this" like Jennifer wants. I have to take action now before I lose my grip.

I check my face in the mirror, grab my things, and get out of the car. With each step toward the front door, I shut down.

I take in a deep breath and knock. The door opens almost immediately. He greets me with a huge smile on his face.

"Hey Bright Eyes," Ten says, as he steps back, gesturing for me to come in. "I'm so happy you finally came to your senses and called."

I look up at his overly pleased face and my reaction is exactly what I was hoping for... Indifferent. Detached. Numb.

CHAPTER 19

Brad

My heart is pounding so violently against my chest it feels like it's about to break through. I grip the steering wheel and try to focus on my driving as I speed down the road, but my thoughts are scattered. I've been completely ignored for the past couple of days by Mabry. I've been swamped with clients' cases as well as my own, but have still tried to reach out to her with no luck. Somehow she's been able to avoid me at the office. She hasn't answered her phone or returned a single text. I've been patient and have given her the space. Fuck that. It ends today.

I screech into the driveway and jump out of my car. I don't even bother to check to see if her car is here. Running up the steps, I let myself into her place without warning, and slam the door behind me.

"Mabry!" I yell. There's no response.

My eyes scan the room and then zero in on the two boxes sitting on her dining table. I walk over and open one. Some books, her diploma, her mom's picture, and the one of the two of us are all inside. Clenching and unclenching my fists, I feel the vibrations and heat take over my body. My hand clamps down on the back of a chair. I'm hoping to ground myself before I ram it into a wall.

"Brad…" A soft and timid voice says behind me.

I don't turn around. I'm not sure I want to look at her right now. "When were you going to tell me?" I ask through grinding teeth. Silence fills the room. "Answer me now, goddammit!" The decibel level of my voice is deafening.

I hear the click of the front door as it closes and then footsteps coming farther into the room.

Hesitantly, she says, "I wanted to wait until things were finalized."

"You didn't think this was something *we* needed to discuss?"

"It's my career, so it's my decision."

Tremors run through my body as anger overtakes me. My grip tightens on the back of the chair. Every bit of strength and willpower I have is focused on staying planted in this spot, because right now all I want to do is go grab her by the shoulders and shake her.

"Why?" I ask.

"Why what? Be specific." There's a tremble in her voice, but also the hint of a challenge.

At that moment something in me snaps. I slowly turn toward her, piercing her eyes with mine, and fire off questions. "*Why* are you pushing me away? *Why* won't you talk to me? *Why* are you leaving the firm? *Why* are you going to work with that fucking douche bag? Are these "whys" fucking specific enough for you?"

"It's a good career move for me. Plus, I need some…" I see the tears appear behind her eyes.

"Don't say it. I'm so fucking sick of hearing you say you need time." I bite out. "How much *time* do you need, Mabry?" I start walking toward her. Each step corresponding with my words. "Be specific. An hour, a day, a week, a motherfucking year?! Exactly, what do you *need* time for, Mabry?"

There's a struggle in her eyes. She's trying desperately to replace the love in them with a numbing coldness. Her expression goes slack when she answers, "I need time away from you."

I try taking in a deep breath, but the air feels thick in my lungs, as I choke out, "Why do you need time away from me?"

I watch her bottom lip disappear into her mouth. Her concentration is intense, wanting to choose her words carefully. "Brad…" She doesn't want to tell me the truth. She gives up and allows the tears to fall. Her expression slowly morphs into a weird combination of warmth and detachment.

"Say it, Mabry. I'm a big boy. I can take it." We stare at each other for several minutes until I finally break the silence. "You think I'm responsible for Becca's death."

Her head shakes before any words leave her mouth. "I never said that."

"You didn't have to, I can see it in your eyes. It's been there all week." My throat is burning as I try to hold back my own tears. "Please talk to me."

Her chin trembles so much I can hear her teeth chatter. "I don't want to hurt you more."

"If I'm losing you, then it's not possible to hurt me any more than I am right now." Tears spill out of my eyes.

"You used to make everything bad in my life disappear."

"And now?" The words stick in my throat.

"You remind me of all the pain in my life. I found out about the bets you used to make and how you humiliated the girls. Did you do that to Becca? Is that why she finally killed herself?"

I'm frozen in place by her words. Somehow she's learned the details of my past. I never wanted her to know how disgusting I used to be. "I don't have an excuse for what I did to those girls. I didn't mean to hurt Becca, Mabry. She was getting too attached. She was sick," I trail off.

"In her email she seemed so happy. She was in love with you. She wasn't thinking about killing herself until you left her. She slit the radial artery in her wrist. Did you know that?"

"Yes," I whisper. The memories of the last time I saw Becca come rushing back to me. The way her arms clutched on to me, not wanting me to leave her. The sad, vacant look in her eyes. Her tear-stained cheeks. Mabry's voice forces me back to the present.

There's a distant tone in her voice. "My mom used Dad's box cutters. You have to cut lengthwise along the radial artery if you're serious about killing yourself. It's a painful death. You know physical pain sometimes relieves the pain inside. Maybe that's why my mom did it that way. People think it's a quick death, but that's not true. First, your heart rate goes up, then you become pale, clammy, lethargic, dizzy, and lightheaded. You start to become short of breath, like you're starving for air and you can't get a full breath. Eventually your blood pressure drops until you lose consciousness. Finally, you lose so much blood that there's not enough left to circulate to your organs and you die. That's how Becca died that night."

"I didn't kill her, Mabry." I can barely get the words out.

"I know, but I feel like you did." Her body convulses as sobs gush out.

I instinctively take a step forward, getting ready to wrap my arms around her. I'm still not ready to admit this is coming to an end. She takes a step back away from me and my world shatters.

"I'm a different person now. You have to believe me. I'd never treat you that way. I love you." The plea pouring out of me.

"Our pasts will always be a part of us, Brad, no matter how much we want or try to escape from it. The way my mom was… I have that in me. There have been times in my life I didn't want to get out of bed, the pain was so stifling. And what's to keep that part of you that you've tried to bury in the past from resurfacing? I can't take that chance on either one of us."

"God, don't do this, Mabry," I beg.

"I knew from the very beginning we were a mistake." The words are barely audible through her sobs.

A mistake. The word echoes through my head.

"Don't say that. Everyone has always looked at me as a fucking mistake. I thought it was true until I met you. You give me meaning and purpose, Mabry. You're the only person who has ever wanted me in their life. That can't be a mistake. What I feel for you isn't a mistake. Let me spend the rest of my life proving that to you."

We stare at each other for several seconds. Both our faces streaked with tears and desperation. My gaze pleading once again with Mabry's. I think I see a flash of indecision in her eyes right before she closes them. She's reconsidering. Hope fills me. It will be difficult, but I know we can get through this.

Her head slowly shakes and she whispers, "No." I stand, frozen, not believing that this is really happening. Her eyes remain closed as she clears her throat, and says in a more commanding voice, "I need my key back."

My entire body feels weighed down in defeat. I take a couple of steps toward her, placing me at her side. I see her body visibly react to our closeness, sending a shiver through it. I bend down close to her ear, my breath causing wisps of her hair to swirl away from her cheek. "I don't know how to be without you," I say, my voice deep and low.

I fish my keys out of my front pocket and slide hers off the keychain, tossing it on the coffee table. She still won't open her eyes. I stare at her for as long as she'll allow.

"Mabry…," I whisper, my voice strained.

"Please just go, Brad."

My hand raises on its own accord toward her cheek. I want to wipe her tears. I want to take her sadness and pain away, like I had once before. Sensing my movement, she steps to the side, putting more distance between us. I head toward the door, not looking back, but also not giving up.

Mabry

Three days have passed since I looked into his eyes and told him we were a mistake. Since then each day bleeds into the next with no beginning or end. My body constantly aches and I'm never fully awake or coherent. I manage to move and make it through a work day, but that's about it. I'm becoming like my dad. Since I started the new job, my main assignment has been research and collecting data for cases. This suits me because I don't have to interact with anyone.

I've looked to my usual reliable coping skills to get me through this, but nothing seems to be working. When I'm home, I attempt to keep moving, keep busy, and keep my mind occupied. My self-harm is a daily ritual, more so now than ever before. I've even scouted out restaurants and stores close to my new office that have single restrooms so that I can go there during lunch or on breaks and inflict pain privately. No longer does yanking a few strands of hair even register as pain to me. I'm so tired of feeling, of hurting. I lay my head down at night, praying that sleep will come and give me some relief, but it doesn't. I end up sobbing most of the night dreading that there will be another tomorrow that I'll have to live through.

I'm wrapped in my comforter cocoon when the continuous banging on my front door startles me out of my weekend catatonic state. I ignore it, hoping whoever it is will just go away. The loud banging finally stops, but is replaced by the loud voice of Sylvie.

Shit! I forgot she had a key.

"Mabry Elizabeth Darnell!" My name bellows through my place just before I hear my bedroom door fly open.

A cool breeze hits my face as the comforter is pulled off of me.

"It's two in the afternoon on a Sunday, what the hell are you doing in bed?" Sylvie asks in a stern voice.

My eyes stay closed. Stretching my hands out in front of me, I feel for the comforter, so I can return it to its proper place, over my head. "Why do you sound so pissed?"

My hand lands on the edge of the comforter and I pull on it when suddenly it's yanked from my grip.

"When was the last time you showered or ate anything, Mabry?"

"What's today?"

"Sunday," Sylvie answers, annoyed.

"Then Friday. I went to work Friday, so I showered then."

"And food?"

"I haven't been hungry. Sylvie, go home. It's been a long week and I'm tired."

I feel a dip in my mattress as she sits next to me. "I talked to Brad." Her voice sounding more sympathetic now.

"Good for you." I make another effort to claim my comforter back, unsuccessfully.

"What are you doing, Mabry?"

"Trying to get some rest." I jerk my body, turning away from her.

Huffing out a deep breath, Sylvie talks, not caring whether or not I respond. "He told me what happened. He sounded as miserable as you look. I understand you're scared, but to push him away like this is insa…"

She stops herself from finishing the word, but the damage has already been done. Sylvie of all people knows how those words affect me. I shift my body, trying to get farther away from her.

"You can't put Becca's death on Brad, its irrational thinking."

Tossing the comforter off, I quickly jump off of the bed, turning to face her. "Oh, is it?" I snap.

"I understand your fear, but…"

I laugh humorlessly. "Give me a fucking break. You don't

understand shit about my fear. You, with your perfect set of parents, who loved and protected you. Who didn't leave you or forget you existed. Tell me Sylvie, what exactly are you terrified of inheriting from your parents? Teeth that are too straight and white or hair that's too shiny and soft?"

Shock crosses her face as tears fill her eyes. "That's not fair and you know it."

Every muscle in my body tenses and my chest heaves as I struggle to hold in my sobs. "Fuck fair. If life were fair I'd still have my mom and her smiles. My dad would give a shit about me and pick up the phone once in a while. And Brad wouldn't be a constant reminder to me of just how fucking unfair my life is."

She stands and walks to the door without saying a word. When she turns to me the tears are streaming down her cheeks. Strangling a sob, she says, "I know you've had horrible things happen in your life. I wish I could do something to change it because I love you. I know you've fought not to become like your mom, but what do you think is happening now? Your mom was able to function for a while before she holed up in her room, staying in the bed all day. You need help, Mabry. You have for many years. I'm sorry your dad let you down, but you're a grown woman now. You have a man who loves and adores you. And me, who will do anything in the world for you. Work through this, Sweetie. Learn from your past and apply the lessons to your future. Brad did."

We stare at each other for a few seconds. The look on her face tells me she wants to come over and hug me. I stiffen my body wanting to convey that her little speech had no effect on me. My gaze follows her as she makes her way to the front door and out of my place. I let out a deep sigh and climb back into my bed. Sylvie's words play over in my head. Her words of wisdom are easy for her to say. She doesn't understand the depth of pain I'm in. I start to pull my comforter back over my head when my phone buzzes with a text.

Ten: Need u 2 come in early 2morrow.

Me: K. What's up?

I'm barely getting to the office at my regular time.

Ten: Hyams got moved up. Need u 2 take over Robinson.

I knew tomorrow was the meeting between the Hyams and Brad. I planned on staying clear of it by hiding out in my office. In my current state, I wasn't sure if I was the best one to step into the Robinson case, but I had no choice.

Me: K. Will b there.

I toss my phone back onto the nightstand and bury myself back under the comforter, shutting out the world for as long as possible.

I rush out of the bathroom the next morning when I hear my phone go off. I grab it and glance at the screen. It's a number I don't recognize. I tap the screen to answer and place it on speaker, so I can continue getting dressed.

"Hello?"

"Is this Mabry Darnell?" the voice on the other end asks.

"Yes, it is. Who's calling?"

"Miss Darnell, my name is Marilyn Sanchez. I'm a nurse at The Medical University."

"Okay?" I say hesitantly.

"Is someone with you, ma'am?" Her voice is all business, but there is a hint of concern.

"No. Why?"

"Miss. Darnell, I'm sorry to have to tell you over the phone, but your father, Thomas Darnell, overdosed. He passed away earlier this morning."

My reaction comes in waves. The breath is completely knocked out of me and my knees collapse. I feel the tremors start in my hands and make their way through my arms, shoulders, and chest, until my entire body is covered. I don't know if the voice on the other end of the phone is still talking or not. Memories of my dad flash across my mind as the realization seeps in.

"That's it, Sweetheart, keep pedaling. You're doing great."

"All A's, I'm so proud of you, Mabry."

"You were fantastic out on that soccer field today."

"Mabry, I'm sorry. It's just been so hard. I'll try to do better. I promise."

Sobs burst out of me as I desperately gasp for air. I haven't had contact with my father in such a long time, but it doesn't stop the empty ache from growing in the pit of my stomach. I'm all alone now. The phone falls from my hand. Raising my knees to my chest, I curl into myself, as I ease onto my side and allow the loneliness to swallow me up.

CHAPTER 20

Brad

My car has become an early morning fixture in the parking lot across from her office over the past five days. During the day, I attempt to break away at the times I'm most likely to catch a glimpse of her. Already one of Charleston's finest has paid me a visit this morning, asking if everything is okay. Either Mabry's going to have to give in and see me or I'll have to find another vantage point.

Since walking out of her place I've been like a zombie. I haven't slept, eaten, or felt anything. I started trying to get her to talk to me about an hour after I had left that day, alternating between calls and texts. She never responded. I even went by her place the next day, but she wouldn't come to the door. That was no big surprise. Finally, I was able to get in touch with Sylvie and sent her over to check on Mabry. She wasn't exactly met with open arms.

I glance down at my watch. I've been sitting out here for an hour, hoping to see her, before heading upstairs for the meeting with Becca's parents. So far she's been quite elusive. I want and need to see her all the time, but this morning especially. I've had the strangest feeling all morning and I haven't been able to shake it. It's not nerves, just something feels off to me.

My phone buzzes with a text.

Father: Pulling into the parking garage. Meet me in lobby. Me: K.

I check my watch one last time before looking around, hoping to spot Mabry, with no luck. I let out a deep sigh of disappointment as the strange feeling intensifies. Maybe she got here super early and is already up in her office. I haven't seen her car, but I could have just missed it in the parking lot. I take my keys out of the ignition, grab my suit jacket, and head inside to the Law Offices of Clarkson and Ross.

As I enter the lobby, I'm met with the intense disdain of my father.

"What took you so long? I've been standing here waiting for…"

"About five seconds," I shoot back at him.

"When we get up there, I'll do all the talking."

"Well, good fucking morning to you too, *Dad*," I say as sarcastically as possible.

Leaning in, he glowers at me, and mumbles, "Don't start shit with me, Bradley, not today." I simply return his look. "Now, that little prick McGuire never did send us a copy of the suicide note. He kept giving lame excuses. No matter what that note contains, you are to keep your mouth shut. Do I make myself clear?"

"Crystal."

You motherfucking asshole.

The ride up in the elevator is silent except for the thrashing sound of my heartbeat in my ears. My body tenses up, starting with my jaw, then my shoulders, quickly moving downward until it reaches the muscles in my legs. I want to see Mabry, I'm excited at the possibility, but I'm also anxious. Plus, the unidentified feeling keeps gnawing at me. Tilting my head from side to side, I try to loosen up a little. The elevator doors open, revealing a classic-looking waiting room with dark woods, large bulky leather furniture, and dim lighting. It's the polar opposite of our firm, which is modern and sleek. As my father steps out of the elevator and approaches the smiling receptionist, my eyes dart around, looking for Mabry's name on an office door.

"Good morning," the receptionist drawls.

"Good morning," my father returns. "William Johnson here for a meeting with Tennyson McGuire."

"Please have a seat and I'll let him know you're here. Can I get you anything, coffee or tea?" she offers.

"No, thank you," my father answers.

She picks up the phone to alert Sir Douche as my father heads toward one of the huge leather chairs. I stay back at the receptionist's desk, waiting to ask her which office is Mabry's.

Putting the phone down, she announces immediately, "Mr. Johnson, Mr. McGuire is waiting for you in the conference room."

I open my mouth to get information on Mabry when I hear the low controlled rumble of my father summoning me. The receptionist and I exchange weak smiles, before I follow *dear Dad* into the other room. We are met at the door of the conference room by Sir Douche himself. I glance at him briefly before my eyes are drawn to the older couple sitting quietly at the long table. Becca's memorial service was only a few years ago, but her parents look as if they've aged fifteen years since then. Mrs. Hyams looks directly at me. Slight recognition flashes across her face. The sorrow that fills her eyes is as intense, if not more so, than two years ago. Mr. Hyams keeps his gaze focused straight ahead, not giving the slightest bit of acknowledgment that we've even entered the room.

McGuire reaches his hand out to my father and they shake. "Mr. Johnson, welcome."

"Mr. McGuire," my father returns.

"It's nice to see you again, Sir. I only wish it were under better circumstances."

Kiss ass, motherfucking douche bag.

Tilting his chin up, my father nods his head marginally in reply. McGuire extends his hand in my direction. I lower my eyes down to it, but quickly glance back up to him. I know I should shake his hand. It's the professional mature thing to do. I don't feel like being either one of those things at the moment, so I end up engaging in a staring contest with him instead. His face gets increasingly more self-righteous the longer I look. Keeping my hands down, I shift them slightly behind me, attempting to hide the fists that are forming. He takes a step back and gestures for us to move farther into the room.

"Mr. and Mrs. Hyams, this is William Johnson, and his client Brad Johnson," McGuire introduces. We all simply nod in recognition as McGuire, my father, and I take our seats. Looking at us, he asks, "Would you gentlemen like anything, coffee perhaps?"

"No. We'd like to get down to business." My father's answer is precise and stern.

McGuire's posture adjusts from hospitable southern lawyer to match my father's. "My client is asking for damages for your client's part in the death of their one and only daughter, Rebecca Hyams."

"With all due respect to the family, this claim is absurd. It's well documented that the young woman had a history of mental problems. To even imply that my client is responsible in some way is ludicrous."

"Maybe you should take a minute to read the note Rebecca left just before she took her own life."

As the note slides across the shiny dark wood, I can feel my pulse pick up. It's more than the final thoughts of a troubled young woman. It represents my regrets, my shame, and my guilt. I take in a deep breath before allowing my eyes to fall on it.

"You didn't have to tell me you loved me, but why did you have to be so mean about it."

"When you walked out of my door everything went with you—my breath, my heart, and my strength."

I finish reading the note, but my gaze remains fixated on the paper. Reliving the events of that night is like looking at a stranger. I'm so far away from the person I was back then. I keep my head down and avoid making eye contact with Mr. and Mrs. Hyams, pretending to scan Becca's words one more time. But it's not her words or even what took place that night in her room that causes me to freeze in this position. What happened after the door closed two years ago is why I can't bring myself to look across the table at them.

My father's voice sounds distant as he tries to discredit the note. "You can't be serious, McGuire, using the words of a mentally unstable girl, right before she kills herself, with a known history of attempting suicide." I sense movement next to me as he shifts, aiming his attention toward the Hyamses. "Look folks, I'm sorry for your loss. Truly, I am. I don't know what your ambitious and arrogant lawyer has told you…"

"Excuse me," McGuire says abruptly.

"The fact is, my client and I could walk out that door right now, no discussion, no settlement, and be completely done with this. There is no judge in this country who will allow this case to go to court. You'll just be wasting your time and money pursuing this any further. I realize you've had a loss, but it's been two years now. You need to get over it and move on with your life."

The audacity of my father's words has all eyes in the room turning in his direction, dumbfounded. The rough clearing of a throat breaks through the silence in the room. Mr. Hyams's voice is low and despondent. "He's your son, right?" Out of the corner of my eye, I see Mr. Hyams nod his head indicating me.

"Yes." My father's voice strains as if he's having a hard time admitting the fact.

"How would you feel if one day you got a phone call telling you that the son you dreamed about having, the one you taught how to catch a baseball, or took on camping trips, was dead? That death was more appealing to him than living because he was so broken inside." He pauses, trying to swallow a sob before continuing. "How would you feel knowing that because of your choices your child suffered his entire life? When Becca was about twelve her doctors recommended we place her in a treatment facility where she would live. We didn't even consider it. It felt as if we'd be abandoning her. She was our little girl to raise and protect. If we hadn't been so selfish, maybe she'd still be here today. I don't know how to get over the guilt and heartache of losing my little girl."

Little does Mr. Hyams know that my father never dreamed about having me and would probably get over that phone call in record time. The tension and silence in the room is suffocating. I force my gaze up toward Becca's parents. Her dad is desperately trying to hold on to his composure while her mom has a steady stream of tears running down her face.

"I'm sorry," I whisper, but then my voice gets stronger and louder. "I'm so sorry."

My father leans into me and mumbles, "Shut up, Brad."

Ignoring him, I direct my attention solely to Mr. and Mrs. Hyams. "The night Becca died, there was something in her eyes that told me leaving was going to devastate her. The last time I looked at her she was crying. She wasn't making any noise, tears just ran down her face. When I walked out and closed the door, I waited to hear her scream or yell. They all screamed or yelled at me." My chest heaves up and down heavily as I try to contain my emotions. "I never heard Becca. All I heard was silence. I should have been a friend and gone back in." A few tears manage to escape my eyes. "Instead, I left her to go be with someone who never even wanted me to exist." I inadvertently glance at my father, who's staring straight ahead, expressionless, and having no intention of making any eye contact with me. "Your daughter impacted my life more in one month than those who'd been around me since day one. She made me want to be a better person. I *am* a better person because of Becca. I'm sorry I wasn't better for her. I'm not to blame for Becca's death, but I'm not blameless, either. It's something I have to live with for the rest of my life."

Warm and compassionate eyes meet mine as Mrs. Hyams raises her gaze to me. "We don't blame you, Son."

"Susan," Mr. Hyams mutters. There's a warning tone to his voice.

"Mrs. Hyams, please," McGuire interrupts.

"Susan, we need this," Mr. Hyams says in a low voice.

Becca's mom places her hand on top of her husband's and turns to him. In a soft soothing voice, she says, "She's not coming back, John, and no amount of money is going to change that."

She squeezes his hand once before shifting an apologetic gaze in my direction. "When someone you love dies, especially your child, you want answers. You convince yourself that once you know the reason, peace will come, and fill that empty space in your heart. You need it so badly, that you will latch on to anything that comes close to an explanation. But an explanation doesn't bring peace. The only thing that does is realizing she's happier now than when she was with us. The more you love a person, the more you miss them, and the longer it takes to accept that they're gone." She looks back at her husband. "Let's go home, John."

Mr. Hyams hesitates for a moment before pushing his chair away from the table, stands, and helps his wife up. The rest of us follow suit. As the Hyamses reach the door, Mr. Hyams turns toward McGuire, extending his hand. "Thank you, Mr. McGuire, for everything. I'm sorry if we wasted your time." McGuire shakes the man's hand, but doesn't say anything.

The couple is almost out the door when Mrs. Hyams stops and

steps closer to me. Looking up with the eyes of a loving mother, she says, "I'm glad my daughter was a positive influence in your life. *You* be that for someone, so that all of this might make a little more sense."

"Yes ma'am. I will."

She rejoins her husband and takes his arm, before leaving the room.

"Well, McGuire, better luck next time," my father quips, victorious sarcasm coating each word. He grabs his briefcase, throwing me a quick glance, and walks toward the door. "See you back at the office."

McGuire heads back to the table. "Well, this day is completely fucked and it's not even noon."

"Where is Mabry's office?" I ask while he gathers up his files.

"It's the fifth door on the left, down the first hallway, but she's not here."

"Do you know what time she'll be in?"

"I don't think she'll be coming back after the little stunt she pulled today." My eyebrows knit together in confusion. "She was supposed to be in early this morning. We were to go over the details of a case she was taking over for me, because I was stuck in here at fucking Forgive Fest. She never showed and never called."

The hair on the back of my neck stands at attention as a prickling sensation covers my skin. The strange feeling that has been with me the entire morning intensifies. It's not like Mabry to blow off a commitment, especially a work-related one.

"When was the last time you talked to her?"

"She was here yesterday. And to think, I stuck my neck out for her."

"What are you talking about?"

"I get a text from her one night, asking me if she could come over. I think, finally, I'm going to get what I've been wanting. All she wanted was help getting a job here." He shakes his head, laughing humorlessly. "I talked her up, big time too."

The idea of Mabry going to this prick for anything causes my body temperature to rise. My fingertips dig into the palms of my hand, coiling into tight fists. I can feel the spurts of air, coming from my nostrils, wash over my lips as my breathing accelerates.

Walking to the door, he mutters, "She was such a waste. I didn't even get a blowjob out of the deal."

I charge toward him, grabbing a handful of his shirt, causing his files to take a nosedive to the floor. Kicking behind me, the door closes as I shove him up against the wall. I get right up in his face, teeth grinding when I threaten, "If you ever refer to her as a waste again, I will fuck you up so badly, you won't have a dick left to blow." I leave him nodding his head in silent agreement.

I rush across the waiting room. Passing the receptionist, I shout, "Stairs?!"

She simply aims her finger in their direction. I swing the door open and fly down them, taking two at a time. I run across the lobby while texting Sylvie.

Me: Call Mabry. C if she's ok.

My phone buzzes with her response by the time I reach my car. I shrug off my jacket, throwing it in the car as I read her text.

Sylvie: Why?
Me: DO IT NOW!

Several seconds pass before I get a response.

Sylvie: Straight 2 vmail.
Me: Meet me @ Mabry's NOW!
Sylvie: Something wrong?
Me: I don't know.

In one continuous movement, I jump in my car, turn on the ignition, and peel out of the parking lot. The ache in my heart spreads across my chest. My lungs feel as if they are filling with cement, making it harder and harder to breathe. I raise up a trembling hand, undoing my tie and the first two buttons of my shirt. As I weave in and out of traffic, sweat trickles down my forehead and into my eyes. I rake the sleeve of my shirt over my face and force my lungs to pump oxygen into my body. It feels like it's taking hours to get to Mabry's, everything is moving in slow motion.

Finally, Mabry's place is in sight. Her car is parked in the driveway, so I know she's at home. Sylvie isn't here yet. Bringing my car to a screeching halt, I jump out, not bothering to turn it off. I run up the steps to the front door and start pounding. My fist makes contact with the door several times before I stop to listen for any movement. Even if she gets pissed off and yells at me, I'll at least know she's not hurt. Everything is quiet inside.

"Mabry!" I yell, accompanied by another round of rapid pounding. "Mabry, open the goddamn door!"

Silence.

I run down the steps and search around the outside of the place for a window to look in to. Mabry owns the downstairs condo of a converted historical home with sizable crawl space. All the windows are too high above ground for me to reach. I text Sylvie one more time, asking where the hell she is, as I head back to the front door. I pound a few more times and still I'm met with silence. I place both hands on either side of the door frame to brace myself. I step back as far as possible without removing my hands and ram my foot into the spot just under the doorknob. I'm so obsessed with getting inside I don't hear Sylvie come up behind me.

"Brad!" she shouts, as she touches my shoulder.

I whip around to face her. The second she sees the look in my eyes panic floods over her.

"Open the door," I choke out.

"What's going on?"

"Open the goddamn fucking door!" I scream.

With a shaky hand she slips the key into the lock. I don't wait for her to turn it before I burst through, Sylvie following close behind.

My eyes dart around the living room. "Mabry!" I yell.

"Brad, please tell me what's going on?"

"Check all the rooms!" I demand.

I head straight for Mabry's bedroom. There are clothes flung around, the comforter is crumpled into a heap on the bed, but no Mabry. I hear a soft whimper come from the direction of the bathroom. I run over, my body comes to a grinding stop in the doorway. It takes a second for my brain to register what I'm looking at. Mabry is on the floor, in front of the sink, laying curled up on her side, with only a towel wrapped around her. She's perfectly still except for the twitching of her eyelids. Her hair falls over the side of her face and there's a trail of blood leading from the back of her head, across the tiles, and up to the sharp corner of the countertop. I lunge toward her, dropping to my knees. I slide my hand across her cheek, brushing her hair off her face and then run them over her, looking for any other injuries.

"Mabry, wake up, baby. Please," I shout.

I adjust my body, so that I'm sitting down, and cradle her in my arms. Grabbing a towel from the floor, I put it behind her head, trying to apply pressure to stop the bleeding. I place my shaky index finger to her neck to check for a pulse. It's weak.

"Oh my god!" Sylvie yells. "Is she...?" Sobs take her over before she can finish the sentence.

My eyes stay completely focused on Mabry. "Call 911."

I hear footsteps as she runs to the other room to make the call. I shift Mabry slightly. Blood covers the towel and my sleeve where her head rests.

Lowering my lips to her cheek, I place a soft kiss, and whisper against it, "Sweetness, can you hear me?" Tears pour down my face as I heave out sobs. My lips never leaving her skin. "Mabry, wake up. You promised you wouldn't leave me."

I hear a strangled sob from the doorway. "The ambulance is on its way," Sylvie says gently.

I trail soft kisses along Mabry's cheek until I reach her lips, my tears falling down her face. "I love you, Mabry," I breathlessly whisper against her lips.

"Brad?" I feel the movement of her lips before I hear her voice. Her eyes struggle to open.

I don't want our lips to lose contact, but her voice is extremely soft and quiet, making it hard to hear. I angle my head so that our cheeks are together, placing our lips at each other's ears. "I'm here, Mabry."

"He's dead," she breathes.

"Who, Sweetness?"

"Daddy. He killed himself, just like Momma."

"I'm so sorry."

"I'm just like them. I don't have a chance," she says, groggily. I know it's wrong, but at this moment, as I feel her breathing slow down, I curse Mabry's parents for doing this to her.

"I got you, Sweetness. Everything's going to be okay." I lift my head to look at her beautiful face. I try desperately to hold my sobs in, wanting to convince her that I'm telling the truth, but they bursts out of me uncontrollably.

"I love you, Brad."

"I love you, Mabry."

I place another gentle kiss on her lips and watch her eyelids close as the roar of the siren fills the air.

CHAPTER 21

Brad

Everything's frantic; my movements, my breathing, my heartbeat, and my thoughts. The only thing that's in slow motion is getting an update on Mabry. I'm going out of my mind. It's been a half hour since we arrived and still not one doctor has come out to give us any information. Sylvie and I followed the paramedics to the hospital in her car. I was told I couldn't stay with Mabry because I wasn't a family member. I started to put up a fight, but realized that wasn't going to help Mabry. I stayed by her side, letting her know I was there and wouldn't leave her, right up until they closed the ambulance doors.

The image of her lying on the floor bleeding is in constant rotation in my head. My shirt is soaked in her blood. One of the nurses brought me some scrubs to change in to, but I haven't done it yet. I know it's sick, but having this shirt on reminds me of how it felt to hold her in my arms. Today was the first time I've held her in two weeks. I'm not ready to let go of that sensation yet.

In the empty waiting room, I continue to pace back and forth, while Sylvie sits quietly, staring down at the clipboard covered in hospital forms that was shoved at us when we arrived. I try to convince myself that no news is good news, but I'm struggling. My mind keeps moving in that dark direction. I force myself to concentrate on the positive. We got to her in time and she's at one of the best hospitals in the state. If I consider the alternative, it will completely destroy me. I have to keep it together for Mabry. She needs me to be strong for her. Out of the corner of my eye, I notice Sylvie's head pop up quickly. Her face is completely void of all color.

Following her gaze, I turn my head and spot the ER doctor standing in the doorway. When his words finally register I understand Sylvie's reaction.

"Who's here for Mabry Darnell?" he asks.

The moment I've been impatient for, the one that seems to have taken a lifetime to arrive, the one that will answer my question, is finally here, and I can't move or speak. I want to freeze this moment now. I don't want to go any further. In this moment, Mabry loves me and is alive. In this moment, I still have the feel of her body in my arms and her lips on mine.

"We both are." I hear Sylvie's trembling voice answer.

As the doctor approaches, I feel the air being sucked out of the room and a low hum swirl in my ears. Sylvie stands next to me, looping her arm around mine tightly to give us both support.

The doctor stops in front of us, his expression unreadable. "I'm Dr. Roberts. Are you next of kin for Miss Darnell?"

Next of kin? Why did he say next of kin?

My knees buckle and suddenly I'm suffocating, I feel myself sag into Sylvie. She clutches my arm even tighter in an attempt to keep me upright as well as herself. I don't respond to him. I'm not sure if it's because I can't or I won't, either way, I'm unable to form any words.

Sylvie does the talking. "Yes, we are."

"And what's your relationship to Miss Darnell?" he asks, looking between the two of us.

"I'm a close friend, but Brad is...," she takes a slight pause.

"…her husband," she states with confidence, looking at me with raised eyebrows, indicating for me to play along. She obviously did a little creative writing when filling out the admissions forms. Sylvie knows they won't give us information on Mabry if they know we aren't family, even though we are all she has now.

"I'm sorry, I didn't realize she was married. Mr. Darnell, your wife sustained significant trauma to the back of the head, causing an extremely severe concussion. In fact, it's one of the worst I've seen. She's lost a good bit of blood, due to the large gash on the back of her head. The blood vessels on the head are very close to the surface of the skin, so with any head laceration, there's a lot of bleeding. We're transfusing her now."

"Is she going to be okay?" I finally manage to say.

"She's in stable condition. Fortunately, the skull is intact."

Relief takes over and my body collapses. Sylvie and the doctor catch me before I hit the floor and guide me to a chair. Sitting, I attempt to breathe normally, as I rub my hands over my face and through my hair.

"Are you okay, Sir?" the doctor asks.

Pulling my face from my hands, I answer, "I will be." I finally feel my lungs expand as I inhale deeply a few times.

"We've stitched up the laceration on the back of the head." He glances around the room, making sure it's still empty. "Can either of you tell me what happened to cause this?"

"We found her lying on the bathroom floor. There was blood on the tile and the edge of the counter. She must have slipped and hit her head," Sylvie replies.

"Does Mabry have a history of self-harm?" he questions.

Sylvie and I exchange glances, not understanding what he's asking.

"Self-harm?" I've never heard the term before, but its meaning is obvious.

"When I examined Mabry's skull, I saw a lot of scar tissue in the surrounding area from healed lacerations and there are also scratch marks on her upper thighs. We found skin and blood under her fingernails."

I look at Sylvie for some explanation, but her expression is as puzzled as mine.

"There has to be another explanation. I would have noticed something like that going on," I say.

"Why would she do something like that?" Sylvie asks.

"It's a coping mechanism some people turn to because of a traumatic event in their lives."

"Her mother committed suicide after a long bout with depression when Mabry was young." Sylvie informs.

"She just found out that her father killed himself." My voice trails off.

"Oh my god," Sylvie breathes out.

I flash back to Mabry's words.

The way my mom was... I have that in me. There have been times in my life I didn't want to get out of bed, the pain was so stifling.

My stomach twists in knots and I blurt out, "Christ, does Mabry want to kill herself?"

"Usually, those who self-harm don't have a desire to end their lives. They use it to numb themselves and distract from the emotional pain. They cut, burn, embed, or hit. From the way it looks and the area that's been affected, it appears as if Mabry's been hitting her head for quite a while. She has a few marks on the side of her skull that could have been caused by hitting with a hairbrush, but the back of her head is too damaged for it to have been done by a brush. My guess is she slams the back of her head against hard surfaces like a door or edge of a counter."

I'm still having a hard time believing Mabry would do this to herself. "You said she had scratches on her legs?"

"Sometimes self-harmers alternate between multiple methods to inflict pain. The tolerance levels keep rising, so they have to intensify the pain to get the same rush of endorphins. Maybe one day, the head banging wasn't giving her the desired effect, so she cut or scratched."

"But she's going to be okay, right? I mean, she'll heal from today." Sylvie's voice trembles.

"I have her scheduled for a CT scan," he informs.

"A CT scan? For what?" I ask.

"To see if there's any brain injury. If she's been doing this type of thing for several years there's a good possibility that today's episode caused lasting damage. Look, Mabry's physical wounds will heal eventually, but she needs to get into counseling and learn how to deal with things without hurting herself. I'll have the nurse come get you when you're able to see your wife." He gives us a slight smile before turning and leaving.

Sylvie takes the seat next to me. As I lean back, closing my eyes, I rest my head on the wall. When I make contact, the thought of Mabry performing this same action, only with more force, sprints across my mind. I tighten my eyes, lift my head off the wall slightly, and then let it fall back hard. I know my lame attempt at trying to understand what Mabry feels from hurting herself comes nowhere near to her experience. The thought of her feeling this desperate and in pain is unbearable. My breathing is deep and rapid, gasping for air, as I fight off the tears.

I feel the touch of a warm hand covering mine. With a shaky voice, Sylvie says, "You better change before you go see her."

Placing the ball of my hand over my eyes, I nod, choking back a sob. "Why would she do this to herself, Sylvie?"

"I don't know. She was a lost and lonely little girl. I guess this was the only way she knew how to handle being left and forgotten." Tears stream down her face.

The sound of squeaky footsteps join our sniffles and throat

clearing as the nurse comes into the waiting room. "Mr. Darnell, you'll be able to see your wife in about a half hour."

Looking up at her, I say, "Thank you." I steal a quick glance at Sylvie and we exchange smirks.

Grabbing the scrubs beside her, Sylvie tosses them to me. "Change before you go see your *wife.*"

I take them and we both stand. Before leaving, I turn to her, place a soft kiss on her cheek, and whisper, "Thank you for being such a good friend to Mabry and me."

She gives me a small smile in response, emotions overflowing in her eyes, as I turn and head out of the room.

I take a deep breath before entering Mabry's room. Inside, the atmosphere is quiet and still except for the rhythmic beeping of the heart monitor and an occasional hiss from the IV pole. Mabry looks like a little girl lying in the bed. She's asleep, her head supported by a neck pillow holding it up slightly off of the bed to protect where they stitched up her injury. From the front, her hair looks untouched, but as I approach, I see the large bandage peaking over the top and around the side of her head. She's going to be pissed when she sees the haircut they gave her.

My throat tightens as I think of the pain Mabry's endured, emotionally as well as physically. I wish I could take everything bad that's happened to her and make it disappear. Memories invade my mind. The headaches, the glassy eyes, and the times I felt her body stiffen when I placed a kiss on the back of her head or when my hands would move too close to the area.

Why didn't I say something? I promised to protect her and I failed.

Her features are relaxed and peaceful. I lean down, with every intention of placing a quick light kiss on her forehead. But once my lips touch her skin they won't move. After several seconds, she inhales deeply, a small whimper escaping on exhale. I remove my lips and look down, meeting beautiful azure blues.

"Hey Sweetness," I say softly.

"Hey." Her voice is breathless and groggy. Gazing at me, she slowly scans the scrubs I'm wearing. "When did you become a doctor?"

"While I was waiting to see your gorgeous face." The corners of her mouth curl up slightly. "The CT scan was clear. You're going to be okay. How are you feeling?" I trail my fingertips from her temples down to her jaw.

"Sleepy." She casts her gaze down. "I'm sorry."

I place my index finger under her chin, guiding her eyes to mine. "No reason to be sorry. I love you."

"I'm so embarrassed and ashamed." Misty azure blues look back at me.

Shaking my head slightly, I swallow the lump in my throat. "Don't be. I love you," I say, running my thumb mindlessly over her cheek.

"I didn't want you to see me like this." Her chin quivers in my hand as the tears threaten to spill from her eyes.

Intensifying my gaze, I say, "I love you." Unable to keep the emotion out of my voice.

"I... um... I can explain," she stammers.

"I love you."

Her eyebrows crinkle together and she asks, "Is that all you're going to say to me?"

"Yeah."

"Why?"

"Cause it's all that matters right now."

"Brad, I..."

I lean down, stopping her words with a light brush of my lips across hers. Our foreheads rest against each other's as I whisper on her mouth, *"I love you. I love you. I love you."* My emphasis gets stronger with each word. "Nothing has changed that for me. You don't owe me an explanation or an apology. I want to be here for you. Please let me."

She nods her head. The movement is so faint it's almost imperceptible. "I love you."

The remainder of the day I watch Mabry dose on and off. When she's awake we chat, but not about anything serious. There will be plenty of time for that later. Right now I just want to be near her and let her know what she means to me. I haven't taken my hands off of her since entering the room. I'm either holding her hand, trailing my fingers down her face, or placing soft kisses from her forehead to her lips. At one point, she invites me to climb into bed next to her. I spend the entire night holding her close to me. For the first time in two weeks I feel settled and know I'm where I belong, doing what I was put on earth to do.

Mabry

"Mabry, are you in here?" Sylvie calls out from the door of my hospital room.

The parade of tiger lilies started first thing yesterday morning. Beautiful arrangements of varying sizes had been delivered the entire day. Every surface that's available in this room is covered in lilies, including the over-the-bed hospital table that sits directly in front of me. There are so many lilies that the bright orange reflecting off of the stark white walls gives the room a warm glow. I push the table as far to one side as possible, revealing myself to Sylvie, who still has a shocked look on her face from all the orange.

"Hey," I say, peeking around the huge arrangement.

"It looks like a pumpkin threw up in here," she jokes.

"Brad may have gone a little overboard."

She glances around the room again, shaking her head, still not believing the sight in front of her. "So, where is Hottie McGee? He hasn't left your side in two days."

"He looked exhausted, so I finally convinced him to go home, shower and get some rest. He'll be back later."

Sylvie takes the chair next to my bed. We sit in awkward silence. She and Brad discovered my self-harm two days ago. I know both have questions they want to ask me, but they have both been sweet and patient, letting me decide when to talk about it. After several seconds, we both open our mouths to speak and then close them, to allow the other to go first. We break out into giggles at how silly we look.

"Sylvie, I want to tell you how sorry I am..." I start.

She raises one hand up stopping my words. "There's no need to apologize to me."

"But, I want to. Please let me just say this."

"Okay."

I look down at my hands fidgeting with the edge the sheet. "When we were younger, I didn't tell you about my self-harm because I thought I was a freak and was afraid that you would stop being my friend. As we got older, I was too ashamed and embarrassed to say anything. Plus, I knew you'd try to talk me out of doing it and I didn't want to stop."

Water fills her eyes. "I'm sorry I wasn't a better friend to you," she chokes out.

Sitting up, I lean over and reach for her hand. "Sylvie, you've been a wonderful friend to me. A good friend is someone who's there to get you through things. You did that for me, every time you invited me over for dinner and let me spend time with your family, when you would experiment on me with makeup and different hairdos, or we would just sit around giggling at silly things. Being with you gave me a break from the pain and loneliness. It was because of you that I survived."

She moves to sit on the side of my bed and we wrap our arms around each other as the tears flow. The love and caring that we had for each other over the years is pours out in that hug.

We give each other a tight squeeze before pulling apart. Sylvie leans over and snatches a few tissues from the bedside table, handing one to me. For a few seconds, the only sound in the room is the blowing of our noses.

"So, when are they going to spring you from this joint?" she asks, clearing her throat.

"Tomorrow. That's another thing I need to tell you." I glance away, avoiding eye contact.

Her eyebrows furrow together in worry. "Is everything okay?"

Looking back at her, I nod my head. "I've talked with my counselor, Jennifer, about setting up a treatment plan."

"That's fantastic, Mabry."

"Yeah and a long time coming." I return to fidgeting with the sheet, my eyes alternating between looking at my hands and Sylvie. I'm not sure why I'm so nervous to tell her this. Maybe because with each person who knows, it becomes more real.

"Mabry, what's wrong?" she asks.

"Jennifer recommends that I enter a treatment facility for a little while. You know, just so I can focus and get on the right track."

Sylvie's hand comes up to cover my restless ones. "It sounds like a good idea."

"Yeah. With the money my parents left me, I'll be okay not working for several months, so I can focus on treatment. She found a facility that has an immediate opening in North Carolina." My eyes dart up to see her reaction.

"Wow, you're going to be moving?" Sadness evident in her voice.

"Right now, being in town and…" My words come to a halt as tears take over and pour from my eyes.

Sylvie scoots closer to me, brushing my hair back over my shoulder. "Sweetie, what is it?"

"Being here and being around Brad right now is still a pretty strong trigger for me." The pain that shoots through me having to admit that Brad is a strong trigger is almost unbearable. I take several deep breaths, trying to get my sobs under control.

Sylvie's hand cups the side of my face, making me look into her sincere and compassionate expression. "It's going to be okay. We're going to make it through this."

"I love him so much, Sylvie. I want to spend the rest of my life with him, but…"

"Does he know?" she asks.

I nod. "Jennifer explained everything to him."

"And?"

"He agrees it's the best thing for me. He's not happy, though. I can't imagine not being with him, but I won't ask him to wait. I can't do that to him." I choke out.

"Mabry, that man adores you. I saw it the minute he walked up to the table during book club. I doubt you'll have to ask him to wait. I think it's a given that he will."

A slight chuckle escapes through my sobs as I wipe away more tears. "I hope so."

Waving her arms around the room indicating the hundreds of flowers, she says sarcastically, "How could there be any doubt?"

The next hour, Sylvie did what she always did, made me feel better. We talk about all the positive outcomes to me going to the treatment facility. She's already planning our first girl's weekend. Logically, I know these are the steps I need to take right now in order to move forward. I'm scared of reliving my past, losing my safety net of self-harm, and Brad disappearing from my life. But I know if I don't take this drastic step, nothing will change for me. I've tried so hard to escape from a life I was terrified of inheriting that I'm running straight toward it unless I change my trajectory.

CHAPTER 22

Brad

We drive to the airport in complete silence, the result of a combination of not knowing what to say and having said everything we needed to. The second I pulled the car out of the driveway, our hands clasped together between us and have been that way since. I measure how close we're getting to the airport by the growing intense ache in my chest. Glancing at Mabry, I give her a weak smile and squeeze her hand slightly. Her eyes are already misting and I have to quickly look away before I beg her not to go.

She has to go.

There's no question or doubt in my mind that this is what's best for her. Being here with me holds too many triggers for her right now. She needs to completely focus on dealing with the issues of her past and learn how to cope with her feelings, without physically hurting herself. I've chanted these words daily like a mantra since we met with Mabry's counselor, Jennifer, and she explained why Mabry needed to seriously consider this option. My brain is totally convinced, but my heart is completely shattered.

As we pull into the parking lot, I'm hoping there are no spaces and we end up circling for a long time. I spot an empty one down the first row.

Fuck me.

Hesitantly, I let go of Mabry's hand while I pull into the space and turn off the car. We sit in more silence. My insides are a jumbled mess and the outside of my body is paralyzed. I take in several long deep breaths before I feel brave enough to look at her. She stares straight ahead.

I reach over and place my hand on her thigh. "Hey," I whisper.

That's all it takes before the tears start flowing down her face. Turning to me, she tries, but loses the battle to keep her composure. A faint tremble takes over her entire body. I fight the urge to pull her into my lap and wrap my arms around her. If I do, I know I won't let her go and I *have* to let her go. I blow out a deep breath. Giving her thigh a quick squeeze to draw her attention up to me, I gaze directly into azure blues, trying to convey to her that everything is going to be okay.

"Let's do this," I tell her.

Her chin trembles uncontrollably and tears continue to flow for several seconds before she takes in a few deep breaths of her own, trying to calm down. I get out of the car and walk to Mabry's side. Once the door is open, our hands immediately reconnect. Mabry hesitates before getting out of the car. I can feel the nervousness radiate off of her body as her gaze darts around.

Leaning down, so that we're only an inch apart, I reassure her, "You look beautiful. No one can tell you have stiches." She's pinned her hair up in such a way to conceal the large spot the doctors had to shave when they stitched up her injury.

"Okay. Thanks," she whispers.

We grab her luggage from the trunk and head slowly into the airport. As we approach the ticket agent, I look up to see if the flight schedule is on time. Unfortunately, it is. As Mabry finishes getting checked in, I produce a ticket from my pocket and hand it to the agent. Mabry's eyes shoot up to mine when she notices what's happening.

"You're going with me?" For a moment her sadness fades away and is replaced with a sparkle of hope.

"No, Sweetness. I bought a ticket, so I could go through security with you. I want to spend every second I can with you until I can't anymore."

Tears fill her eyes in a split second and the sadness returns.

We make our way through security as quickly as possible. There's a little time left before her flight. We sit quietly, our fingers still laced together. Mabry and I have expressed all our dreams, our fears, concerns, desires, and how we feel about each other over the past few days. But there's one thing I haven't been able to say to her and I have to tell her before she leaves.

I've been concentrating so hard on the feel of her hand in mine, the smell of vanilla, and how beautiful she is, that time slips away, and before I know it her flight is being called. I've run out of time.

We stand to face each other and I can't pretend anymore. I shut my eyes as tight as possible, trying to keep the tears from falling, but there's no use. I can't hold it together any longer. Mabry's tears match mine. We still don't say a word to each other. We just hold hands and stare through blurry eyes.

I attempt to speak several times, but my emotions stop me before I can get the first word out. Roughly clearing my throat, I finally start. "This is the hardest thing I've ever had to do." I pause, swallowing my sobs. "God I'm so in love with you."

Raising her hand, she traces the stubble along my jaw with her fingertips. "I love you too. I'll come back as soon as I can."

I close my eyes again, trying to summon the courage to say what I need to say and not chicken out. "Mabry, I desperately want you in my life, but I want you happy in your life more."

"What are you trying to tell me?" she says between sobs.

I stare at her for several seconds. "I don't want you to come back here and be with me if it's too hard for you. I want you happy, healthy, and safe more than anything else, even if that means I have to let you go forever."

"I *will* come back to you. I promise."

A voice blasts from the speakers announcing her flight.

Mabry launches herself into my arms. I wrap them tightly around her, burying my face in her neck. Our bodies shake with sobs.

With her lips to my ears, she whispers, "Thank you for saving my life."

"Thank you for saving mine, Sweetness."

I place kisses frantically up her neck, over her cheek, to her forehead, and back down the other side until I reach her lips. My hands move, framing her face as hers grab hold of my upper arms for balance. When our lips touch all the franticness of the previous moment evaporates and everything slows. Our tongues take turns slipping into each other's mouths, exploring the space we both know so well. I commit every detail of the moment to memory. The placement of her hands on my arms and how firm the grip is. How many times she allows a whimper to escape from the back of her throat. The sweet scent of vanilla. The smoothness of her skin as my thumbs run over it. How soft her lips are.

The voice blasts through the speakers again for final boarding. We linger for a split second longer and then hear the voice of an actual person, "Miss, you need to board now or you'll miss the flight."

Reluctantly we pull away from each other. Mabry's face is drenched in tears and blotchy, her eyes are red and swollen, and she's still the most beautiful woman I've ever seen.

Taking one step back, she says, "I'm coming back to you."

"I'll be right here with open arms." I do my best to give her a smile.

She grabs her purse and slowly steps backward. Our eyes remain locked on each other. She walks this way until she's forced to turn the corner and disappear. I stay in that spot for I don't know how long. Part of me was hoping she'd walk around that corner and back into my arms. It wasn't until I noticed the plane taxiing past the window that it sunk in, she wasn't coming back. I walk to the window and watch the plane glide down the runway. Resting my forehead against the window, I whisper, "Have a fantastic life, Sweetness."

THE END

EPILOGUE

THE FUTURE

The honor of your presence
is requested at
the marriage of

Mabry Elizabeth Darnell

to

Bradley Michael Johnson

Saturday, the eighth of October
two thousand and sixteen
at
five o'clock in the evening

Brad

I can't keep my foot from tapping while I stand here and wait. I tug the cuff of my white shirt out from under the black material of my suit jacket, fiddling with my silver cufflinks for a few seconds before moving to obsessively straightening my tie. Every part of my body that has a gland is sweating. I thought I was nervous the night I planned on telling Mabry I loved her, but those nerves are nothing compared to what I'm experiencing right now. I pace, alternating between checking my watch and the end of the aisle. She'll be here any minute. We have everything planned out to perfection for tonight.

There was never a question as to where our ceremony would be: Middleton Place Gardens, at sunset, down by the lake, between two large moss-covered oak trees. The decorations are simple and minimal. The surroundings are already breathtaking, especially with the fall colors. Four huge arrangements of tiger lilies are placed at the four corners of the space, as well as two smaller ones upfront where Mabry will meet me. Different size lanterns and candles outline the perimeter of the grounds. A handful of white chairs with big orange bows tied around the back of them are placed on either side of the orange runner. It's a small gathering, but frankly I couldn't care less who else is here, as long as Mabry shows.

My hands run through my hair a few times as I try to breathe. I glance at my best man, who is focused more on flashing *the smile* at the single women here than helping calm my nerves. With Mabry's prompting, Peyton and I have made more of an effort to be closer over the past couple of years. I slap the side of his arm and he reluctantly turns his attention toward me.

"What is it?" he whispers, glancing back at some blonde in the third row.

"Is everything tucked in and smoothed out?" I ask, as I continuously lick my lips and swallow.

Leaning in close to my side, confusion crosses his face. "What the fuck are you talking about, tucked and smoothed?"

"Do I look okay?"

"Yeah, you look like a million bucks." Scrunching up his face, he asks, "What's with the lip lickin'? You look like a goddamn lizard."

"My mouth is so dry. I can't get any spit going."

Peyton slaps me on the back and says, "Well, hock up some lubrication, brother, because it's show time."

Boyce Avenue's acoustic version of "A Thousand Years" flows through the air. I turn and look up the small hill leading down to where I stand. I notice Sylvie for a split second before I see the reason I'm here. That day I let her go at the airport, I was terrified I'd never see her again, but she was determined, and worked hard to overcome her past. She fought for us and our future together. No one has ever done anything like that for me before. She kept her promise and came back to me.

My breath and all nerves simultaneously leave my body when I see her. She's exquisite. The white dress is poofy from her hips down, but hugs her upper body perfectly, exposing her creamy shoulders, and the very top of her phenomenal rack. Her hair is pulled back at the sides and has a slight wave to it as it falls over her shoulders and down her back. I guess she's got makeup on, but all I see is a gorgeous glow radiating off of her. My heart pounds faster against my chest the closer she gets to me. Our eyes lock and everyone else disappears from my awareness. It's just me and Mabry.

After she takes her place by my side, I lean in and whisper, "Wamfu, baby."

A small giggle escapes her lips, and then she whispers back,

"Wamfu to you too."

She's so close and smells so damn good, I just need a quick taste. I close my eyes and let my lips skim across her cheek. Before I know it, they've moved to her lips and the tip of my tongue slips into her mouth. A loud clearing of a throat startles me. I straighten up, look at the minister, and give him a sheepish grin.

"Sorry, Father," I apologize.

Smiling at me, he says, "I'm not a priest, Son."

"Oh, yeah. Right."

"I'll get through this as quick as possible." Directing his attention to our guests, he starts the ceremony. "We are gathered here today to take part in that most time-honored celebration of the human family, uniting a woman and a man in marriage. Mabry and Brad have come to witness before us, telling of their love for each other. We remind them that they are performing an act of complete faith, each in the other; that the heart of their marriage will be the relationship they create. In a world where faith often falls short of expectation, it is a tribute to these two who now join hands and hearts in perfect faith." He looks between the two of us. "I believe you've each written something." He nods in my direction, indicating I'm up first.

I turn and look into beautiful misty azure blues. I haven't said one word yet, and I can already feel the moisture build up in my eyes and my throat close up. Taking her hands, I start. "Mabry, when I met you, the world changed for me. I was able to breathe easier, see clearer, and feel for the first time. You opened my heart and entered my soul. The moment I looked into your gorgeous eyes I knew why I was put here on earth. It was to be with you. I will protect you, support you, and catch you if you fall. I promise to be the best husband to you. I'll try not to embarrass or annoy you too often." I could hear chuckles coming from our guests. "You're not just the love of my life, Mabry. You *are* my life."

Tears run down her cheeks as she mouths, "I love you."

We stare at each other until the minister clears his throat and says in a low voice, "Mabry, it's your turn."

She swallows hard, trying to compose herself. "When I was a little girl I would dream about my Prince Charming. The boy who would eventually come rescue me. He didn't have a name or a face, but I knew in my heart that I'd recognize him when we met. The very first time I saw you, I felt a connection. The first time I met you, I knew I had found my hero. Not a fictional character who would make all the bad things disappear, but someone who would love me through whatever life handed me. Someone who'd be strong when I couldn't be. Someone who'd hold my hand, letting me know I wasn't alone. I promise to be the best wife to you, Brad. I'll learn how to cook more than spaghetti sauce from a jar and soup from a can." More chuckles fill the air as I raise my hand to her cheek, wiping away her tears. "I will show you every day how much I love you, want you, and need you in my life."

"Every day?" I ask flirtatiously. I can't help the huge grin that crosses my face.

"Every day," she says, smiling back at me.

Not taking my eyes off Mabry, I instruct, "Let's wrap this up, Rev. My wife has *things* to show me."

"Certainly. Will you now give and receive a ring?"

"We will," Mabry and I say in unison.

"May I have the rings, please?" the minister asks. The maid of honor and best man hand him our rings. "The circle of this precious metal is justly regarded as a fitting symbol of the purity and perpetuity of marriage, having neither beginning nor end; and cannot be tarnished by use or time. Brad, please place this ring on Mabry's left hand and repeat after me."

He feeds me the words. Gazing at Mabry, I not only see my future, I see exactly where I belong. "Wear this ring forever, Mabry, as a symbol of my love and of all that is unending." I let out a deep sigh as I slip the ring on her finger.

Mabry repeats the same words to me, her voice and hand shaky with emotion as she glides my ring on.

The minister speaks again. "In the years which shall bring Mabry and Brad into greater age and wisdom, we pray that their love shall be ever young; that they shall be able always to recover from moments of despair, and they will forever hold on to the passionate ways of youth."

I wanted to jump Mabry and devour her the second I saw her today, but managed to control myself up until the word "passionate" came out of the minister's mouth. I don't know what happened, but something in me snapped, and I could no longer keep my hands or lips off of her. Cupping the sides of her face, I brought our lips together and invaded her mouth.

The minister's pace speeds up and his volume rises over the laughter of the crowd as he finishes up the ceremony. "In this hope, may they keep the vows made on this day... *bah, bah, bah...* Inasmuch... *bah, bah...* Mabry and Brad have declared their love and devotion to each other before family and friends, by the authority vested in me by the State of South Carolina, I pronounce them to be husband and wife. You may now... *um...* continue to kiss the bride!"

Mabry

"It's a four bedroom, three and a half bath, with the master on the main floor. Hardwood floors throughout. The kitchen has top of the line, stainless steel appliances and granite countertops. There is also a fantastic bonus room upstairs that would be great for a playroom," the realtor says, tilting her head to one side as she smiles at us.

"Hear that, Sweetness, our very own playroom." Brad flashes a sexy grin my way. "Tell me, Mrs. Taylor, is the ceiling sturdy up in the playroom? Say, if we needed to hang chains and whatnot," he says, deadpan, swatting me on the ass before walking away to look around.

I don't know whose face was redder, mine or Mrs. Taylor's.

"He's joking. We aren't into that kind of... um," I stammer.

Thankfully, her phone rings, breaking the awkward silence. "Excuse me for one moment," she says, walking away.

I walk up to Brad, who is looking out the French doors into the backyard. "Thanks for leaving me back there with that, buddy."

Leaning down to my ear, his warm breath floats over my neck, as he whispers, "I bet she's picturing us doing things right now."

"Brad!" I say, popping his arm. We continue to stare out to the backyard. "I love this house," I tell him.

"It is an awesome place."

"I've fallen more in love with it each time we've driven by it. And, there won't be anything built behind us. The woods will stay as is. It's very private."

"That's good to know. Means we can swim nekked anytime we want." He sends a wink and *the smile* my way. I simply shake my head in response.

"Oh my god, Brad! Look! There's a joggling board out there. I wonder if it comes with the place." I don't even pretend to try to contain my excitement.

We hear the click of Mrs. Taylor's heels on the floor as she walks back in the room, causing us to turn around.

"I'm sorry folks for the interruption. That was another client. They're able to come now and see a house in the neighborhood right down the street. I don't want to rush you. If it's okay with you, I'll go meet them and then come right back here," she offers.

"That would be great," I tell her.

Once the front door closes, Brad turns to me. He has that look in his eyes that causes my heart to beat faster and heat to spread over my body. I try to divert his wayward thoughts.

"So, what do think about putting in a bid?" I ask.

He leans in and nibbles across my jawline and down my neck. My head swirls, but I stay in control, completely mindful of where we are and the fact that Mrs. Taylor will be back soon.

"Brad...," I say, breathlessly.

I feel his hands slip under the bottom of my shirt and graze over my bare stomach. "Let's christen the place, Sweetness," he says against my neck as he backs me up toward a wall.

I shove on his chest, but he doesn't budge. "Brad! No."

"Unbutton your shirt," he growls.

My back hits the wall and I feel the snap of cool air touch my skin as the bottom of my shirt pulls apart. All coherent thoughts fly out of my head as my fingers find their way into his hair. More air hits my bare skin as the rest of the buttons come undone. I feel the lace of my bra slide over one of my hard nipples just before Brad's lips close around it, sucking hard.

I shut my eyes as my back arches off the wall, and I moan, "Brad... Baby, we need to stop. She'll be back any minute."

He pulls away from my nipple, but continues to place slow open-mouth kisses across my breasts. "She's not coming back," he mumbles.

Brad's hand travels up my side to my chest. Suddenly, I feel something cold and hard between my tits. He gives me one deep kiss before backing away from me, leaving me completely disoriented and breathless. Opening my eyes, I see him standing in front of me, desire still evident on his face, but amusement now accompanies it.

"What?" I ask, confused.

"I said, she's not coming back here."

He tips his chin toward my chest. I reach in my bra and pull out a set of keys. I look up at him, still confused.

"I signed the papers this morning. Welcome home, Sweetness," he says with a huge smile on his face.

I blink at him a few times, trying to let the news sink in. "And the joggling board?"

"A housewarming gift."

I launch myself into his arms, crashing my lips to his. I feel his hands move down to my ass. As he lifts me up, I automatically wrap my legs around his waist.

He pulls away from the kiss slightly. "So, buying the house meets your approval, Mrs. Johnson?"

"Yes, it does, Bradley. I'm extremely impressed with your acquisition. Now I want you to take me in our kitchen, bend me over that island, and give me a proper homecoming."

"Yes ma'am."

We welcome with love
Brandon Michael

Born June 19, 2018
7 pounds 12 ounces
20 inches
Proud Parents
Brad and Mabry Johnson

Brad

The emotions I'm experiencing right now either are impossible to describe or I'm just not smart enough to find the words. I can't get over how much I already love him. I've been sitting here holding my sleeping son for the past half hour while his mom gets some much needed rest. Looking down, I'm mesmerized by his chubby cheeks and the way his tiny lips purse together as if he's concentrating on something. I wonder who he gets that from. His sapphire eyes open wide, looking up at me, as his little hand grips my finger.

"Hey Buddy," I whisper. "Remember me? I'm Dad. We met a few hours ago."

A big yawn escapes him. I shift, propping him up slightly in my arms. "You might think I'm boring now, but wait until you get older. I've got big plans for us. I'm going to teach you how to ride a bike and drive a car. You don't know what those are yet, but trust me, chicks love when you have cool ones. I'm going to coach your little league baseball team. Now, you don't have to play baseball just because I did. You can play football if you want or if you don't like sports, that's okay too. It doesn't matter, I'll be there to support and cheer you on."

Brandon takes in a deep breath, his mouth forming into a little O, as a small bubble of saliva appears. That's the cutest spit I've ever seen.

"Wow, that was a mighty deep breath, little man."

A huge smile crosses my face as I watch his eyes blink in wonderment. "You know what? I already have a room picked out in the house for our man cave. That's where we can watch sports and action movies while we eat junk food. No girls allowed. Well, except maybe for your mom. She's pretty awesome, but you'll find that out soon."

Another yawn escapes from my son as his eyes close. I notice his grip around my finger hasn't lessened this entire time. My thoughts drift to my own father, wondering if there was ever a time, even for a millisecond, that we shared a bond. I can't imagine ever labeling this little boy in my arms as a mistake.

I ease my head down towards him, placing a soft kiss on his forehead, and whisper, "I promise to be the best father to you, Brandon. I didn't have one, but I've watched enough TV to know what one's supposed to be like. I'll be fucking Heathcliff Huxtable and Mike Brady rolled into one."

"Brad." Mabry's soft sleepy voice drifts over to me.

"Hey Sweetness."

"Did you just cuss in front of our son?" she asks, sounding offended.

"Shit! I don't think so."

"Shhh, Brad!"

"Fuck. Sorry. I'll do better," I whisper.

I carry Brandon to Mabry and place him in her arms. I slide into the bed next to them.

Looking up at me, a smirk crosses her beautiful face, "You're going to be a wonderful father."

"Thank you for giving me the chance." I kiss her forehead and say, "I love our family, Mabry."

Mabry

She comes bounding down the stairs, completely ignoring the last one, and lands in the kitchen. "Mom, does this outfit look awesome, because I need to look awesome for this party." Her words come bursting out her mouth so fast, I'm only able to understand every other one.

I stop cutting the vegetables I'm working on for tonight's dinner. My breath hitches when I look up at her. I can't believe my little girl is going on her first date. Sadness sets in a little. Both Brandon and Paige are growing up faster than I'm ready for them to. They're both healthy and happy though, and that's what matters. The fear of them inheriting my family's mental health issues has subsided a little over the years. Brad and I have always made it a point to be open and honest with the kids, encouraging them to come talk to us no matter what the problem or concern. Paige's exacerbated voice breaks me from my thoughts.

"Mom?"

"Paigie, even if you didn't try, you'd look beautiful," I tell her.

"Thanks, Mom, but do I look awesome enough for the party?" she asks.

"You're covered in awesome sauce."

"Yay!" she says, with a huge smile on her face as she teeters up and down on her toes with excitement.

The back door suddenly flies open. Brandon comes barreling in, sweaty, twirling his basketball on the tip of his finger, and bumps into his sister.

"Brandon!" Paige shouts.

"Sorry squirt, didn't see you there."

"Mom, do I have Brandon ick on me?" Paige asks, as she double-checks her outfit.

"No ick," I answer.

Seconds later, Brad comes through the door, drenched in sweat and breathing heavy. A shiver runs through my body as I glance at him. The T-shirt is weighed down with sweat, clinging to every dip, curve, and edge of his well-defined muscular torso. Not only is he still the hottest guy around, he's also been an incredible husband and father over the years. He wipes his face with the bottom of his T-shirt, as he walks to the fridge and grabs two bottles of water. Tossing one to Brandon, he leans against the counter and says, "You kicked my ass out there, Son."

Brandon's chest visibly expands with pride as *the smile* crosses his face. "Yeah, I did, didn't I?"

Brad returns our son's smile and pushes off of the counter. He comes up behind me, his chest grazing my back, as he peers over my shoulder. Placing a quick kiss on my neck, he nuzzles the spot right below my ear and whispers, "I love you," before grabbing a carrot and popping it into his mouth.

"Ew, Dad. You're getting ick all over Mom," Paige says in disgust.

"Your mom likes my manly juices," Brad tells her.

Brandon laughs as Paige scrunches up her face in response. Her expression drops when she hears the doorbell. "Oh my god, he's here. Harry is here." She turns in my direction with a look of terror in her sapphire blues.

"Who the hell is Harry and why is he here?" Brad asks.

I look at Paige. "Take a deep breath, go answer the door, and bring him in here to say hello."

"Who the hell is Harry?" Brad repeats.

Paige takes two deep breaths before turning and walking to answer the door.

"He's a douche bag that goes to our school," Brandon chimes in.

"Brandon!" I scold.

"What? He *is* a douche and he *does* attend our school."

"Who. The. Hell. Is. Harry?" Brad's tone is full of frustration and annoyance.

"He's the boy Paige has a date with tonight," I finally answer, glancing up at him.

I see all the blood drain from his face and his jaw go slack. He stands there in silence for several seconds as the realization sinks in. "A date? She's not old enough to date."

"She's sixteen," I inform him.

"Since when?"

"Since her last birthday, five months ago," I remind.

"Do we know this kid?"

"Harry Ford. They've been in the same class since preschool."

He continues to look at me dazed and confused. It's not as if Brad was unaware that this day would eventually come. He started worrying about Paige dating when she came home from first grade one day announcing that she was in love with Jonathan. I remember the sheer look of relief on Brad's face when he found out Jonathan was the class's bunny. To say he's overprotective would be an understatement. He wants to shield her from anyone or anything that would cause her pain like a good father would, but the idea of his little girl dating terrifies him. We have drilled it into the kids to always have self-respect and never let anyone force them to do something they didn't want to do. Brad remembers how easy it was for him to charm girls back in the day and doesn't want our daughter to fall for a smooth talker.

Hesitantly, Paige escorts Harry into the kitchen. He's a sweet boy who comes from a good family. My heart goes out to him for what he's about to endure.

"Hey Harry. How are you?" I say, trying to break the nervous tension.

"I'm good. Thanks," Harry answers, his gaze quickly darting back and forth from me to the icy glare of Brad.

Brad walks on the other side of me, placing him directly in front of Harry, who stands on the other side of the kitchen island barely breathing. Brad places his arms across his chest, deliberately flexing his muscles so they strain against the material of his sleeves. It's meant to intimidate Harry, however it's turning me on.

"So, you go to school with my daughter?" Brad says as if he's accusing the boy of wrongdoing.

Swallowing hard, Harry answers nervously, "Yes Sir, since preschool."

"How old are you?" Brad continues his interrogation.

"Um… seventeen, Sir."

Brad eyes him suspiciously. "And you're in Paige's class? How's that work? She's sixteen. Did you get left back?"

Harry shoots Paige a helpless glance. "No Sir. It's just the way my birthday fell during the school year."

"Why is it I don't remember you?"

"Um… I'm taller and um… my voice is deeper and um…"

"Mom," Paige pleads.

"Y'all have fun tonight and be careful." Raising my eyebrows, I nod at Paige, letting her know now would be the time to leave.

"We will." She grabs Harry's arm and pulls him toward the living room.

Brad follows behind them, until they are out the front door. He stands at the window in silence, watching as his little girl grows up. I walk up behind him to wrap my arms around his waist when his words stop me.

"Brandon!" Brad yells.

Brandon comes rushing in from the kitchen, stopping at Brad's side. "Yeah, Dad?"

"I'll give you fifty bucks if you follow your sister and keep an eye on that Harry."

"Wamfu, yeah."

"Brad!" I say.

Giving me an innocent look he asks, "What?" I narrow my eyes at him and smile. He turns back to Brandon and continues, "Don't let your sister see you."

"I'll be like a ninja," Brandon announces before heading out the door.

I snake my arms around Brad as he instinctively drapes his around my shoulders. Looking up, I tell him, "It's going to be okay."

He brings his forehead to rest against mine. "Promise?"

"Mmmhmm. I talked with her. She's a smart girl."

He nibbles along my bottom lip before slipping his tongue inside. A moan escapes me when our tongues make contact. The kiss is slow and deep. Brad's hands travel down my back to my ass. Squeezing gently, he grinds himself against me.

Breaking the kiss, he says on my lips, "We have the whole night. Which room you want to start in?" *The smile* crosses his face as he throws me a wink.

"The shower. Definitely the shower." I back away, looking at him through my dark lashes.

"I thought you loved my man juices?"

"Do you really want to discuss this or do you want to shove me against the shower tile and do *things* to me?" I slowly unbutton my shirt.

"Fuck juices."

Loud squeals and laughter ricochet around the room as Brad rushes toward me, ducks, and throws me over his shoulders before heading into our bedroom.

Brad

I'm standing in the doorway of the kitchen, with one shoulder leaning against the frame, gazing at her. Sitting at the table, she flips through one of our many photo albums. I watch as a bright smile breaks out across her face looking at a particular picture. She's wearing a black dress that fits her form perfectly. Streaks of silver gray mix with her chestnut brown hair that's swept up into a tight bun with several pieces falling to frame her face. The diamond drop earrings I gave her for our fortieth anniversary hang down to that spot just below her ear that I love to drag my tongue across. My eyes scan over the rest of her body, down to her shoes, black patent leather with a ribbon tied at the ankle. The heel isn't as high as it used to be, but the sight of Mabry in heels, no matter what height still makes my dick twitch. She's as beautiful and sexy today as she was the first time our eyes met.

Clearing my throat, I say, "Hey, Sweetness."

She looks up and narrows her eyes at me. "What are you doing?"

"Drooling over you." I flash her *the smile* as I push off from the door and walk toward her. "What are *you* doing?"

She tilts her head up and I'm met by happy azure blues. "Looking at what an amazing life we've had together."

Leaning down, I place a soft kiss on her pale pink lips. "It has been pretty amazing."

Pointing to one of the photos, she says, "Look at how little Bren is in this one."

I rest my hands on Mabry's shoulders, peer over them and chuckle. "It's hard to believe we've had five more grandkids since Brenny."

"She had you wrapped around her tiny finger from day one."

"Well, it was my responsibility as a new granddad to spoil the first one rotten."

Shaking her head, she informs me, "You've spoiled all of them rotten."

I simply flash her *the smile.*

"The kids want us to bring all our photo albums to the party. I have them sitting on the table by the front door, so we won't forget them."

She flips through a few more pages as I bend down and press my lips just under her ear and start nibbling.

Tilting her head to the side, exposing more for me to taste, she sighs, "And where do you think you're going with this?"

My hands travel over her shoulders, moving across her collarbone, and head straight to my intended targets. "You still have one of the all-time best racks, Sweetness."

She giggles. "I don't know about that. They've been traveling south for quite a few years."

"My hands have always enjoyed the trip." I smile against her neck.

"Brad…," she moans. "We can't do this right now." A small whimper escapes her lips. "We're going to be late to our own party. The kids will be worried." She exhales a deep sigh.

I know she's right. The kids have put in a lot of time planning this party for us. A low growl rumbles from my chest. "At least dance with me," I whisper in her ear.

"But Brad…"

"I need you in my arms right now."

She smiles up at me as I take her by the hands and lead her away from the table.

"There's no music," she says.

"I always have a song in my heart for you, Sweetness." I throw her a sexy grin and wrap my arms around her waist.

Her hands find their way to the back of my neck as she gives me an exaggerated eye roll. "I was wondering when I'd get my daily dose of calcium."

Our foreheads rest against each other's as we sway, slightly. "I gotcha covered, baby."

"Your hip action is still top-notch."

"Yeah, especially since I got the new one," I say.

Mabry softly hums one of our favorite songs, "I Said" by Michelle Featherstone. As we continue to move in sync, I close my eyes, soaking in the moment with the love of my soul. My life has been imperfect at times, and I've made a lot of mistakes, but if that's what it took to have Mabry in this moment, then it was all worth it. My hands glide down and over her little ass.

She lets out a long slow sigh. "Maybe I can call the kids and tell them we're going to be just a little late."

Our eyes open at the same time and connect. The corners of my mouth turn up into a huge grin, and I say, "Wamfu yeah, baby."

The American Foundation for Suicide Prevention

http://www.afsp.org/

Crisis Hotline

tel:18002738255

http://www.suicidepreventionlifeline.org/

Self-Injury Foundation

http://selfinjuryfoundation.org/34222.html

The Keith Milano Memorial Fund was established to help raise awareness about the devastating and deadly disease that is mental illness.

Keith's spirit and laughter is kept alive through our efforts to increase awareness about mental illness and to raise money for education and imperative research. Keith often struggled with society's perception of mental illness. Our hope is that by having the strength to say that Keith was "Bipolar" we can strip away the stigma and help others to be more open about their disease.

http://www.keithmilano.org/

The Keith Milano Memorial Fund benefits the American Foundation for Suicide Prevention (AFSP). AFSP is the only national not-for-profit organization exclusively dedicated to understanding and preventing suicide through research and education, and to reaching out to people with mood disorders and those affected by suicide.

ACKNOWLEDGEMENTS

Acknowledgments are so hard to write. You want to make sure you not only include all those who have made an impact on you, but also express how grateful you are to them without sounding repetitive. Here's my attempt.

This past year, 2013, has been one of the most incredible years of my life. The incredibleness (I know, it doesn't sound like a real word) started in mid-January before anyone even knew I was attempting to write a book. I took out my iPhone and wrote the first scene of *Present Perfect* (the blind date). It's one of my favorite scenes. It spurred me on to write the next scene and the next, and then a chapter. As the words appeared on the computer screen (my late father's netbook) I started to rediscover something that I used to love but had put to one side when life got in the way.

We all go through periods when we get overwhelmed by doubts, lose ourselves a little as the years pass, and have negative situations that leave us exhausted. We wonder where the person we used to be disappeared to and crave relief from the negative, even if it's momentary.

I let a couple of close friends read a few chapters of *Present Perfect* in late January/early February, then I got a small group of betas to start reading. With each note of feedback things began to change for me and I'm not referring to just the words on the screen. Not only did I want to write this story but I needed to write this story. As the months went by I continued to work on *Present Perfect* every day. I'm blessed to be able to write full-time. During those months I met and became friends with some wonderful people—authors, avid readers, publishing professionals and bloggers.

A publish date was set, ARCs (advanced reader's copies) went out, bloggers blogged, and readers read. Notes started coming to me from people expressing how the book touched them. I hope every one of you has at least one experience in your life in which someone tells you how something you did, wrote, or said impacted them in a positive way. It leaves you speechless, humbled, and grateful.

The folks listed below have all touched my life in a meaningful way. Some I've known for years and others are new friends. Some I talk with several times a week and others I've talked to only a few times. The time spent with an individual is irrelevant. It only takes a second to leave a lasting impression on a person and these folks have all done that with me. I will always remember and be grateful to them for helping me regain my confidence, find a lost passion, and for bringing so much positivity back in my life.

Thank you!

To my loving and supportive family: Jef, Momma, Kelley, Frank, Brandon, Paige, and Jerry.

To my friends and the fantastic Smurfettes: Beth Hyams, Kristina Amit, Tina Bell, Sandra Cortez, Leslie Cox, Stacy Darnell, Tamron Davis, Nicki DeStasi, Jennifer Diaz, Alexis Durbin, Christine Estevez, Michelle Grad, Carrie Horton, Stephanie Loftin, Christine Mateo, America Matthew, Marilyn Medina, Mia Michelle, Jennifer Mirabelli, Tracey Murphy, Stacia Newbill, Kim Shackleford, and Tabitha Willbanks.

To the groups who are always there to answer my questions and make me smile: Author Support 101, Book Babes and the *Present Perfect* Support group.

To the amazing creative professionals who have guided, advised, and encouraged me: Amy Tannenbaum, Linda Roberts, Robin Harper, Abigail Marie, Angela McLaurin, Nadine Silber, A. L. Zaun, Helen Wheeler, Daniel and Sheena Cobb.

To the extremely supportive blogging community.

To my incredible readers.

To the young women who shared their experiences of self-harm and suicide with me while researching *Past Imperfect*. You are strong, brave, courageous, and not alone.

ABOUT THE AUTHOR

Alison was born and raised in Charleston, SC. She attended Winthrop University and graduated with a major in Theater. While at school Alison began writing one-act plays, which she later produced. Her debut novel, *Present Perfect*, landed on Amazon's Best Seller List and appeared on many "Best Reads of 2013" Book Blogs. The novel won Best Book at the 2014 Indie Romance Convention Awards. Her second novel, *Past Imperfect*, was published in February of 2014 and appeared on several best books of 2014 lists as well. *Presently Perfect*, the third and final book in The "Perfect" series, was published in December 2014.

AUTHOR LINKS
Website
http://alisongbailey.com/

Facebook
https://www.facebook.com/AlisonGBaileyAuthor

Goodreads
http://www.goodreads.com/author/show/7032185.Alison_G_Bailey

ALISON G. BAILEY

Twitter
https://twitter.com/AlisonGBailey1

Pinterest
http://pinterest.com/alisongbailey/present-perfect-by-alison-g-bailey/

Past Imperfect Playlist
http://bit.ly/pastimperfectplaylist

OTHER BOOKS BY ALISON G. BAILEY
Present Perfect (The Perfect Series #1)
Presently Perfect (The Perfect Series #3)

Turn the page for an excerpt of
Worth It
By Nicki DeStasi

WORTH IT

NICKI DESTASI

When she reaches my door, I swing it open and lift her up for a kiss, just like always. With her legs wrapped around my waist, I don't think I'll ever get sick of this ritual.

"Hey, baby," I greet her, smiling. I let her slide down my body, loving every second of her perfect tits pressed against me.

She smiles brightly up at me, lighting up my world. "Hey, you. I love Tuesdays."

"Me, too." I bend down to plant another kiss on her lips. Everything on this woman is perfect, perfect for me.

I step back, so she can take off her coat. "How was your day?" I ask, knowing she's gonna have some funny stories.

Her beautiful smile makes an appearance. "Do you know what Sarah said today?"

"I'm sure you're going to tell me," I tease.

We head to the kitchen to make dinner together, which has become a habit on Tuesdays.

She opens the fridge to find the ingredients, making her black skirt stretch tightly over her fantastically rounded ass. *What do people call it? Apple bottom?*

"Hello?" she says, annoyed.

I move my gaze from her ass to her eyes, and give her *that* smile. Her lips twitch, fighting laughter

"Hey, you can't blame me when you're bent over while wearing that skirt."

She stands and turns, so I can see her breasts encased in a light pink blouse that fits her just right, not helping my ogling problem.

"Eyes up here, buddy."

"Sorry."

But I'm not sorry at all, and she knows it.

"Can you stop for two seconds?" she says, rolling her eyes.

I know she loves it though. I tilt my head up in thought, teasing her. I look back down at her and say, "Nope."

She rolls her eyes. "Fine, then veggie casserole it is," she says, returning to the fridge.

Panic flares through me, and I reach out and turn her to me. "Wait—what? Let's not get hasty here."

She bursts out laughing, laying her head against my chest. She circles her arms around my waist and looks up at me. "I knew a meatless dish would get your attention." She laughs.

I give her a half-stern look. "That wasn't funny. I mean, seriously, you don't joke about food. That's just wrong."

She only laughs harder. "I was asking you before if chicken stir fry was okay, but you were too busy leering at my ass to listen."

"Hey! I was appreciating the perfection that is your ass," I say. "There was no leering involved whatsoever."

She rolls her eyes again, still smirking. "Whatever you say, buddy. So, does stir fry work for you?"

"Absolutely, baby."

She turns back to the fridge to gather the ingredients.

"So, what did Sarah say today?" I ask, trying hard not to get distracted again. It's not an easy task, considering I have a sexy woman wearing a teacher outfit while cooking for me right now. It's like someone reached into my head and pulled out my fantasy.

She turns after gathering what she needs, and she kicks the door closed with her stocking feet. "Can you grab me a cutting board?"

"Sure," I say and turn to grab one out of the cupboard for her.

"So, we were talking about what makes us happy, and she goes, 'The sun shining down on my face when I'm with my mommy.' I mean, come on, is that not the sweetest thing you've ever heard?"

I laugh and shake my head. "That's cute," I agree, handing her the cutting board and kissing the top of her head. "What else can I do?"

"Why don't you get out a wok?" she say, pulling out a knife and starts to chop up the chicken.

"What the hell is a wok?"

She looks at me and rolls her eyes. "The big frying pan that looks like a bowl."

I pull out something resembling what she's talking about. "This?"

"Yes, perfect. Thanks. Oh, and guess what Ian said?" She laughs as she turns her attention back to chopping

"I bet it's good," I say, laughing with her. "What can I do next?" I ask as I walk up behind her and close my arms around her waist.

She tilts her head back, and I brush my lips against hers.

"You can start the rice if you want."

"Okay," I say, backing up to find a pot to start boiling water.

"So, we were talking about senses, hearing specifically, and I was asking the kids what makes a sound. Ian shoots his hand up and starts waving it around frantically. It's obvious he must have this brilliant idea, right?"

She glances over at me where I'm filling the pot with water, and I nod.

"So, I call on him, and he says, 'Tick tock.' I'm like, 'Good, Ian. A clock makes the sound tick tock.' Then, he starts shaking his head back and forth and goes, 'No, Miss M. I mean"—and he starts singing—"tick tock, on the clock, but the party don't stop.' " She starts laughing.

My gut squeezes at seeing her so happy, especially since I've seen her so full of anguish.

"You know that Ke$ha song, right?"

I chuckle as I walk over to the stove and set the pot down to start boiling the water. I lean down and kiss her cheek. "Yeah, I know which one you're talking about, and that is pretty funny. I'm glad you're enjoying yourself."

She grins and turns her head, so she can kiss me quickly on the lips. "Oh my gosh, I almost forgot the funniest thing," she continues as she tosses the chicken she cut up into the woky-pan thing. Then, she takes the cutting board and knife to the sink. "Can you wash these for me real quick?"

"Sure, baby," I say, coming up behind her before she has a chance to turn back to the stove.

I press myself against her ass with my hands on either side of her, and I duck my head to kiss along her neck and shoulder. She tilts her head to allow me better access.

"Mmm, you're distracting me," she murmurs.

I kiss up her neck until I reach her ear, and I flick my tongue out to lick just underneath her lobe. "Payback," I whisper.

She spins around, wraps her arms around my neck, and brings me down to kiss me hard. I fucking love how fast I turn her on.

"Payback for what?" she whispers against my lips.

I press my hard-on against her stomach. "You're walking around while looking so fucking sexy that it's distracting me," I say against her lips. I kiss her again, slowly but deeply stroking her soft warm tongue with my own.

She moans and squeezes her arms tighter around me, pressing her curvy little body against mine, and it's a green flag at NASCAR. I pick her up, put her sexy-as-fuck behind on the edge of the sink, and shove my mouth into her mouth like my life depends on it. She claws at my shoulders and kisses me back just as hard. I rub my rock-solid length against her center, which is now at the perfect height, only making it more difficult not to strip her and fuck her now, right at this fucking second. I rub against her again, harder this time, and I deepen the kiss further than I thought possible. I reach down and inch my fingers up the inside of her thigh where her skirt has ridden up. My hand moves slowly, building the anticipation until I reach something I did not see coming.

I break the kiss and glance down. "Jesus! Fuck, you're wearing garters!" I pant while trailing my fingers along the edge of her stocking, not taking my eyes off her toned smooth thighs.

I watch as goose bumps erupt along her skin, and she lets out a soft whimper. My eyes shoot to hers, and she bites down on her lower lip and hoods her eyes. I watch as a slow, seductive smile spreads across her lips.

My cock jerks. I'm so fucking turned-on right now from seeing this woman turn on the seduction for me.

Jesus Christ, I don't think anything could be hotter.

I keep my eyes on her face as it starts to soften and a flush spreads across her cheek bones. Her breathing get heavier as I inch my fingers up, edging closer, closer, almost there—

"Oh fuck, the chicken!" she shouts, pushing me back, drawing me out of my stupor.

Now, I'm starting to smell the burning food. She hops off the counter, rushes to the stove to remove the pan from the burner, and starts scraping the charred chicken off the pan in an attempt to salvage dinner.

She glances over at me where I'm still recovering. She tries to look annoyed, but her breathing is still erratic, and her face is still flushed.

"You ruined dinner, hornball."

I smirk and saunter over to where she's standing. With her back to me, I wrap my arms around her and nuzzle my face into her neck, breathing her in. "If you're looking for an apology, you're not getting one," I say. Then, I nibble her earlobe. "Let's finish what we started and order take-out."

She groans and pushes her backside against me. "Okay," she breathes. "I like that plan."

66219518R00184

Made in the USA
Lexington, KY
07 August 2017